## Last tango in Savannah . . .

"Gina, what's wrong?" I asked, pushing her gently away, holding her by the shoulders. "Do you want to come upstairs and sit down? You're shaking like a leaf."

She was so pale, I was afraid she might faint right on the spot. I tried to edge her toward a bench by the front door. She wriggled out of my grasp and started twisting her hands together like she was wringing out a towel. I was struck by the anguish in her dark eyes, and I knew that whatever had happened, it had shaken her to the core.

She shook her head violently. "No, there's no time to sit down. Just call nine-one-one. Please, do it now."

"What's this all about?" Ali said sharply. I had been so focused on Gina, I hadn't even heard Ali slip down the stairs behind me. "Gina, what's going on? Tell us right this minute."

"It's Chico," Gina gasped, gesturing to the studio across the street. I could see that the front door to the dance studio was wide open and music was pouring into the street.

"What about Chico?" Ali demanded. "Gina, please! Pull yourself together. You're frightening me."

Gina swallowed and closed her eyes tightly, her lips quivering. Then she opened her eyes and tugged at my hand. "Come, come right now!" she rasped. "There's no time to waste. He's . . . he's on the floor and he's not moving." She drew in a long, shuddering breath, her voice catching in her throat. "I think he's dead."

*Titles by Mary Kennedy*

*Talk Radio Mysteries*

DEAD AIR
REEL MURDER
STAY TUNED FOR MURDER

*Dream Club Mysteries*

NIGHTMARES CAN BE MURDER

# Nightmares Can Be Murder

Mary Kennedy

BERKLEY PRIME CRIME, NEW YORK

THE BERKLEY PUBLISHING GROUP
Published by the Penguin Group
Penguin Group (USA) LLC
375 Hudson Street, New York, New York 10014

USA • Canada • UK • Ireland • Australia • New Zealand • India • South Africa • China

penguin.com

A Penguin Random House Company

NIGHTMARES CAN BE MURDER

A Berkley Prime Crime Book / published by arrangement with the author



For information, address: The Berkley Publishing Group,
a division of Penguin Group (USA) LLC,
375 Hudson Street, New York, New York 10014.

ISBN: 978-0-425-26805-6

PUBLISHING HISTORY
Berkley Prime Crime mass-market edition / September 2014

PRINTED IN THE UNITED STATES OF AMERICA

10 9 8 7 6 5 4 3 2 1

Cover illustration by Bill Brunning.
Cover design by Lesley Worrell.
Interior text design by Kelly Lipovich.

*To Carolyn Hart, gifted author and dear friend*

# Acknowledgments

A big thank-you to my wonderful, creative, and energetic agent, Holly Root, who makes everything possible. I also want to thank Michelle Vega, who loved the idea of the Dream Club from the very start and has been my champion. And special thanks to my husband, Alan, plot genius and computer guru, who smoothes over technical (and creative) glitches for me. A grateful shout-out to Jill and Bob Ten Eyck and Lisa Schieferstein, who love all my books and are my most devoted fans. The world would be a boring place without you!

# 1

**Friday, June 2, 8:00 p.m.**

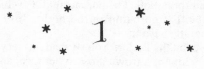

"You know I don't believe in dreams." *How can I? I'm one of the small percentage of people who never dream. I fall into bed and it's total oblivion for the next eight hours. My brain powers down to sleep mode. No fragments of memories, no images, no dramatic storyline to analyze when I wake up. No dream content, period.*

*And I have to confess, I like it that way.*

"I'm not trying to convert you, sis. You say you don't dream, and you don't believe in dreams. Okay, I get it. Some of us feel differently, you know. I think of a dream as a little window into my subconscious."

Allison looked distracted as she scurried past me, putting the finishing touches on a platter of delectable-looking petit fours. The bite-sized cakes were calling to me with their sugary little voices, nestled in a checkerboard pattern on a hand-painted porcelain tray. Ali strategically placed dark chocolate truffles in between them and stepped back to admire her work.

*Very Savannah*, I decided. Elegant, sophisticated, with a cosmopolitan flair. I was dying to grab a tiny cake and pop it in my mouth, but I knew it would ruin the look of the platter. As Ali says, it's all about presentation.

"I'm totally out of my element with this stuff," I went on. "Dream interpretation. The paranormal. Psychic phenomena. Things that go bump in the night. Tarot readings. Voices from the beyond—"

"Okay, enough, Taylor! You've made it very clear how you feel." A hint of a frown crossed her face, and she blew out a little sigh. I couldn't tell if she was exasperated with me, or just a tad stressed out over playing hostess. We've had this conversation dozens of times and have never come to a meeting of the minds. "Here's the deal. I won't ask you to share your history of childhood night terrors, and you don't have to be a believer to enjoy yourself tonight. Anyway, it's not as woo-woo as you think. Scout's honor." Ali quirked an eyebrow and held up three fingers in the Girl Scout salute.

"I'll take your word for it."

"Just think of the Dream Club as an experience, an entertaining evening. It's a fun way for me to socialize with my friends. Not everyone takes it seriously, but we do have a couple of die-hard psychics and intuitives in the group. Everybody has dreams, and all we do is try to make sense of them."

"Okay, you win," I said, pushing myself to sound positive. "You've certainly put out a nice spread. And the sitting room looks great."

Ali had gone all out tonight. My sister seems to have inherited a Martha Stewart gene, and sadly, I didn't. My Chicago condo is positively spartan compared to Ali's place. I took a moment to appreciate the creamy taupe walls, the glossy white woodwork, the old brick fireplace with the white marble mantelpiece.

The whole room was bathed in a golden glow thanks to fat amber candles she'd placed on nearly every flat surface.

Soft cello music was playing in the background, and the faint scent of lavender danced on the air.

"So tell me you won't be grumpy and you'll try to enjoy yourself." Ali turned, flashing a smile that has melted my heart ever since we shared a crush on Bon Jovi, growing up in Muncie, Indiana. "Please? For me?" Her voice was warm, entreating, and she had little crinkles around her eyes.

"I'll do my best."

"That's all I'm asking—just keep an open mind." She gave me a friendly fist bump.

"You got it," I agreed, giving in to temptation and snagging one of the petit fours. And then I took a second one, because the whole platter looked off-kilter with just one cake missing. I nudged the remaining cakes toward the middle and grabbed a third.

*There, you can hardly see there's a gap in the platter*, I decided, chomping happily away. *Melt in your mouth delicious. At least the food will be good, even if the rest of the evening turns out to be a snooze.*

The petit fours were just the beginning. A crystal decanter of iced "sweet tea" flavored with fresh mint was the star attraction, along with two kinds of gourmet coffee, exotic Asian teas, and an assortment of French pastries heaped high on a silver platter.

Tiny triangles of chess pie were arranged on a hand-painted antique tray along with fragrant lemon bars and mini cupcakes frosted in Easter egg colors. And for die-hard vintage candy fans, there was a blue and white Limoges bowl filled with pastel Necco Wafers. It was enough to make a sugar junkie salivate with pleasure. I was getting a buzz just inhaling the heavenly aromas.

And then the doorbell rang, and the Dream Club was in full swing.

"Last night I dreamt I was walking stark naked down the produce aisle in Publix." Lucinda Macavy folded her French-manicured fingernails demurely in her lap and let her gaze wander around the circle, waiting for a response. A long beat passed. "Anybody have any thoughts?" she added hopefully.

Nobody jumped in to offer an interpretation. Lucinda was so prim and uptight, I could hardly imagine her naked in her own shower. Plus, this was the third "naked" dream of the evening, so the shock value had lessened considerably. Persia Walker had regaled us with a hilarious story about finding herself in the altogether at choir practice, and Dorien Myers had confessed to being "au natural" on the Savannah Hills Golf Course.

Why do so many people dream of being naked in a public place? According to Ali, this is a fairly common dream theme, usually related to anxiety or a fear of being "exposed." It's a "worst-case scenario" type of dream and usually happens during a time of great stress or emotional upheaval.

I have to admit I was having trouble relating to the "buck naked" dream template.

I stifled a tiny yawn and pulled my attention back to the group. The Dream Club members were gathered around a white wicker coffee table in the cozy sitting room attached to Oldies but Goodies, my sister's vintage candy store.

"Tell me more about the dream." Sybil Powers leaned forward, her bright eyes keen as a ferret's. "Were you shopping with anyone? Did you recognize any friends or relatives in the dream? Maybe someone significant in your life?" I'd met Sybil earlier in the week, and I knew she favors bold colors, flowing tops, and chunky handcrafted jewelry she buys from local artisans. Tonight she was wearing a caftan that looked like hand-printed batik in a sapphire blue and snowy white pattern.

"I'm pretty sure I was alone." Lucinda shrugged. "I remember pushing my cart down the aisle, all by myself. It didn't seem to bother me in the least that I was completely naked," she said, flushing bright pink.

"You didn't feel uncomfortable?" I asked.

Lucinda hesitated. "Uncomfortable? No, not really. I was chilly all over, though. I remember I had goose bumps when I turned into the frozen dinner aisle. They had the AC cranked up full blast."

"I know what you mean, my dear," an elderly woman in a bright floral dress offered.

She was wearing orthopedic shoes with little ankle socks, and her face was framed by a cloud of fluffy white hair. "It's downright freezing in that aisle. It's cold enough to lay out a body in there. I've complained to the manager several times, to no avail." Her companion—who resembled her so much I wondered if they were twins—nodded in agreement.

I decided that they must be the Harper sisters. Ali had mentioned that her elderly neighbors, Minerva and Rose, would be attending the group tonight. The women were well into their eighties, longtime Savannah residents and history buffs.

Someone snickered and quickly covered it with a cough. "Well, I think we have to look at the subtext here," Sybil went on. She gave me a quick glance. "You probably don't know this, Taylor, but the subtext is the hidden emotional content in a dream."

"Ah yes, the subtext." I tried to look suitably impressed even though I'm pretty sure dream interpretation isn't rocket science. In fact, I'm inclined to think it's a bunch of hooey. A dream can mean anything you want it to, right? Like reading tea leaves or tarot cards. The meaning is in the eye of the beholder.

"Now Lucinda," Sybil said, "I'm surprised that appearing naked in public didn't bother you. In the majority of these cases, the dreamer experiences a certain degree of embarrassment and humiliation."

"Well, I certainly didn't *want* to have this sort of dream," Lucinda said, looking chastised. "I'd rather dream about something sweet, like kittens or babies."

"No one dreams about kittens," Dorien cut in. "Unless they're rescue dreams, and that's another whole issue. Rescuing animals is a very common theme. I have those dreams all the time. It's always late at night and—"

"Let's not get sidetracked," Sybil cut in swiftly. "We need to focus on Lucinda's dream and her feelings about it. That's the path to enlightenment."

*The path to enlightenment?* Sybil and her fortune cookie platitudes were beginning to grate on my nerves. "But why do people have dreams like this?" I cut in. "Where do they come from?" I felt my BS register rising, and I suppose I may have sounded sharper than I'd intended.

Sybil turned to me. "Well, it can be related to the imposter syndrome, wouldn't you agree, Ali?"

"Yes, I do. Being naked is a metaphor. Having no clothes means your smooth veneer is stripped away and people will see right through you. They might discover that you're a fake, an imposter." Ali paused, passing a plate of lemon squares.

"Yes, exactly." Sybil waved her hand dramatically, and her bangle bracelets clanked together. "Lucinda, is there something you need to overcome in your personal life? Maybe you're facing a dilemma, or something left unresolved?" She arched her eyebrows, and her voice spiraled upward in a question.

"I don't think I'm struggling with anything," Lucinda said doubtfully. "No more than usual, I mean." Lucinda has so many phobias and neuroses, she makes Monk look like a model of sanity.

Lucinda is a quiet woman in her mid-forties who took early retirement from her headmistress position at a private school to become a patron of the arts. Her brown hair was pulled back in a tight chignon, and she wore a beige linen sheath that was probably expensive but hung shapelessly on her bony frame. She's pleasant but colorless, the kind of woman who could easily blend into the wallpaper.

I'd heard she's well connected in Savannah, serves on the boards of several charities, and volunteers at a homeless shelter once a week. Ali told me that Lucinda was a trust fund baby before anyone had even invented the term, so she's never had to worry about taking a paying job. Instead, she can devote herself to philanthropic work and live off her considerable assets.

The only sound was the lazy whirring of the Casablanca fan high above us, suspended from the tin ceiling with its distinctive fleur-de-lis-patterned squares. It had been a sun-baked June day, but the thick walls of the old building warded off the Georgia heat and the sitting room was cool and pleasant.

The contrast between the cream-colored walls and dark wood floors added a light, airy feeling to the room. Ali had covered the fussy antique furniture with white cotton slip-covers and had made her own throw pillows from scraps of blue and white gingham. A crystal water pitcher filled with blue hydrangeas, a few artfully arranged seashells on a steamer chest, and suddenly the once formal living space looked fresh and inviting.

Shabby chic, Savannah style.

I was torn between the mille-feuilles and the napoleons when I heard Samantha Stiles blow out a low sigh. Samantha, who was sitting right next to me on the settee, is a rookie detective in Savannah and new to the group. She'd been drumming her fingertips impatiently on the armrest for the past ten minutes, sneaking an occasional glance at her watch.

I figured she'd already decided Ali's little Dream Club was sheer hocus-pocus and couldn't wait to make her escape. I'd heard from Ali that Samantha had been dragged into the group by her close friend, Dorien Myers, a self-proclaimed psychic and tarot reader.

"Maybe this fear, or whatever it is, is buried deep in your subconscious," my sister offered. "Outside your awareness. Your conscious awareness, I mean."

There was Ali, back on her Freud kick again. Ali reads a lot of books on psychodynamic theory so her suggestion didn't surprise me. According to Ali, the unconscious is a boiling cauldron of unexplored fears, wishes, and desires. We manage to keep a lid on the pot during waking hours, but at night, all bets are off and the repressed material comes bubbling to the surface in the form of dreams.

An interesting idea, even though I'm not sure I agree with her. Poor Ali, I think she's a frustrated psychologist.

Lucinda nodded politely, but I could see my sister's analysis didn't strike a chord with her, either.

"You say it was the produce aisle? I'm not sure what that brings to mind, but I'd certainly like to hear more about it." Persia Walker scored a tiny glazed fruit tart from the tray. Our eyes met and she gave me a sheepish grin before adding a cream puff and two double-chocolate brownies to her plate.

I knew Persia was doing Weight Watchers and idly wondered how many points those pastries would cost her. I squashed the thought and tried to focus on the discussion. Some things are better left unexamined.

Persia had told me before the meeting that she has the strong feeling there's a mystery man buried somewhere in my past. She said it could be the remote past, going back several centuries. I raised my eyebrows and Persia looked disappointed when I told her that I don't have any loves—lost, found, recent, or long ago. Persia promised to loan me the DVD of *Somewhere in Time* and said that it would all become clear to me. She predicted that true love was waiting right around the corner.

*Wrong.* At thirty-two years old, I'm happily single and I intend to stay that way for a long time.

"I just remembered something," Lucinda piped up. "One of the workers in the produce aisle told me they were having a special on mangoes." She frowned. "Or maybe it was the manager who told me. It's probably not significant, but—"

"Oh, for heaven's sake, of course it's significant, Lucinda,"

Dorien cut in. "You should have mentioned you spoke with someone in your dream." She shook her head and blew out an exasperated sigh. "You have to be precise about these things. Every detail counts, you know. I'm not sure what mangoes represent, maybe the tropics, or exotic places. Perhaps something you're striving for, that's just out of reach." She paused. "Does that strike a chord with you?"

Dorien has a thin, angular face, and her heavy dark brows knitted together as her chin jutted forward like a bulldog's. Her sleek black hair was cut chin-length, on the diagonal, and one side fell forward, covering her cheek for a moment.

"I simply don't know. I just have a vague sense of the big picture. It's really hard to get every little detail straight." A defensive note had crept into Lucinda's voice, and I noticed she was twisting her hands together in her lap, probably regretting she had ever mentioned the Publix dream.

Dorien brushed her hair back from her face with a choppy gesture and tucked it behind her ear. "Details are important, Lucinda. *Everything* in a dream has meaning. I've said that a thousand times. *Everything!*"

Dorien has the reputation of being prickly, and from my brief acquaintance with her, I can see that she's the kind of person who always has to be right. She glanced around the group, as if daring anyone to disagree with her. Our eyes met, and I did my best to look intrigued by her latest pronouncement. This was my first introduction to the Dream Club, and I wasn't going to risk opening myself up to Dorien's scathing tongue.

"I just remembered something else," Lucinda said, brightening. "I noticed the floor was black-and-white tiles. An Art Deco pattern, like something you'd see in the foyer of a mansion."

"That's interesting." My sister leaned forward, her expression rapt with interest. "Black-and-white tiles. Are we talking symbolism here?"

*Symbolism. Again.* Ali and I are polar opposites.

Sometimes it's hard to believe we're biologically related. She's a soft-spoken, creative type, and I'm a high-level bean counter with an MBA from Wharton. I have to admit, Ali loses me when she prattles on about universal symbols and Jungian archetypes. I'm a bottom line kind of girl ("Show me the money"), and Allison has her head in the stars. As a freelance business consultant, I specialize in taking failing businesses and turning them into success stories.

I usually work with Fortune 500 companies, but I flew in to Savannah to help save my sister's vintage candy shop. It might take a few weeks or a few months, it's hard to tell. Ever since both our parents passed away, Ali is my only family and I feel like it's the two of us against the world.

"Yes, I think you nailed it. It's highly symbolic." Sybil Powers nodded her head. Ali told me Sybil was one of the early members of the group and she likes to call herself a "dream-hopper."

I'd never heard the term, but Sybil claims to be able to interject herself into other people's dreams. It doesn't seem to matter if the dreamer is dead or alive, and the dream can have taken place ages ago. Apparently time doesn't have any relevance in dreamland.

According to Sybil, dreams go on forever. They continue to exist, somewhere in the cosmos, and astute dreamers can tap into them. I know it sounds crazy, because, after all, how can you tune into someone else's dream?

I have a hard time wrapping my head around that idea, but as Sybil says, "If love is eternal and the universe is infinite, why shouldn't dreams continue to exist as well?" The whole question is a little too metaphysical for me, but the other Dream Club members seem to eat it up.

Earlier in the evening, Sybil had treated us to a dream she'd "visited." The dreamer was a Confederate soldier, sleeping in a field tent near Leesburg, Virginia, longing to see his beloved once more. He dreamt that the two of them were reunited and walking hand in hand down a lovely, magnolia-lined path that led to a mansion right out of *Gone with the Wind*. Sybil described the dream in great detail. She said she was simply a bystander; she observed the soldier's dream and didn't interject herself in any way.

"I'd look for the subtext in the dream about the supermarket," Sybil said, pulling me back to the present. "Black and white, that's an easy one. It clearly means good and evil." She paused a moment to let that sink in. "The produce aisle is just incidental, it's the opposing forces angle that interests me. Black and white, good and evil, yin and yang."

She pushed her rimless glasses down on her nose and peered at Lucinda. "Is there anything you feel guilty about, Lucinda? Anything that's troubling you? It could be you're repressing something, and the material is coming out in dream form."

"No, I don't think so," Lucinda said, shooting a nervous look at Dorien. "I can't imagine what it could be." She hesitated, as if she were tempted to say more, but like many people, she seemed a little intimidated by Dorien's high-voltage personality.

I haven't made up my mind about Dorien, but Allison swears she's a softie under that hard shell. When Allison first arrived in Savannah, Dorien had gone out of her way to be kind and welcoming. She'd brought her a gift basket and taken her to a local merchants' association dinner. She even brought organic fish treats for Barney and Scout, Ali's adored cats, who were napping in the front window, oblivious to the discussion going on around them.

Of course, her motives might have had more to do with good business than friendship, I thought with a certain degree of cynicism. Dorien's tarot-reading shop is right down the street from Ali's candy shop, and I know that Dorien is also trying to launch a separate business as a personal chef. Many of the businesses in the district try to cross-promote each other, and she may have decided that she could target Ali's customers for her new business ventures.

Samantha was growing restive beside me, and I hoped Ali was getting ready to conclude the meeting. "C'mon, let's wrap this up, it's time to go," the young detective muttered under her breath.

Samantha grabbed a handful of Jordan almonds and inched over to the edge of the settee as if ready to bolt out of the room. She'd already mentioned that she was working the evening shift for the Savannah PD tonight and was reporting for duty at ten o'clock sharp.

"Anybody have any final thoughts?" Allison asked, glancing at the antique schoolhouse clock that graced the back wall. "It's almost nine thirty."

"I had a very strange dream," Persia piped up. "More of a nightmare, actually. It was all about a murder right here in Savannah."

# 2

*Bingo! Now we're getting to something interesting.* I found myself coming out of my sugar rush and snapping to attention. *A murder in Savannah!* Finally, a dream that I could relate to. With my extensive knowledge of TV crime shows, I might actually be able to contribute something to the discussion.

Persia perched on the edge of the sofa, her eyes glowing with excitement. The room fell silent and she wriggled expectantly in her seat, thrilled to be the center of attention.

I noticed that Gina Santiago froze in her chair. Her hand was trembling so much, she had to put her cappuccino down on the glass-topped coffee table. Gina is a flamboyant young woman who works as an instructor in the Latin dance studio right across the street.

"A murder?" Samantha Stiles asked sharply, shifting into detective mode. "When did it take place? Was the perpetrator caught and convicted?"

Persia shook her head. "Oh, it hasn't taken place yet, that's what's so confusing. It's a vision from the future. I have a very strong image of the victim, but the details of his death are a little fuzzy. I'm sure there's some evil force at work, though. There's a dark presence in the dream, but I can't get a handle on it." She gave a little shudder. "I have the strange feeling the killer is someone I know, even though that makes no sense to me. I'm sure I've never met anyone who's capable of murder."

"Everyone's capable of murder," Gina said, her voice barely a whisper. I glanced at her to see if she was kidding, but she looked dead serious. Her expression was stony, impassive.

"Wait a minute, Persia, you said *his* death," Samantha cut in. "So the victim is a man? You're sure of that?" This was the most enthusiasm Samantha had shown all evening. I almost expected her to whip out her tiny tape recorder to capture Persia's remarks, but I sensed an undercurrent of doubt in her tone.

Persia nodded. "Yes, it's definitely a man. That's the one thing I can say with complete confidence."

"But you don't have any idea of when it's going to happen? Or where?" Now Samantha's tone had turned skeptical, and I wondered if she was writing off Persia's dream as pure fantasy.

"No idea at all, I'm afraid." Persia spread her hands dramatically in front of her as if she were peering into an imaginary crystal ball. "I could see him quite clearly, but his back was turned to me. He was tall and well built; I'd say he was a man in his thirties or forties, in the prime of his life. I remember vivid colors and flashing lights. There was a pack of wolves circling him, they looked terrifying, menacing. I saw flashes of red everywhere, and there was loud music playing in the background." She paused for a moment. "I'm positive about the music. I remember wishing someone would turn the volume down. The noise level was awful, and I was getting a splitting headache."

"Someone was murdered, and you heard loud music. What kind of music?" Samantha's tone had flattened to the verbal equivalent of an eye roll.

Persia flushed. "It was very loud Latin music. I wasn't at all fond of it. I prefer classical music, you know. It helps me concentrate when I meditate and do my dream work."

"What else do you remember about the dream?" I asked, intrigued in spite of my doubts.

"Not much," Persia admitted. She squinted her eyes tightly shut for a moment as if she were trying to re-create the scene in her mind. "I did see a silver serving tray and a lovely dinner laid out on a snowy white tablecloth. It might have been in a restaurant or it might have been someone's home. The lighting was soft and there were candles. First everything was fine, and then"—she gave a little shudder—"the dream turned into fragments. I saw the man eating dinner, and the very next moment, he just keeled over and collapsed on the floor." She put a hand to her chest and made a fluttery gesture. "It gave me quite a start, and I sat straight up in bed, my heart beating like a rabbit's."

For a moment there was dead silence while we all absorbed this.

"What makes you think the man was murdered?" Ali asked. "He might have had a heart attack, or maybe had low blood sugar and blacked out. There are loads of possibilities besides murder." She gave a little shrug. "He could have had a seizure or he could have fainted."

"I'm not really sure how I know this," Persia said vaguely. "But I absolutely am convinced he was murdered. I wish I could remember more details. I did notice something strange, though. There was a serpent in the dream—a black snake on a red background."

"A serpent," I said under my breath. "That could mean anything, right?" I happen to like snakes and think they've been given bad press. The majority of them are harmless and just want to sun themselves on a warm rock and live out their lives undisturbed by spade-wielding humans.

"I think it would indicate evil. There I go with more symbolism," Persia added with a light laugh. "And I'm not sure what the red and black meant, maybe something Satanic? I'm not clear on that."

Persia fell silent then and Allison looked at her watch. "Well, I guess we should stop for tonight," she said. "That's certainly a fascinating dream, Persia. Maybe we should pick up at that point next week. I think there's a lot of material here for us to work on. So if that's all . . ."

"Just one more thing . . ." Dorien began. She held up her index finger in a move that reminded me of Columbo, the television detective from years ago who always had one more question. "Before we go, I have some advice for Lucinda. I'd like you to try to dream about shopping in Publix again."

Lucinda blinked. "How would I do that?"

"Just remind yourself to think about the supermarket as you drift off to sleep. See the produce aisle in your mind's eye. It would be really helpful if you could have another dream so we can analyze it more carefully. And try to pay more attention this time," she said, a snide tone creeping into her voice. "Notice the surroundings, the weather, the time of day, your emotions, everything you're feeling and experiencing. Think of taking a mental snapshot of the image and then locking it in your memory banks." She gave Lucinda a sharp look. "Do you think you can do that?"

"Oh, I see what you mean. Well, I can certainly give it a try," Lucinda said quickly, grabbing her purse. Like Samantha, she seemed eager to make her getaway. "Thanks for the goodies, Ali," she added, standing up. "Everything was delicious, as always."

"My pleasure," Ali said. Our eyes met and she gave a tiny frown and then an almost imperceptible nod toward Dorien. I knew we both were thinking the same thing: sometimes this woman is simply impossible!

Sybil was the last to leave, stopping for a moment to pet Barney, who'd roused from his slumber and gave her that slow blink that cats do when they're fond of someone. "Such a handsome boy," she murmured, running her hand over his glossy coat. She turned and touched my arm. "So nice to have you with us, Taylor. I expect you'll be in town for a while?"

"Oh, I certainly hope so. I think it would be easy to fall in love with Savannah."

"Indeed it is," she agreed. "I've spent my whole life here and I'm still discovering beautiful places to visit and things to do." She moved closer and I caught a whiff of her delicate lavender perfume. "Anytime you want a guide, I'll be happy to give you a tour of the city."

"Thanks, that's really nice of you."

"Have a good night's rest and try to think pleasant, healing thoughts before you go to sleep," she said in a low voice. "You don't dream at all anymore, do you?"

She caught me by surprise. "Well, no, actually I don't." My mind zinged. *How does she know this about me?*

Sybil nodded. "I think I know why. I have the feeling that you don't allow yourself to have dreams"—she paused—"because you had a bad experience sometime in your life. Maybe you had night terrors as a child. That would be my best guess, my dear. At some level, I think you're afraid to dream so you're blocking them. Your fear is holding you back, and that's not healthy."

I blinked in surprise. Her best guess? She was right on target. It's true that I suffered from night terrors as a child, but there was no way in the world Sybil could have known this. I walked her to the front door, wondering if the woman really could be psychic.

"I know the night terrors were disturbing to you," she said softly, giving me a keen look, "but it's best not to read too much into them. Just try to put them out of your mind, if you can. Everyone has vivid, disturbing dreams from time to time, and I don't recommend dwelling on them. By keeping yourself from dreaming, you're not letting your subconscious mind do the work it needs to do. "

"Thank you, I'll be sure to remember that." I felt a little chill go through me, but I tried to keep my tone neutral and plastered a bland expression on my face.

"Bad dreams happen for a reason, Taylor," she said carefully. Her voice was now barely a whisper, her eyes were full of shadows. "They have something to tell us, and the message becomes apparent soon enough. You know what they say, the truth always comes out in the end." She paused. "Oh, and tell Barney he can find that little catnip mouse—the blue one with the orange tail—under the refrigerator. He lost it a week ago, and I finally had a dream about it last night."

"I'll be sure to tell him." My eyes widened, and I caught myself wondering if this woman was for real. "I know he'll appreciate it." *She dreams about cats and their lost toys?*

On that very odd note, I said good night and decided to ask Allison if she'd said anything to Sybil about my nightmares. I felt uncomfortable thinking she might have discussed my personal life with her friends, and I vowed to get to the bottom of it.

And I decided to ask her about Barney and his missing catnip mouse. Just in case.

# 3

"Oh my gosh, you've must have gotten another shipment of Chunky bars and Mallo Cups, Allison. And what are these? Chocolate Ice Cubes! I haven't seen these in years. I didn't even know they still made them."

"They came in yesterday, I just put them out this morning. Do you think the bins look too crowded?"

"No, they look perfect. Like something out of a magazine photo shoot."

I ran my fingertips over a glass display case in the shop area of Oldies but Goodies. The shop was bright and appealing, with sunlight streaming in the front windows from Clark Street and zigzagging across the bleached oak floors. A pot of hazelnut coffee was brewing and a selection of fresh croissants was nestled on a serving tray along with a jar of Ali's homemade blueberry jam and sweet cream butter.

Ali's shop has neatly stocked rows of candies that were popular half a century ago. Red Hots, Scottie Dog licorice, hot dog bubble gum, jawbreakers, and candy buttons line the top shelf divided by colorful partitions. Circus Peanuts,

Chuckles, Bit-O-Honey, and Juicy Fruits are arranged in neat compartments along the bottom.

I couldn't resist reaching into an antique apothecary jar for a handful of French burnt peanuts. Munching away, I checked the rest of the inventory.

This was a trip down memory lane and Ali had been thorough. She hadn't missed a thing. Swedish fish and Jujubes, sold by the pound, were there, along with Necco Wafers and Sen-Sen packets. I saw all my old childhood favorites. Clark Bars, Fifth Avenue Bars, and Mounds Bars were neatly arranged in wicker baskets on top of the counter.

The shop had a delightful, sugary aroma and reminded me of a real-life version of Willy Wonka's Chocolate Factory. I wondered why business wasn't booming. Why was Oldies but Goodies one of Savannah's best-kept secrets?

The building is tucked away on a side street a few blocks from the Historic District, and as I looked out the front window, I could see the heat already rising off the sidewalk. The sun was climbing high in the sky, signaling another scorcher on the way. I had the wild thought that Ali would be more successful selling frozen treats—ice cream, sherbets, and sorbets—than vintage candy.

"Everything looks tempting, but think of the calories." I read the fat count on a chocolate bar and nearly gasped aloud. In the old days, manufacturers didn't print nutritional listings on wrappers, but now they're required to by law.

I checked out a row of glossy wax lips nestled close to a little mesh bag filled with chocolate coins wrapped in gold foil. I had a sudden flashback to my childhood home in Indiana when my parents were alive and we were still a family. Nostalgia time.

"I don't think an occasional splurge hurts anyone. Candy is a feel-good food; it gives you a little boost when you're feeling down. Necco Wafers and Mallo Cups are two of my biggest sellers." Ali looked up from her laptop, a tiny frown creasing her face. The AC was cranked to the max but the outdoor temperature was already in the nineties and Ali glanced up at the Casablanca fan as if willing it to spin faster. "Does that surprise you?"

*Oops.* I gave myself a mental head slap. I'd been tactless and it was time for a little damage control. "I just figured that since everyone is so health-conscious these days, they might want to cut down on sweets. And especially white sugar," I finished lamely.

"You're not in Chicago anymore, sis. This is the South, remember? Home of sweet tea, lemon pie, and blueberry cobbler. Think of the spread I put out last night for the Dream Club. There was hardly a crumb left."

"That's true," I agreed. Everyone had practically inhaled the pastries, and Persia Walker had even asked if she could bring home some chess pie in a plastic container.

Ali chewed on the end of a pencil and ducked her head back to the computer screen. After a quick breakfast, she'd spent the past hour going over last month's receipts and tallying up the vendors' bills. From time to time she gave a little sigh, and her forehead was wrinkled in concentration.

Or maybe it was quiet desperation.

Oldies but Goodies had been in operation for nearly a year, and I suspected she was barely breaking even. Allison had accepted my offer to stay with her for a while to get things in the black, but glancing around the shop, I wondered if I'd been fooling myself. Maybe this was a business that was doomed to fail. It needed a major infusion of something, but what? It doesn't help to throw money into an operation unless you have a solid business plan. I wasn't convinced that Ali did.

Ali continued, "When people come here for the evening, they expect a nice spread. It's part of the enjoyment, you know. Sampling goodies and exchanging recipes."

"I suppose you're right," I said, aiming for a positive note.

I poured myself a glass of lemonade from the crystal pitcher she kept on the counter for the customers. "Retro is in and Southerners certainly do love their sweets."

Ali keeps a well-thumbed copy of Sandra Lee's *Bake Sale Cookbook* on the counter, and I idly flipped through it. "Sandra always manages to come up with a modern twist on all the old favorites."

"She certainly does. That book is my inspiration." Allison nodded. "Nostalgia is the name of the game here in Savannah. Southerners have long memories and a passion for old-timey things. People remember all these candies from the good old days, and they buy them for their kids and grandbabies. Of course it wouldn't hurt if I could figure out a way to draw in the younger crowd, as well. Maybe you can help me with that, since you're going to be in town for a while."

I bobbed my head up and down in a show of enthusiasm. "You know I'll do my best." I paused, glancing at the street as a middle-aged couple in plaid Bermuda shorts stopped in front of the shop. They took a quick peek at the window display and then moved on.

Not a good sign.

I made a mental note to talk to Ali about revamping the window display. We needed something eye-catching that would draw in the tourists. Maybe a selection of vintage candy advertisements, blown up poster-size and mounted in old-fashioned frames? I might be able to find some online, I decided. Or perhaps a display of antique candy presses? A collage of vintage candy bar wrappers was another possibility. Something fun and colorful that would make people take notice and step inside.

And then another idea hit me. *We should be running a weekly special.* Ideas started ricocheting back and forth, and I couldn't wait to get started with a marketing plan.

We could offer bagged candy that people could eat on the go, perfect for tourists as they took in the sights. Nothing that would melt in the sultry summer weather, maybe Broadway

Licorice Rolls or Red Hots, or even those crunchy Boston Baked Beans. We could give away free samples, offer two-for-one coupons, anything to draw in more traffic.

Or maybe we could run a contest? Kids could guess the number of gummy bears in a glass jar or jawbreakers in a bin?

We could even do something interactive, maybe have an old-fashioned taffy pull on the sidewalk in front of the shop? I grabbed a notepad and started scribbling before the ideas got away from me.

"You're still not operating in the black, right?" I said, writing madly.

I had the feeling Ali was putting a good spin on things, as usual, and leaving out half the story. Ever since our parents died in a car crash ten years earlier, I'd stepped into the parental role with my headstrong younger sister. I wanted to know the details on Oldies but Goodies, because in the end, I'd be the one picking up the pieces and maybe even bankrolling Allison's next venture.

Ali had pulled her streaky blond hair into a ponytail and was wearing a black apron over her burgundy tank top and skinny jeans. She was tall, slim with the kind of good looks that turn heads. With her golden hair, china blue eyes, and finely chiseled cheekbones, she could have stepped out of a Victoria's Secret ad.

Ali hesitated, a little frown flitting across her perfect features. "Well, I guess you could say I'm in the black, but barely."

*Barely. That meant she wasn't at all, just what I'd suspected.* "So you're just breaking even; you're not turning a profit," I said flatly.

She held up a finger for silence. "Okay, here we go. I've finally crunched the numbers, and here's the deal." She gestured to a spreadsheet she'd plucked out of the printer. "If I meet all my expenses by the end of the month, I'll have enough to pay the rent till September, or possibly October. It's cutting it close, but I think I can do it."

"It sounds like you're going to have to step up your

marketing," I said as gently as I could. The situation was worse than I'd expected. I don't think Ali realized how dire things really were; her sunny personality seemed to protect her from some of life's harsh realities.

"I'd like to do more promotion. I just never seem to have the time or the budget for it. What I really need is some national attention."

"National attention?" That seemed like a stretch, but I didn't want to burst her bubble.

"Yes," she went on in a dreamy voice. "If I could just persuade the *Daily News* or one of the major metropolitan newspapers to do a feature on me, I'd have it made. Or if I could get on *The Today Show*, that would be incredibly cool."

"I think it's very hard to land those spots," I said mildly.

"Who knows? Maybe Matt Lauer will visit the shop and bring along a camera crew. Now that would be sweet!" Ali pumped her fist triumphantly in the air like a boxer. She smiled but then her expression turned pensive. "I've sent out tons of press releases, but so far, no takers. I'm not sure what the problem is. No one's beating a path to my door. The national media seems to be ignoring me."

*The* Daily News. The Today Show. *Always thinking big, that's Allison.*

I let my gaze wander around the shop, trying to be objective. Trying to look at it dispassionately, through an investor's eyes. It's a charming brick building dating back to 1895, with wide-planked wood floors, a tin ceiling, and wonderful architectural details like eight-inch crown molding and hand-carved chair rails. The candy shop and lounge area are on the first floor, along with a small kitchen and bathroom. A shaded patio area is in the back, housing a few tiny bistro tables and wrought iron chairs.

Upstairs, there's a cozy two-bedroom apartment that's been completely renovated. Ali plans on eventually buying the building and using the apartment for rental income. Her goal is to buy a small house for herself, but at the moment, she and I are both living in the apartment above the shop.

Ali told me that the building used to be a jam factory at the turn of the century, a neighborhood lending library in the fifties, and more recently, the office of a community newspaper that had folded. The upper floor needed some paint and refurbishing, which is why Allison got a very good deal on the rent.

But would she be able to keep the place going? It seemed as though people weren't beating down the old-timey door with the hand-painted lettering and brass fittings, clamoring for sweets. She definitely needed a gimmick, and maybe she should expand her offerings. Old-timey candy is nice, but why not add desserts and beverages?

The patio area in the back was pleasant, and perhaps she could start serving tea and pastries? Or would that require a different sort of business license? That was something I needed to investigate right away. The shop was in a downward spiral, and only a new business model could save it.

Who eats "retro candy" anyway?

As far as I knew, this was Ali's fifth career move since graduating from art school. A brief stint working for a graphic designer, a freelance marketing gig for a textile museum, an event planner for a couple of local galleries, and the proud owner of a glass-blowing shop that opened and closed within the same month.

And now a retro candy shop.

There was a pattern here—no doubt about it.

Part of it was the economy, of course, but I had a sneaking suspicion that Ali, with her spontaneity and her devil-may-care attitude, was partly to blame. Maybe she just didn't have the soul of an entrepreneur—the confidence, the relentless drive, the unstoppable ambition.

I'd earned a business degree with a combination of scholarships, student loans, and two waitressing jobs. But Ali wasn't like me; she didn't have any specific career goals and always seemed to be searching for something just out of reach. The brass ring, maybe.

If only Ali knew what she wanted, maybe I could help her get it.

# 4

Later that evening, Ali and I decided to share a pizza at Luigi's, a little bistro across the street from the shop. It was barely six thirty, and I wondered if Ali had closed up early in my honor. After all, it was a Saturday night and I figured the tourists would be out in full force, exploring the trendy shops and restaurants in the nearby Historic District.

*So why are we sitting here instead of working?* I finally broached the subject with my sister.

"Oh, I never stay open in the evening," Ali explained, "even on a weekend. Most of the traffic comes during the morning and early afternoon hours." She swirled her Pinot Grigio in her glass before raising it to her lips. "Plus I like to have the evenings to myself, you know? I'm working on a couple of art projects that might pay off down the road."

"What sort of art projects?" My guard was up and little alarm bells were clanging in my brain. Ali always has trouble staying on task, and I worried she was veering off track once again, not focusing her energies on her business.

"I've been thinking about doing graphics and web designs as a sideline. I'm helping a few friends with their websites, just to see if I can get the hang of it. I don't charge them for my services, because I'm new to this and there's a pretty steep learning curve." She gave a breezy wave of her hand. "I like to keep a lot of irons in the fire. That way if something doesn't go well, I always have a plan B to fall back on."

I took a deep breath and let it out slowly, feeling like my head was going to explode. This was just what I was afraid was going to happen. The candy shop would take a backseat to whatever new project had caught Allison's fancy, and she'd have her head in the clouds once again.

"Really, Ali, it might be better to work on something that actually increases your revenue right now. You don't have time for sidelines like web design. I think you should concentrate on the candy store. That should be your one and only goal at the moment." I gritted my teeth, trying to keep the edge out of my voice and failing miserably.

"I suppose so," she said, flushing. "You know me, I always go off in a dozen directions at once. I've always had trouble focusing on just one thing. Maybe that's part of the problem."

She blew out a little breath, and our eyes met across the table. She looked very young and vulnerable in her green and white boho top and skinny jeans. She'd pulled her silky blond hair back from her face with an embroidered headband that gave her an Alice in Wonderland look.

She looked so crushed, I felt my heart melting. The waiter placed an enormous veggie pizza on the table, but neither of us reached for a slice, and for a long moment, you could hear a pin drop.

I knew I'd hurt her feelings, and it was time to backpedal. Swiftly.

"Ali," I said in a softer tone, "I didn't mean to criticize you. Let's put our heads together and come up with some really fun ideas to boost your business. See if we can target customers who are already visiting other merchants in the area. That would be a great place to start."

"If you say so." She heaved a little sigh and poured herself some more wine.

"Let's take a look. Maybe there are some possibilities we're missing out on."

I took another deep breath as I scanned the rows of shops lining the street. Business wasn't exactly booming, but there were a few pedestrians out and about. Were they tourists or just residents heading for home? They probably lived in the area, I decided. They were walking quickly, with a sense of purpose, not window-shopping or dawdling.

We were sitting outdoors at an umbrella table, and suddenly I noticed an old-style movie theater directly across the street from us. The marquee advertised a French film I'd never heard of and the movie posters in the display cases looked pretty retro themselves with their faded yellow backgrounds.

"Here's a possibility. Vintage movies, vintage candies," I said, "right in your own backyard. Maybe you could sell bags of candy to people as they head into the movies. What do you think?"

Ali followed my gaze, and a little smile twitched at the corners of her mouth. "Nice try, Taylor, but there aren't any customers. That theater has been closed for thirty years."

She rested her chin on her hand, staring out at the street scene. It was a lovely evening in Savannah, and the air was soft, filled with the intoxicating scent of gardenias.

*Oops.* "I should have noticed the marquee wasn't lit up," I said with a sheepish grin.

"This street is off the main drag and it's not booming with traffic. That's why I got such a good deal from Trent, my landlord. He warned me it would be a challenge to launch a thriving business here, but he figured I could make a go of it. They're always talking about revitalizing this section of town, but nothing ever comes of it."

"I see." I pressed my lips together, wishing I hadn't sounded so judgmental. Ali would have to find her own way in the business world, and maybe the best thing I could do was to cut her some slack. After all, the candy shop was her baby, and I was here as a consultant, not a silent partner or an investor. And more important, I was here as her sister.

"Tell me about your other neighbors on the block," I said, eager to strike a positive note. "The flower shop looks interesting. Do you get much business from their customers?"

I'd spotted a flower market called Petals just a few doors away, and I pictured yuppie types buying fresh blooms and then dashing into Ali's shop for a sugary treat. The shop was older, but neatly maintained with a green canvas awning, a cascade of pink and white petunias tumbling out of matching window boxes, and a stunning violet clematis climbing up a trellis near the front door.

I felt encouraged and immediately wondered if there was any way to attract the Petals customers to Allison's shop. Maybe do some sort of joint promotional effort?

*Flowers and candy.* They were a natural combination. All we had to do was find a way to link these two products together. Holidays would be easy, of course. Everyone loves flowers and candy for Valentine's Day and Mother's Day, but we needed to think big. We needed to focus on a more general promotion, something that could run throughout the year. But what?

"There has to be a way we can capitalize on the flower shop being so close to your store," I said. "At the moment, I'm drawing a blank, but I bet there are loads of possibilities there."

"Don't get your hopes up. I don't think I can get any business from Petals." Ali looked wistful. "Two elderly sisters run the place. They came to the Dream Club last night, the two ladies in the flowered dresses? You probably didn't get a chance to chat with them. Minerva and Rose Harper are very nice but they've got to be in their eighties if they're a day. They mostly do wreaths for funeral homes, and they seem to sell a lot of potted plants."

"That doesn't sound too encouraging," I admitted, playing

with my tossed salad. "And I don't see any customers over there. That's not a good sign, especially on a Friday night."

"I'm sure they do a lot of home deliveries because I see them loading flowers into their van all the time. There's not much foot traffic into the store. Petals has been here forever, and I don't think they even have to advertise. Everyone in the district just knows about them."

"It doesn't sound like a good match for your business, after all," I admitted. A failed movie theater and a flower shop run by geriatric owners. This was going to be a tougher job than I'd thought.

"Anyway, their customers aren't the right people to target for vintage candy," Ali said. "I can't imagine anyone stopping to buy Mallo Cups on their way to a funeral."

"No, I suppose not." I smiled, pleased to see that Ali was at least thinking about coming up with a marketing strategy. "What about the dance studio over there? Look, there's some people going in there right now." Offhand, I couldn't think of how a dance studio could help promote the sale of vintage candy, but I liked to look at all the possibilities.

Ali followed my gaze and her expression hardened. "That's Chico's place. Chico Hernandez. He's offering a special on tango lessons this month, and he's drawing quite a crowd. Mostly women, as you can see."

I took a good look. The doors to the studio were open, and salsa music was pouring into the soft night air. "Tango lessons? That could be interesting. Have you met him? What's he like?"

"Oh, I've met him all right. He's quite the Latin lover," Ali said shortly. "Thinks he's God's gift to women, an Antonio Banderas wanna-be. You know the type."

"Sadly, I do." I took another peek as a darkly handsome man with longish hair and flashing black eyes stepped outside, talking on his cell phone. He was wearing black pants so tight they could have been spray painted on him, along with a white shirt, a black vest, and Cuban heels.

A middle-aged woman brushed by him to enter the studio. We watched as he shoved his cell phone in his pocket, pulled her close to him, and planted a kiss on her cheek. He then executed a few tango steps before bending her backward in a spine-crunchingly low dip. You'd think he was auditioning for *Dancing with the Stars*.

He finished his little performance by pulling her upright and kissing her hand. Ali rolled her eyes, but the bystanders standing on the sidewalk seemed impressed by his impromptu performance and broke into delighted applause.

"That's Chico in action," Ali said with a rueful laugh. "Always on the move, always on the make. And the crowds eat it up."

"Quite the ladies' man."

She nodded, her lips thinning in disapproval. "He tried to hit on me the day I opened the shop. He has a sort of superficial charm, you know."

"Yes, I can see that," I said wryly. His dance partner was giggling like a schoolgirl and blushing furiously as he bowed to her.

"I was crazy enough to go out with him a couple of times until someone told me he has a wife and four kids back in South America, so I ended it. I'm not even sure it was true, but things were headed downhill anyway. That was the last straw." Ali's tone was thoughtful. I wondered if she had actually cared about Chico but was putting on a brave front for me. It's very possible he'd played her, and she'd been hurt by him. My sister's track record with men was as dismal as her success as an entrepreneur.

I chuckled sympathetically. "A wise move." I was helping myself to a slice of mushroom pizza when I heard Ali suck in a quick gulp of air.

"Oh no," she muttered. "Chico's spotted us. And he's crossing the street, heading right this way."

"Maybe he wants one last tango with you," I quipped.

# 5

But Chico seemed to have more in mind than dance steps. He darted nimbly through traffic, leapt over a low concrete planter filled with coral and white petunias at the edge of the curb, and quickly crossed the space between us. He was flashing a thousand-watt smile, playing to the crowd, radiating a kind of rock star cockiness. A group of diners at a nearby table turned to stare at him, and he gave them a jaunty wave, basking in the attention.

"*Mi muchacha querida!*" he cried dramatically when he reached our table, bending to kiss Ali's hand. "It's been so long, I've missed you, I'm desolated without you." He pulled over the extra chair in one swift motion and planted himself on it, his eyes never leaving her face. "I was getting ready to open my studio, and then I saw you sitting here as beautiful as a painting. I couldn't believe my *fortuna*, my luck, and I couldn't wait *un momento mas* to tell you how you make my heart race."

Nothing subtle about Chico. He was laying on the compliments so thick, he could have been using a trowel. I winced, wondering if any woman in her right mind would really fall for his spiel.

Up close, I could see that he was a little older than I'd originally thought, with a few lines around his eyes and a certain softness blurring what was probably once a finely chiseled chin line. I noticed he was wearing a flashy ring with an insignia on it, but no wedding ring. I assumed that was deliberate; appearing single would be good for business.

"How are you doing, Chico?" Ali said evenly. Two little pinpricks of color appeared on her cheeks, the only sign that she was feeling a bit rattled by his attention. He tried to hold her hand, but she pulled it away and wrapped her fingers around her wineglass.

"How am I doing?" he repeated soulfully. "I'm lonely without you, my lovely Ali," he said. He placed his hand over his heart, and his dark eyes flickered to me, shooting me a look that I couldn't begin to decipher. "Who is your bee-oo-tiful *amiga*? Please to introduce us?"

Ali hesitated for a moment, and I saw a shadow of indecision in her eyes. "Chico, this is my sister, Taylor Blake, from Chicago. Taylor, this is Chico Hernandez." She sent him her frostiest stare.

Chico immediately laser-locked me with his sultry gaze. "Taylor, a lovely name for a lovely woman." He leaned across the table and touched me gently under the chin. "I can see very much the family resemblance." I drew back slightly in my chair, shrinking from his touch. A heavy wave of cologne hit me, and I wrinkled my nose, drawing back even farther. He wasn't easily dissuaded and gave a throaty chuckle. "You will be staying long in our city, I am hoping?"

"I'm really not sure," I said vaguely.

"If you need someone to show you the city, I am here for you." He licked his lips, staring at me as if I were a Big Mac and he were a hungry hound. "I can show you things you've never seen before," he said suggestively. I glanced up to see

Ali giving me a delicate eye roll over the rim of her wineglass. I assume this was Chico's standard line when talking to women.

"I'm afraid I don't have much time for sightseeing," I said curtly. I decided it was better to be blunt with the man. It was obvious he wouldn't take a hint; only a verbal two-by-four would put a dent in his gigantic ego.

Chico grinned, reaching for my hand and running his thumb over my palm before I yanked my hand away. "Well, you never know, you may change your mind. And I'll be here, waiting for you." He gave me another soulful look, like a B-list actor in a cheesy Spanish soap, and I bit my lip to keep from laughing.

An awkward silence fell between us, and I noticed a slow flush creeping down Ali's neck. Chico's unwavering gaze and blatant come-on were making both of us uncomfortable. I kept my eyes focused on my quickly cooling slice of pizza, hoping he would get the hint and say *adios*.

"Chico!" a flashy redhead yelled from across the street. I recognized her from the Dream Club meeting. Gina Santiago. Her hair tumbled almost to her waist in soft waves, and she had a knockout figure with curves in all the right places. She was wearing a white ruffly peasant blouse with a full cotton skirt and black strappy dance shoes. "What are you doing over there? Class is starting, everyone is in the studio!" She waved her arm in the air, frowning, pointing to her watch.

"*Un momento, por favor!*" he called to her, holding up an index finger. He turned back to us, his lips tightening into a thin line. "My assistant is driving me crazy," he said with a dismissive wave of his hand. "She lives by the clock; no wonder her husband divorced her. She should be working in a factory, not a dance studio. She does not have the soul of an artist, like you, my beautiful Ali." He gave a short bark of laughter. "But I'm afraid for once she is right. I must take my leave of you ladies. What is it you say in English? Duty screams, or is it duty shouts?"

"Duty calls," I said flatly, willing him to be on his way.

"Ah yes, that is it, duty calls." He stood up slowly, and I quickly grabbed my napkin in case he was going for the fingertip-kissing routine again. "I wish I could join you for dinner, my lovelies, but I'm having a special meal prepared for me later tonight. Veal scallopini, you know it?"

Ali gave a delicate shudder. "I'm a vegetarian, Chico. No meat, no fowl, no fish."

Chico slapped his head. "Ah, *querida*, how could I forget? You don't eat the animals, you eat the tofu and bean sprouts, of course I knew that. I was distracted by looking at you and your *hermana*, so much loveliness at one table."

"Really?" Ali said, barely holding back a snort.

"*Sí!*" Chico replied, bobbing his head up and down. "My mind cannot take in such a sight! It's too much *belleza*, how you say, beauty, for one man to grasp." He slapped his forehead in a spot-on Ricky Ricardo imitation.

"Chico!" the redhead trilled. "We're waiting for you!"

"Coming!" he shouted. He pushed back his chair and jumped to his feet, a scowl marring his handsome face. "Ladies," he said, giving a little bow before darting back across the street.

"Wow. So that's Chico," I said the moment he was out of earshot.

"In the flesh," Ali said wryly. "I think I made a narrow escape when I dumped that guy."

I raised my wineglass and clinked it against hers. "I'll drink to that, sis!"

# 6

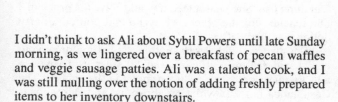

I didn't think to ask Ali about Sybil Powers until late Sunday morning, as we lingered over a breakfast of pecan waffles and veggie sausage patties. Ali was a talented cook, and I was still mulling over the notion of adding freshly prepared items to her inventory downstairs.

I was toying with the idea of serving homemade pastel mints along with gourmet coffee and breakfast sandwiches. Maybe we could even add a few interesting soups and salads to draw in the lunch crowd. I wanted to find recipes that were regional and representative of the Deep South, delectable dishes you wouldn't see anyplace else.

"You didn't happen to mention anything to Sybil about my nightmares, did you, Ali?" I kept my voice deliberately casual. Ali is often impulsive, and I didn't want to lay a guilt trip on her in case she had blurted something out without thinking.

Ali looked up from the Sunday paper, blinking in surprise. "Tell her about your nightmares? Oh, gosh no," she said, looking shocked. "You know I'd never discuss your personal life with anyone, Taylor. And especially not with

Sybil. Everyone in Savannah knows you can't trust that woman not to blab. She has no sense of boundaries, none at all."

"Is that so?" Scout was winding around my bare feet, looking up hopefully for a morsel of veggie sausage. I wasn't even sure if cats could digest soy protein, but the smell clearly had him hooked and he looked as if he were dying to sample it. I broke off a tiny corner of a sausage patty and slipped it to him under the table.

She gave a little snort. "Absolutely. Anything you tell Sybil is all over town by dinnertime. Last week I told her Barney had a hairball, and three people called me up that day with homeopathic remedies for him. One woman even dropped by the store with a little bottle of castor oil flavored with tuna fish. She guaranteed it would solve the problem." She reached for the blueberry syrup and poured a hefty dollop over her waffles.

"I'm glad you didn't say anything about my dreams to her," I said, feeling a little relieved. "It must just have been a lucky guess on her part." It was quiet in the kitchen. The Casablanca fan was whirring above us, and Barney was sleeping on the window ledge of Ali's second-floor apartment. Ali didn't open the shop until the afternoon on Sundays, so we had the early-morning hours to ourselves. I took another look and spotted Barney's catnip mouse nestled between his front paws. Had he found it under the refrigerator as Sybil had suggested?

"What did Sybil tell you? Now you've got me really curious."

"I suppose she was trying to be helpful, but she told me not to let the *nightmares* get to me." I frowned. "That it was unhealthy to block my dreams. I guess she meant well, but the whole conversation was a little disconcerting, that's all. She seemed to know I had a history of bad dreams and that I had them for a reason."

"Wow, that's very weird. Creepy, actually."

"I know," I agreed. "I wasn't sure what to make of it."

Ali poured more coffee for us, my favorite, hazelnut cream. "I don't know how she could have figured this out on her own; it's simply not possible."

"Has she made these sorts of pronouncements before?"

"All the time. I've never really believed this dream-hopping talk of hers, but sometimes she seems to be dead-on in her predictions. She sees things other people don't see. Not just in dreams, but she seems to sense things about people. It's almost like she can look inside their souls and their psyches."

I felt my eyebrows shoot up. "So you think she's psychic."

Ali chuckled. "Well, *she* certainly thinks she is. I don't know what to make of her comments," she added with a little sigh. "But I'm sorry she said that to you. It must have felt a little intrusive, but I guess I shouldn't be surprised. Sybil has never been known for her sensitivity. She's like a bull in a china shop, but you probably figured that out from the way she dominates things at the Dream Club. Along with Dorien, of course."

"The two of them have strong personalities," I murmured. "But maybe that's not a bad thing; they keep the conversation going. And they do have some interesting insights. They came up with some interpretations I never would have thought of."

"I just hope they don't drive new members away," Ali said. "We want to keep the group small, but everyone has such busy schedules these days that I think we could accept a few more members. I like to have at least eight people for the meetings, so we can have plenty of material to cover."

"Do you accept anyone into the group?"

"Pretty much. They have to be recommended by a current member, of course. It's a tight-knit community in Savannah, and most of us who are doing dream work know each other. I like to be careful, though, and I don't want to jeopardize the integrity of the group. I don't want someone to show up one time just out of curiosity and never come back. And I certainly don't want any reporters in the club."

"A smart move," I agreed.

Ali nodded. "We insist on discretion in our group; otherwise people won't feel free to discuss sensitive material. I even ask members to sign confidentiality agreements. They probably wouldn't hold up in court, but it just makes me feel better to have a signed document."

"I can understand that. It sounds like you have a good plan." I was surprised at how thorough Ali had been; it looked like she'd anticipated problems and covered all the bases.

Ali nodded. "My goal is to have a base of a dozen or so regulars with maybe two or three drop-ins. That way I can always be assured of eight people showing up on any given week."

"Was Friday night a pretty typical meeting?"

"I suppose so," Ali said thoughtfully. "No group is perfect, of course. You have to take the good with the bad, and Dorien pretty much hogged the discussion, as usual. Other people might have had different ideas, but everyone is afraid to disagree with her."

"There was Persia and her murder dream," I reminded her.

"Yes, and I wish she hadn't waited until the very last minute to drop the bombshell about that dream. She does that deliberately, I think. Maybe it's a bid for attention, but she always seems to come out with something really spectacular, just as we're getting ready to wrap up the meeting."

"What's your take on Samantha Stiles?" I asked, referring to the young detective, who seemed a bit out of place in the group.

"Oh, Dorien drags Sam to the meetings from time to time," Allison said. "I think Sam is ready to pull her hair out in sheer frustration, but she and Dorien have been friends for years, and I suppose she feels she has to tag along."

"Maybe she'll become a believer."

"I wouldn't count on it. I bet she thinks it's all a sham. I noticed she was interested in Persia's dream, but that's only because she thought an actual crime had taken place. Once she realized it was just a projection, something off in the future, she lost interest pretty quickly."

"I agree. I noticed the same thing."

Ali began to clear the plates away, and I watched as she cut up a veggie sausage patty and dropped it into a food bowl for Scout and Barney. She covered it with plastic wrap and stashed it in the refrigerator for their late-night treat.

"I remember Sam told me once that the police do use psychics occasionally in solving crimes and finding missing persons, but this is different," she continued. "As far as we know, there isn't any crime to solve or mystery to uncover because the whole thing only exists in Persia's dream. There's no evidence it will ever happen."

"Do you really believe all dreams are significant?" I've never really understood Ali's fascination with dreams. I've never looked for any deep psychological significance. I figured they were just a quirk, like a glitch in the brain. I'm content with my life, and I'm certain I don't have any deep dark secrets lying beneath the surface.

"Oh yes, I do," Ali said swiftly. "Our dreams are messages from the subconscious. And even animals dream, did you know that?" She gestured to Barney and Scout, who were now both curled up side by side on the sunny windowsill.

"They look dead to the world," I noted. Neither one of the cats was a barrel of energy, even during their waking hours. And sleeping, they appeared almost comatose, impervious to street noises and music, as they sacked out, motionless, for hours at a time. They reminded me of Gallagher's description of a cat as "a pillow that eats." Only a cat owner could come up with such a colorful phrase.

"A lot of people don't understand about cat dreams," she said seriously, "but an energy healer explained it all to me. A cat's brain is working all the time, processing information and trying to make sense of things. Just like our brains do. They want to make sense of their environment—it's all based on evolution, the survival of the fittest." She paused. "Think about it, Taylor. Thousands of years ago, if you didn't understand the world around you, you could end up as someone's dinner." Barney woke up, raised his head, and shot her a look of pure alarm. "Not you, sweetie," she called out to him.

"Really?" Now my skepticism was kicking in big-time. How could anyone really tell what a cat was thinking? "I wonder what they dream about?" I said carefully. "I can't even hazard a guess."

"Why, they dream about the same things we do. They have likes and dislikes and regrets and plans for the future."

"They do? Plans for the future?" I tried not to smile, picturing Barney signing up for an online MBA course and Scout attending summer tennis camp. "I find that hard to imagine."

"And some of their dreams revolve around fantasies, of course," Ali said, skimming over my objections. "They dream about things they'd like to do, places they'd like to go, people they'd like to meet."

"Is that so?" I poured myself a final cup of coffee before she whisked the pot away.

"Absolutely. I think a lot of cat dreams are based on wish fulfillment. I'd love to know what Barney and Scout dream about," she said wistfully. "If we could just tap into a cat's thoughts, the world would be a better place."

According to Ali, Barney and Scout are not only sensitive souls but excellent judges of character. She believes they can read minds, understand human conversation, and have amazing insights into the world around them.

Glancing at them snoozing away so blissfully, I found that hard to fathom, but who was I to challenge her belief system? If she found comfort thinking that her four-footed friends had paranormal abilities, I wasn't about to take that away from her.

# 7

Allison had warned me that business was usually slow on Sundays. I was helping her unpack a box of root beer barrels when a young woman with high cheekbones and glossy black hair pulled back in pigtails burst into the shop. She was model-thin and wore a tie-dyed shirt and skinny jeans with Teva sandals. Her eyes were a captivating river green, and her grin was infectious.

"Sorry I'm late," she called to Ali before zipping back to the lounge area. "I'll just grab some sweet tea and then I'll get right to work in the storeroom, I promise!"

"Take your time, Dana," Ali called. "There's not much to unpack, we're still waiting for those black licorice ropes to come in. I may put out some cherry Twizzlers instead. They're not exactly vintage, but everyone likes them." Ali turned to me. "Dana Garrett, my new assistant," she said in a low voice. "She's a criminal justice major at the university, and she helps me out a few hours a week. She's doing a minor in marketing, and she'll get credit for her work here, if I write an evaluation for her professor after six weeks."

"Really? She doesn't look the criminal justice type. I would have figured her for an arts major."

"She'd like to be. Her family insisted she study something practical, but she's an artist at heart." Ali's lips curved into the briefest of smiles. "I feel a little guilty, because I never seem to have any interesting jobs for her." She paused. "Maybe she could help you with some marketing projects? At least marketing would be related to her minor, and she wouldn't be stuck in the backroom doing inventory. You wouldn't mind, would you? She's really nice and she's willing to learn."

"I wouldn't mind at all. I'll come up with something," I said, just as a group of tourists wandered in. "The more the merrier. It's always good to brainstorm ideas."

As I watched Dana waiting on customers later that afternoon, I discovered that she was just as pleasant and enthusiastic as Ali had told me, and I vowed to come up with a project for her.

It was six thirty when we finally closed up the shop and retired upstairs. Ali had made a roasted veggie tray and I was spooning out whole wheat couscous onto our dinner plates when the doorbell rang downstairs. Both Barney and Scout woke up instantly and jumped out of their cat bed, landing nimbly onto the floor, their ears standing up at attention, their dark eyes flashing.

Barney's tail was fluffed out, and I thought I heard Scout growling softly in her throat. Did they suspect intruders? I was surprised they were so jumpy because they seemed accustomed to the constant comings and goings downstairs.

"Another tour bus?" I asked.

Ali shook her head and peeled off her oven mitts. "I don't think so. I've got the CLOSED sign up." She waved a hand at the dinner plates. "You go ahead and start. I'll get rid of whoever it is. I'll be back in a sec."

Almost immediately, Allison came back upstairs and

darted into the kitchen with a red-haired woman trailing after her. "Taylor," Allison said breathlessly, "you remember Gina from the dance studio and the Dream Club?" I certainly did remember. Chico's glamorous assistant. Ali turned to Gina. "My sister, Taylor. You met each other at the Friday night meeting, right?"

Gina nodded and gave me the once-over. "We sat across from each other," she said coolly.

She was wearing a skin-tight black spandex top with a flowing red and black skirt. Her flaming red hair was done up in a loose bun, with tendrils framing her face. She was really quite attractive in spite of the fact that her perfect features were twisted into a scowl and she was popping gum like a teenager.

"Hi." I nodded politely as Ali riffled through a drawer in the kitchen. Gina drummed her fingers on the tiled countertop, her lips pressed together. "Can I help you find something?" I asked Ali after a long moment had passed.

"Gina needs a key to the dance studio, and I know it's in here somewhere," Ali explained. She flashed an apologetic smile at Gina. "I'm chronically disorganized, I'm afraid. This is my junk drawer. Well, it's one of my junk drawers," she amended.

She wrenched the drawer out and dumped the entire contents on the countertop. "Chico gave me a set of keys for emergencies last year," she went on. I raised my eyebrows and she added quickly, "We decided to exchange keys because there was heavy flooding in the district after a storm. I don't think I ever returned the key to him." Her mouth curved in an ironic smile. "Sorry to keep you waiting, Gina. I'm an inch away from being a hoarder."

"No problem," Gina said, cooling down a little and looking around the kitchen. "I should have brought my own keys. I took the kids out for ice cream this afternoon, and I left my house in a rush."

"So you hold dance classes on Sunday?" I asked, just

making conversation. I could see Ali had no luck with the first drawer and now was scrabbling through a second drawer, pulling out a collection of pens, pencils, and sticky notes. Barney and Scout ambled into the kitchen, watching her with interest. I wondered what they found so fascinating and then remembered that Ali kept their catnip in that drawer.

"We just started offering Sunday classes," Gina said, looking supremely bored. "It's an experiment. Chico wants to bring in more working people, and we figured Sunday might draw in some new students. Saturdays aren't so good because everyone's running around shopping and doing errands."

"Got it!" Ali said, holding up a key ring. She passed it to Gina, who nodded her thanks. "The square one's for the front door, and the pointy one is for the back. If you're going in the front door, though, you have to jiggle the handle a little to the left, or it sticks and the lock won't turn."

"Okay, thanks, I'll remember. And I'll bring it right back," Gina said. "I don't know why Chico didn't answer the door, his car's parked behind the studio. He must have walked into town on an errand and he's running late as usual," she huffed. "Once he gets talking, there's no stopping him. Nice to see you again, Taylor."

"Gina, please tell Chico to keep the keys." Ali spoke quickly but Gina was already down the stairs, her dance shoes tapping a noisy staccato on the bare wooden steps.

"How long has she worked for him?" I asked when we finally settled down to our dinner.

"A few years, I think." Ali wrinkled her forehead in concentration. "There's the usual gossip about them. You know, the studly dance instructor and his voluptuous partner, but I don't think there's anything to it. Gina seems really devoted to her kids. Frankly, I don't know how she stands working for him. I guess the secret is that she doesn't put up with any nonsense. He can be a pretty irritating guy with that Latin lover act."

I nodded. "I saw him in action at Luigi's. I suppose he comes on to any female within a hundred miles. Hard to believe that women fall for that, but maybe some do—" I broke off abruptly as Barney and Scout ran under the coffee table doing their hellcat imitation, hissing and spitting, their thick fur coats standing on end.

"What in the world's wrong with you two?" Ali said, shaking her head. "I was going to give you a tiny bit of vanilla ice cream tonight, but if you can't behave yourselves . . ." Her voice trailed off as we heard a furious pounding on the front door of the floor below.

"I'll go," I offered. "I'm closer."

"Maybe it's Gina and the key didn't work," Ali said. "Tell her to come up and have a glass of wine with us. Chico will turn up eventually. They certainly can't start without him." It was Gina but I knew immediately she wasn't worried about the key. I opened the front door to find her white-faced, trembling, and crying uncontrollably as she fell into my arms.

"Taylor, come quick," she said, sobbing. "And get Ali. Something terrible has happened."

"Gina, what's wrong?" I asked, pushing her gently away and holding her by the shoulders. "Do you want to come upstairs and sit down? You're shaking like a leaf."

She was so pale, I was afraid she might faint right on the spot, and I tried to edge her toward a bench by the front door. She wriggled out of my grasp and started twisting her hands together like she was wringing out a towel. I was struck by the anguish in her dark eyes, and I knew that whatever had happened, it had shaken her to the core.

She shook her head violently. "No, there's no time to sit down. Just call nine-one-one. Please, do it now."

"What's this all about?" Ali said sharply. I had been so focused on Gina, I hadn't even heard Ali slip down the stairs behind me. "Gina, what's going on? Tell us right this minute."

"It's Chico," Gina gasped, gesturing to the studio across the street. I could see that the front door to the dance studio was wide open, and music was pouring into the street.

"What about Chico?" Ali demanded. "Gina, please! Pull yourself together. You're frightening me."

Gina swallowed and closed her eyes tightly, her lips quivering. Then she opened her eyes and tugged at my hand. "Come, come right now!" she rasped. "There's no time to waste. He's . . . he's on the floor and he's not moving." She drew in a long, shuddering breath, her voice catching in her throat. "I think he's dead."

# 8

"If something's happened in the studio, we can't go in there," I said automatically. *It could be a crime scene*, I thought, my heart hammering in my chest. The three of us had raced across the street and were peering through the open door into the studio. I noticed that Ali had pulled out her cell phone and was already punching in some numbers.

"But what if he's not dead?" Gina whispered. She was white as a corpse, and her voice was low and shaky. She swayed a little on her feet. "What if he needs medical attention right this minute? He's all alone in there. I was afraid to turn him over. I didn't even touch him."

"It's okay, they're sending paramedics," Ali said, finishing her conversation and snapping the phone shut. I noticed her face was pale, her lips drawn into a thin line. "The ambulance should be here in a couple of minutes; the station is right around the corner." She looked at me and lifted her eyebrows. "The police are coming, too."

I nodded as she peered past Gina to the prone body of Chico. He was lying on his side next to a low sofa in the reception area of the studio. I've always wondered what people meant when they said someone looked "deathly still," and now I knew. Chico resembled a mannequin, his eyes closed and his chest absolutely motionless. There was no doubt about it; Chico had danced his last tango. He no longer was sporting a George Hamilton tan, and his skin had already acquired an unhealthy grayish tinge. His features had lost that finely chiseled look, and his face had a slack expression. I could see china plates and serving dishes as if he had been struck down while eating dinner. Latin music was playing, the upbeat sound at odds with the grim scene before me.

"How could this happen?" Gina wailed. She looked at her watch, shaking her head. "The students will be turning up any minute, and what will I tell them? It's too late for me to call for a substitute teacher."

Ali and I exchanged a look. It was an odd thing to say under the circumstances, but shock does funny things to people and I decided not to read too much into it.

"Gina," Ali said gently, "try to calm down. Listen to me. There won't be any classes tonight. They'll take Chico"—she paused, glancing at the prone figure—"away, and then we can put up a notice that classes are canceled for this evening."

"Yes, you're right, what am I thinking?" Gina asked with a catch in her throat. "Of course there won't be class tonight. You must think I'm crazy—"

"Not at all," Ali said soothingly. She put her arm around Gina's thin shoulders. "It must have been quite a shock to you, finding him like that." Gina was staring at Ali with a dazed expression, her eyes blank. Ali added in a soft voice, "You can come over to our place and have a nice cup of tea and get your bearings."

*Really? She's inviting her upstairs for a nice chat over a cup of tea? This is insane.* If Chico was as dead as he looked, Gina wouldn't have time for tea because the cops would want to interview her immediately at the scene. I decided not to mention this fact, and a couple of minutes later, I heard the ambulance tearing around the corner, sirens blaring.

The paramedics double-parked in the narrow street, unloaded their equipment, and took off at a fast clip into the dance studio. Gina, Ali, and I stood awkwardly on the sidewalk, watching through the open doorway as two female paramedics, one young and blond, the other dark-haired and middle-aged, wordlessly knelt beside Chico. They moved quickly and efficiently, flipping Chico onto his back. One slapped a blood pressure cuff on him while the other checked for a pulse at his throat.

My stomach clenched as one of the paramedics shone a penlight into Chico's eyes and slowly shook her head. She sat back on her heels for a moment, exchanging a look with her partner, her expression grim.

They rose slowly to their feet. "Are you family members?" the young blond paramedic asked in a low voice.

"We're neighbors," I said, surprised that my voice was shaky. I thought I had my emotions under control, but the gravity of the situation suddenly hit me and I felt light-headed.

"You discovered him?" the older paramedic asked.

I hesitated. "Yes," I said. Not exactly true, but I wasn't sure if Gina was up to answering any questions. The blood had drained from her face, and she'd wobbled over to the curb, sitting with her head in her hands.

"I'm the one who called it in," Ali volunteered. She was standing over Gina with her hand resting protectively on her shoulder.

"The police will want to interview you," the older paramedic said, making her way toward us. She looked bone-tired and eager to be on her way. I wondered how emergency workers managed to deal with crisis after crisis and maintain their emotional equilibrium.

"They're here," Ali said quietly. Two squad cars pulled

up fast with lights flashing, and I watched as Samantha Stiles jumped out and headed for the studio. She nodded at us, her gaze sweeping over Gina sitting on the curb. Sam gave me a questioning look, and when I shrugged, she made a sharp gesture with her fingers splayed.

"All of you, stay right here." She was obviously the incident commander and spoke with quiet authority to three uniformed officers who accompanied her. "The ME's on her way. Nobody in or out until she gives the okay." She stepped into the studio and approached the paramedics, who were packing up their equipment. "What do we have here?" she said, indicating the prone Chico. "Any idea on time of death?" I knew the medical examiner would have the final word on this, but I suppose she wanted a rough estimate.

"We got the call eighteen minutes ago," one of the paramedics told her, consulting her clipboard. She turned away from the doorway and I caught the words "dead for some time" and "rigor has set in." I cringed and took a deep breath, determined to hold it together. Gina was crying softly to herself, and I wondered if it was the result of shock, or if she was genuinely upset at Chico's death.

A small crowd had gathered on the sidewalk, and one of the uniformed officers pushed everyone back when the coroner's van arrived a couple of minutes later. "Nothing to see here, folks, nothing to see," he said, which didn't help to dispel their curiosity.

Dr. Ranklin, a petite woman with sharp features, emerged from the van and snapped on a pair of surgical gloves. She walked into the dance studio, pulling the door closed behind her. Now the gawkers turned their attention to the tearstained Gina, sitting unhappily at the curb, just as another wave of dizziness hit me.

"We're going across the street," I said to the nearest officer, who barely looked old enough to shave. I tried to put a little steel in my voice even though I was feeling shaky. "My sister's shop is right there, and we live above it."

"Ma'am," he began uncertainly, "I think Detective Stiles wants you to remain here—"

"My friend is ill," I cut in firmly. "Detective Stiles knows where we live, and she can interview us the moment she comes out." I pointed to Oldies but Goodies for emphasis. "See, we're just across the street. We'll wait for her inside."

Before he could raise another objection, I walked over to Gina, grasped her by the elbow, and briskly pulled her to her feet. "Let's get her inside," I said to Ali, who had tucked her arm around Gina's waist. "Something hot to drink will work wonders for all of us." A good shot of brandy might have been a better choice, but I felt uncomfortable suggesting it, with the young officer listening to my every word.

"Sit," I ordered Gina the moment we were upstairs. The color was slowly coming back to her face, but her features were haggard and drawn.

"Shall I make her some herb tea?" Ali asked, fluttering around. She began pulling strange-smelling teas from the cabinet and piling them on the kitchen table. She's fond of teas I've never heard of, made from exotic herbs and vegetables. Some of them are appealing, but others smell like dirty feet, and I knew Gina needed caffeine in her system.

I studied Gina, who was motionless, her hands resting in her lap, staring blankly at the gingham tablecloth. "Forget the herb tea, I think she needs some strong espresso." Ali raised a questioning eyebrow at me. "I bought some; it's on the top shelf."

Ali made a little moue of disapproval, but began brewing the espresso. In a few moments, a lovely fragrance filled the kitchen. She pulled out a pan of strudel that was homemade from Granny Smith apples and cut generous wedges.

"Eat, Gina," I said, pushing a plate and fork toward her. She held up a hand in protest, but I ignored her. "Sugar, you need sugar," I insisted. "Just have a few bites if that's all you can manage."

I poured her a cup of steaming espresso and she accepted

it gratefully. No one said anything for a few minutes as we sat at the table, lost in our own thoughts, listening to the commotion outside. I noticed that Barney and Scout were awake and alert, ears forward, balancing on the window ledge, watching the scene below.

I expected Sam Stiles to burst in on us at any moment, and I wanted Gina to have a few minutes to pull herself together. My own heart rate had slowed and I was feeling calmer. Just as well because I knew Sam would be in full detective mode when she confronted us, and friend or not, we'd have to be on our toes.

# 9

"Tell me exactly what happened," Sam said minutes later. She was slightly breathless, and her face was flushed after rushing up the stairs from the shop. She sank into one of the ladderback chairs around the kitchen table and waved away the coffee and pastry. "I told Bates to keep you at the studio," she said peevishly. "I'm going to have to have a word with him. He never should have let a material witness exit a potential crime scene." She tsk-tsked to herself, whipped out a notebook and pen, all set to take our statements.

"Gina wasn't well," I pointed out. "Surely you saw her sitting on the curb. She might have been in shock, and I was worried about her health. I thought it was more appropriate to bring her inside."

Sam flashed me a steely look, not prepared to be conciliatory. "Be that as it may, we have certain protocols for these situations. Normally the three of you would be separated, and you would each give your own statement. Witnesses are interviewed independently. That's one of the first rules of investigation."

Her eyes bore into mine, and she waited a moment for

that to sink in. I knew where she was heading. She was annoyed that all three of us had had time to talk to each other and maybe even be in collusion, providing alibis for each other. But we were friends, weren't we? If Chico was the victim of foul play—and I still wasn't sure that was the case—she didn't suspect us, did she?

"Since it's too late for separate statements"—she heaved a sigh—"I'll interview you all together right now."

I spread my hands in a gesture of apology. "I'm sorry if we caused any problems for you, Sam. I'm the one who insisted that Gina come upstairs. It seemed like the sensible thing to do."

She nodded briefly and turned to Gina. "You're the one who found the body. Why don't you walk me through it. What were you doing at the studio today?"

Gina took a deep breath and related how she'd come over to borrow the key and Sam interrupted her. "Ali, you had a key to the studio? That seems odd. How come you had a key and Gina didn't?"

Ali flushed. Her brow furrowed as she considered the question. "Chico and I exchanged keys just in case of emergency. You know, in case there was flooding or a fire or . . . something. In either one of our buildings, I mean . . ." Her voice trailed off and she gave a little helpless wave of her hand.

"We tried to look out for each other."

Sam was eyeing her coolly, as if she didn't believe a word of it. "So Ali, you had a key for"—Sam paused—"emergencies, and Gina, who worked at the studio every day, didn't have her own key." She arched her eyebrows suspiciously.

"I did have my own key a long time ago," Gina said sullenly. "One day Chico forgot his key and borrowed mine. He never gave it back. It wasn't a big deal. He was at the studio night and day; it was his whole life. That's how I knew something was wrong when he didn't let me in." The last words ended in a sob, and she raised a napkin to her eyes.

"So tell me what happened next," Sam pressed on.

Gina continued her story, and I placed the espresso pot on the table. This time Sam accepted a cup and nodded her thanks. Her fingers were flying as she recorded Gina's words in her notebook.

"I'm a little puzzled about something. Gina, you were the one to discover the body, right?" she asked, frowning. "But why did the paramedic tell me Taylor was the first one to find him?"

I gave a dismissive little grunt. "A miscommunication. All of us were peering inside the studio at"—I paused—"Chico." It seemed strange to say "the body."

"But Gina is the only one who actually entered the studio, is that correct?" Sam waited for affirmation and then scribbled some more.

"Do they know what happened to him?" Ali blurted out. She'd been quiet during the entire interrogation, and I wondered where her thoughts were taking her. "You said it was a *potential* crime scene, so does that mean you suspect murder?" Her voice wobbled on the last word.

"I'm not at liberty to say," Sam said, her expression closed, her voice flat. She was all business. "At the moment, we're calling it a suspicious death. That's as much as I can tell you right now. Once we get the ME's report, I'll have more information."

After a few perfunctory questions, Sam decided she had enough to write a preliminary report and stood up. "I'm sure we'll have more questions for all of you," she said. "If anything else comes to mind, any detail, no matter how small, I want you to call me immediately."

We nodded, struck by her solemn tone. This was the first time any of us had seen Sam in action as a Savannah PD detective, and she was impressive. Cool, methodical, and deliberate in her questioning, with a steady gaze and no-nonsense style that guaranteed compliance.

I stood up to walk her downstairs, and she surprised me

by turning to ask one more question. "Does anyone know if Chico had family? A next of kin?" She directed her question to all of us, but I suspected that she was really interested in what Gina would say. Gina steadfastly kept her head down, staring at her plate.

"He mentioned a wife, or maybe an ex-wife back in Colombia," Ali said slowly. "But I don't have the name or any contact information."

"He told you he had a wife?" Sam quirked an eyebrow. Her tone was incredulous. From what I knew of Chico's philandering habits, this seemed totally out of character. I just didn't picture him as a family man.

"No, Chico didn't mention it," Ali said quickly. "Someone else must have told me, but I can't remember who."

"If you think of it, let me know." She snapped her notebook shut and glanced around the table. "I'll let myself out, ladies."

I returned to the kitchen table, and for a moment, we were silent. Gina seemed to have gotten a grip on her emotions and thanked us for looking after her. Ali gave her a quick hug and promised to check in on her later tonight. She asked if Gina would like to stay for dinner but she declined. She said she was exhausted and was eager to go home and take a nap.

"I don't think they'll let me back in the studio to check the computer, will they? I could call the students," Gina offered.

"I'm sure they won't," I said, shaking my head. "But you don't have to worry about that. There will probably be something in tomorrow's paper," I added, "so everyone will know that classes are canceled."

"Yes, of course, I should have thought of that. My brain isn't working today." Gina gave a wan smile and hesitated. "Are they still there?" she asked softly. "The police?" I knew she didn't want to see the coroner's van or, worse, Chico's body lying on a gurney.

"I think they left," I said, walking to the window. Barney and Scout had lost interest in the scene below, and sure enough, the street was empty. "All clear," I told Gina, and she headed down the stairs.

I heaved a sigh when Ali and I were finally alone in the kitchen. Barney seemed to sense my mood and circled around my feet for a moment before jumping into my lap. He nuzzled the top of his head against my hand, giving tiny meows encouraging me to pet him. "I think this calls for something stronger than espresso," I said ruefully.

Ali opened the fridge and poured us both hefty glasses of white wine. "You know what I think we should do tonight?" she asked. Her brow was furrowed, her expression pensive.

My mind went blank for a moment. I felt bone-tired, and all I wanted to do was melt into the couch and have a quiet evening. But people deal with stress in different ways, and maybe Ali needed a distraction. "I hadn't planned on going out, but we could grab some dinner or take in a movie, if that's what you want."

She shook her head and reached for the phone. "Dinner and a movie? Heavens, no, we don't have time for anything like that. We have work to do."

I glanced up as Scout settled companionably on the chair next to me and began grooming himself. "What did you have in mind?"

"We need answers, Taylor," she said, and I could feel the tension in her voice. "We have to call an emergency meeting of the Dream Club." She gave me a sharp look as if I was going to disagree with her, and I raised my hands, palms up.

"Whatever you want, Ali."

She nodded, tilting her chin resolutely. "I'll make the calls right now."

# 10

"Don't you think we should have invited Gina?" Lucinda asked, her face clouded with worry. "She's going to wonder why she wasn't included, and I think she needs us now more than ever."

"This is a time to be surrounded by friends," Dorien Myers agreed. "I can only imagine how shocked and upset she must be."

"It's better to let her rest," Ali said firmly. "I did try to call her, but it went right to voice mail. She looked absolutely shattered when she left here, and I'm sure she's turned her phone off for tonight. We can fill her in on everything tomorrow morning."

Ali had pulled herself together very quickly after the shock of Chico's death just a few hours earlier. I must admit, I was impressed by my kid sister. She appeared to be a lot stronger and more resilient than I'd realized.

She'd pulled out half a dozen casserole dishes from the freezer and had put together a quick supper for the Dream Club members. She'd managed to assemble everyone except Gina and Sam Stiles, and we all gathered in the cozy living room with the shuttered blinds open to the evening air. A fragrant breeze wafted in from the street, and a Mozart concerto was playing softly in the background.

"I don't know how you managed to do all this," Persia said, taking in the cheerful blue and yellow gingham tablecloth and matching napkins. I'd set the table buffet style with bright blue Fiesta ware and poured white wine for everyone. "Especially in light of what's happened, Ali." Persia went on, "After all, you were very close to Chico, weren't you, Ali?" She kept her tone level, but the slight emphasis on the word "close" made me think she was making an effort to be discreet. Southern towns are rife with gossip, and Savannah is no exception.

"Well, of course—we were neighbors," Ali cut in. "Everyone on the street is going to be upset by the news." She glanced at Minerva and Rose Harper, the elderly sisters who ran the flower shop. "You probably knew Chico longer than anyone." I remembered Ali telling me that the Harper sisters and their flower shop had been a fixture in the district for nearly half a century.

"Oh my yes," Minerva said, scooping up a portion of green beans and toasted almonds. "I was surprised when he first moved in. I never thought he'd get much of a following in this neighborhood, but he proved me wrong. Women took to him, you know."

"Like bees to honey," Rose piped up. "How did you get all this food together, Ali? This macaroni and cheese is absolutely delicious. It's better than the one I make."

"It has three different kinds of cheeses," Ali said absently. "That's the secret. And I add a touch of white wine. I'll write the recipe down for you." I noticed Ali had taken a tiny portion of salad greens, but hadn't touched any of the casseroles.

I had no idea the freezer was so well stocked with homemade delicacies, and was amazed when she'd pulled out an enchilada casserole, an artichoke and Gruyère mixture with wild rice, and an amazing roasted vegetable curry.

It was obvious to me that Ali's talent for cooking would be a tremendous asset to the vintage candy shop, and she should be serving light meals and snacks to her customers. I resolved to bring the issue up again once things had settled down with the investigation. This was no time to talk business; everyone's mind was on Chico.

We spent a few minutes talking about being interviewed by Sam, and then Persia jumped in. "You do remember my dream, don't you?" she asked, looking around the group. "It was prophetic, wasn't it?" she said, raising her eyebrows in a V.

"Tell me again," Lucinda said, leaning forward. "You saw a dark-haired man, and there was some loud Latin music playing in the background."

"Exactly," Persia said, giving a smile like the Cheshire cat. "It all fits, you see. The man, the music, and in my dream, the door was open to the street." She widened her eyes and tossed me a meaningful look like someone in a soap opera. "That's precisely what you discovered when the two of you rushed over to the studio, wasn't it? The door was open to the street, and you could see inside?"

"Yes, that's what happened," Ali said, pressing her lips together for a moment. "We could see Chico lying inside and music was blaring away, the salsa numbers he uses for his dance classes. He was lying there still, so still." She winced at the memory, and her voice wobbled a little. Ali had always insisted her relationship with Chico had been casual, yet she was having a hard time dealing with his death, and trying not to show it.

"But there were other points of comparison, isn't that right, dear?" Persia went on. "Maybe you overlooked some elements that are less obvious. Do you remember what I said about the wolves?"

"The wolves?" I asked. I refilled everyone's glasses and

sat down again. Almost everyone was having wine except the Harper sisters. They'd asked for sweet tea, and I'd put a large, cut-glass pitcher on the coffee table.

"Yes, Taylor, the wolves," she said with a touch of impatience. "I saw a pack of wolves circling the man in the dream. They looked menacing, almost bloodthirsty, and their fur was tinged with red. She gave an involuntary little shudder and clasped her hands together in her lap.

"What do you suppose that means?" Sybil asked.

"The presence of the wolves in Persia's dream must have been symbolic," Ali said slowly. "One interpretation is that the wolves represent people who posed a threat to Chico."

Dorien cleared her throat. "Well," she began, "not to speak ill of the dead, but let's face it, ladies, there were plenty of people who wanted to get rid of Chico." She looked around the group as if daring anyone to disagree with her. "They wouldn't be too upset if a pack of wolves had chomped him to death. They'd probably figure he had it coming." She seemed to take a grim relish in the image of Chico being dismembered, and I wondered if she had a particular ax to grind with the dead dance instructor.

"Oh, I wouldn't go so far as to say that," Lucinda said, twin spots of color popping up on her cheeks. "I mean, Chico had his faults, bless his heart, but I don't think anyone really wanted to see him dead. He tried his best, but he was always an outsider here, bless his heart."

Her remark was met with stony silence, and I had to bite back a smile. Whenever a Southerner says "bless his heart," it's usually code for "I'd like to wring his neck."

"There was always something a little off about him, you know?" Persia offered. "Not that he didn't have a certain charm, but he wasn't quite up to snuff."

Sybil blew out a little breath. "Tell us more about your dream, Persia. Anything else you can remember about the wolves?"

"Just that they were circling around a campfire," Persia

said, squinting her eyes. "There was a sort of red haze around them. I remember bright red flames shooting up in the air. The whole scene took on a fiery aura. I could almost feel the heat; it was overwhelming."

"I remember you mentioning the flames, Persia," I offered.

"Fire is an important element in dream work," Ali said. "It's open to interpretation, but it can mean passion, love, or danger."

*That's the trouble with dream interpretation*, I thought. *There are just too many possible explanations. It was all beginning to sound like smoke and mirrors to me, and the truth was hidden under too many layers of camouflage.*

"Fire can also mean something more sinister; it can represent evil," Dorien said firmly. "Think of hellfire. Nothing glamorous about that." She pressed her lips tightly together and sat back with a satisfied smile.

We were all silent for a moment. Ali got up to serve raspberry cobbler—another freezer find—when Persia snapped her fingers. "I just thought of something else, ladies." She paused dramatically, waiting until she had everyone's attention. "The dinner, remember? In my dream, the dark-haired man was surrounded by the remains of a dinner service. There was fine china and crystal. I couldn't tell if it was a private dinner at home or in a restaurant or hotel. But he was definitely in the middle of dinner when he was struck down."

I heard a clatter of silverware and realized Ali had dropped all the dessert forks she was carrying onto the tile floor. "Sorry," she said, scooping them up. "How clumsy of me. I'll be right back with some more."

"Let us help you, dear," Lucinda said, springing into action. "I'll make coffee if you want to slice the cobbler, Taylor."

"I'll do that," I said, reaching for the glass dessert plates that had belonged to my grandmother. I hadn't thought Ali was sentimental, but she'd chosen a few things from the house when my grandmother passed away a couple of years earlier.

"Fresh raspberry cobbler," Persia gushed. "With such a flaky homemade crust. I could practically swoon over it. Your sister is a wonderful cook, Taylor."

"Yes, she is," I said, forcing myself to smile. My thoughts were a million miles away from raspberry cobbler, though, because I'd just remembered something. When I'd glanced into the open door of the studio, Chico had been surrounded by china and cutlery. The whole image registered in my mind like a freeze-frame in a film. The dishes, the glasses, the napkins. And of course, poor Chico lying dead on the floor while the music played on.

Just like in Persia's dream.

Finally, we seemed to have exhausted the subject of Chico and his untimely death, and everyone except Ali tucked into dessert. She seemed pensive, gazing out the windows to the street now and then, a sad look flitting across her face.

When Rose and Minerva stood up to take their leave shortly after, it seemed to put an unofficial end to the evening. Lucinda and Dorien gathered up their things, and Sybil gave Ali a quick hug. We were just about to make our way downstairs when Persia announced, "Before we split up, ladies, I have a very important request. There's something I need each of you to do tonight." Everyone stopped in their tracks to listen. Persia has a forceful personality and a rather commanding presence.

"What is it, dear?" Minerva Harper asked. She stood next to her sister, resting her hand lightly on top of the sofa for support.

"I want everyone to dream about Chico tonight," Persia said. Her gaze moved slowly over all of us gathered at the top of the stairs.

"What?" Lucinda blurted out. "How in the world would

we do that? I can't control my dreams, no matter how hard I try, and I'm sure no one else can, either." I remembered Lucinda's embarrassment when she dreamt she'd been strolling down the produce aisle at Publix, stark naked.

Persia smiled. "Think about him right before you go to sleep. Get an image in your mind of him in the studio, exactly as Ali and Taylor described him. I believe in the collective power of dreams." She paused. "And in the power of suggestion. The mind is always open to instructions from us. Sometimes we fail to take the reins, and we miss a valuable opportunity."

"I'm not sure I can make myself dream about the man," Dorien said snippily. "It's not like I really knew him, after all."

"You don't have to *make* yourself dream about him, Dorien," Persia retorted. "You can *encourage* yourself to dream about him. The mind is a marvelous creation, you know." I heard Dorien, who was standing behind me, give out a little sigh. She was obviously eager to be on her way and didn't feel like listening to a lecture on dream work from Persia.

Persia, while well meaning, does tend to adopt a professorial tone from time to time, and I hoped she would keep her explanation brief.

"So you're saying that if we think about Chico, we can encourage ourselves to dream about him?" I asked, hoping to hurry her along. "That's really all we have to do?"

"Yes, that's exactly it," Persia said approvingly. "Just give your subconscious free rein, and you might be surprised where it takes you. Your mind might go down some interesting pathways and come up with images and themes that will surprise you. I suggest we all give ourselves an opportunity to dream about what we learned here tonight, and meet again midweek for another discussion."

"That's sounds wonderful," Minerva said, clutching the banister and making her way slowly down the stairs. She turned to Ali and patted her hand. "Thank you for the delicious dinner, Ali. I enjoyed every single bite of it. Next week, Rose and I will bring the sweets; you've been doing far too much work." She smiled warmly at my sister. "We'd like to lend a hand."

# 11

"I'm exhausted," Ali said the moment everyone left. Her skin had turned as white as a kabuki player's face, and my heart went out to her as she curled up on one end of the sofa. She suddenly looked very young and vulnerable as she twisted a lock of pale blond hair around her finger, staring blankly at the carpet. Barney and Scout immediately jumped down from their perch on the window seat and snuggled close to her. They seemed to sense she needed the comfort of their warm, furry little bodies, and she kissed the top of Barney's head.

"Would you like me to get you anything? Maybe some hot chocolate?" I remembered all our late-night talks growing up. We'd sit at the kitchen table and drink hot chocolate while we talked about whatever was troubling her, whether it was boys or history class.

"I'll be okay," she said, smiling her thanks. "I just need some time to get a grip on what's happened. I thought I was dealing with it pretty well, but—" She broke off suddenly, and her voice caught in her throat. "Sorry," she said after a moment. "I'll be okay tomorrow, I promise."

"You don't have to put on a brave face for me," I told her. "This has been a huge shock, and it's going to take time to process it." I hesitated. "Part of the problem is that we don't really know what happened."

"I know," she said miserably. "I'd feel better if it was some kind of an accident. I hate to think that someone actually wanted to kill Chico." She shivered as if a chill had gone through her. "But it looks like that could be the case, doesn't it?" She let her blue-eyed gaze settle on me, and I could see she was holding back tears.

"I'm afraid so," I said gently. "Maybe Sam will have some answers for us soon." I struggled for something reassuring to say and came up empty-handed.

I wondered if Ali would ever find "closure," even if it turned out that Chico had died of natural causes. Sudden death—especially in someone so young—is always a shock. It seems to go against the natural order of things and makes us question basic tenets we always took for granted.

It also brings us smack up against our own mortality.

"Do you mind if I turn in?" Ali said suddenly, swinging her feet to the floor and gathering the hand-crocheted throw around her like a shawl.

"No, of course not, but do you think you'll be able to sleep?" I had assumed Ali would want to sit up for a while and might enjoy some company. I felt a little pang of guilt when I realized I didn't know my sister as well as I thought, and time and distance had created a gulf between us. I couldn't seem to find the right words to say to her when she was obviously in pain.

"I doubt it," she said, giving a sad little smile. "But I think I might just rest a bit and listen to music. I'll take these guys with me." Barney and Scout seemed to understand they were being invited into the bedroom. They immediately jumped off the sofa and scampered down the hallway to Ali's room. "See you in the morning," she said softly.

I settled back at the kitchen table and decided to have

another sliver of cobbler with a cup of coffee before turning in. For some reason, caffeine seems to soothe me, even though it's supposed to cause a boost of adrenaline. There's something comforting about holding the warm cup in my hands and breathing in the delightful fragrance of hazelnut or vanilla bean. I'd just finished brewing the coffee when the phone rang. I snatched it off the hook almost immediately. There was always the chance that Ali had fallen asleep and I didn't want her to be disturbed.

"Hope this isn't too late to call." Persia's voice came racing over the line. "I thought of something I need to run by you."

"Go ahead," I said, trying to put a little enthusiasm into my voice. I didn't feel like rehashing the meeting of the Dream Club, but I didn't want to be rude to Persia, who sounded like she was ready for a chat. "What's up?"

"Well, I've been mulling over the imagery in my dream about the dark-haired man," she began. "And I think something stands out. We talked about evil and danger, but we didn't even touch on the jealousy angle. That could be crucial to solving the case."

"Jealousy?" I sneaked a little bite of cobbler in my mouth and tried to chew quietly.

"Yes, remember how prominent the red imagery was in the dream? The color red can signify jealousy, you know. I wondered if Chico could have been involved in some sort of love triangle?"

"A love triangle? I haven't heard anything like that, but I suppose Sam will have to delve into all his relationships, if he really was murdered."

She pondered that for a moment, and I had the feeling she was looking for something more gossip-worthy, probably some spicy details about Chico's love life. "How is Ali holding up?" she said, shifting gears.

"She's exhausted," I said quickly. "She's already turned in for the night." I could hear soft music coming from the bedroom, and I had no intention of disturbing my sister. "I'll tell her you called, though, and I'm sure she'll get back to you first thing tomorrow."

"Oh well, that would be fine," Persia said with a note of resignation. "Some more details may come to light once the news gets around." It seemed obvious to me that Persia was someone who lived for gossip, and the phone lines would be burning up tomorrow morning as she shared the news about Chico. "And Taylor—"

"Yes?"

"Don't forget to allow yourself to dream about Chico. You can nudge the subconscious; it's not at all difficult to do. Your subconscious is just waiting for your command. Remember, dear, you're in control."

I smiled to myself. Persia was relentless. "I'll do that. To the best of my ability, I mean."

"That's all anyone can ask," Persia replied. "Have a good evening," she said before ending the call.

I spent a restless night and was up at six the next morning, greeting Barney and Scout, who'd padded into the kitchen. I noticed the door to Ali's room was firmly shut so I filled their bowls with low-cal, nutritious crunchies while they circled around my feet, mewing softly.

Both cats stared at the pellets in disbelief and then looked back at me, as if to say, "This is it? You've got to be kidding!" Ali had gotten into the habit of adding a few goodies to their dry food—a slice of smoked turkey breast, a spoonful of tuna—but the vet had warned her that the cats were turning into porkers. Barney weighed in at seventeen pounds, and Scout topped the scales at eighteen and a half. Ali had reluctantly agreed to place them on a strict diet. I had to admit the "heart-healthy" dry food she bought from the vet didn't look appealing, but we decided to limit treats from the table.

"I'm afraid that's it, guys," I told them, as if they could understand me. "If Ali wants to spoil you, she'll have to do it on her watch. I've been given my orders." After shooting me an abject look of hurt and betrayal, they tucked into their bowls, resigned, and I brewed a pot of strong coffee. Barney shot me a last, sad look from over his shoulder, and I had to steel myself against adding a handful of tuna cat treats from the pantry.

I thought about how I wanted to spend the day. The shop wouldn't open for another three hours, and I planned to unpack a shipment of gummy bears that had arrived Saturday evening. Ali had a nice selection of gummy fish and gummy worms on display, but gummy bears were a perennial favorite and we'd nearly sold out.

I grabbed a cup of coffee fresh from the pot and a notepad as I settled myself on the chintz-covered window seat. I opened the dark walnut plantation shutters to the warm Savannah air and peered outside. Not a hint of a breeze, and even at this early hour, it was obvious that the day was going to be a scorcher. The air felt soupy, and I could hear the buzz of cicadas from the live oak trees lining the street.

I glanced across the road at Chico's dance studio. The curtains were drawn, and I noticed someone had posted a sign in the window. The pale yellow brick building looked sad and desolate, and I felt a little pang thinking about the vibrant dance instructor whose life was suddenly cut short.

Giving myself a mental shake, I sipped my coffee and began to make lists. I try not to brood over things, and I've found that action is the perfect antidote to ruminating. Ali always teases me about my ABC to-do lists. Items in the A-list are "must-dos," the B-list is for "should-dos," and the C-list is for "would like to do." On a good day, I can hit all three, but I don't let myself fall into bed at night until I accomplish everything on the A-list. Ali thinks this is obsessive, but I can't operate any other way.

I lined up today's tasks in order of priority. I wanted to

help Ali with the stock inventory, work up some publicity ideas with Dana, her young assistant, and think about reorganizing some of the glass display counters for maximum effect. All of these items went on the A-list.

The B-list was easy. I wanted to go forward with my idea of adding a "soup, sandwiches, and snacks" menu to the shop. I knew I'd have to tread carefully, because Ali didn't seem too keen on the idea.

When we'd talked about it initially, she had no idea whether she was even allowed to serve fresh food, or whether she would need a pricey upgrade to her current business license.

Did a shop owner like Ali need a restaurant license to serve soups and sandwiches? She already had a license to sell candy. The fact she hadn't checked this out told me I'd have an uphill battle on my hands.

I was jotting down some menu items—wondering if we should add some classic Savannah favorites like crab cake sandwiches and corn chowder with roasted red peppers—when Ali appeared, looking pale with dark smudges under her eyes. She yawned and stretched elaborately, reminding me of a teenager in her Ralph Lauren striped pink pajama set. I recognized the outfit because I'd given it to her last Christmas.

"I'm glad you're awake, but I bet you didn't sleep well," I said, jumping up from the window seat to pour her some coffee.

She glanced over at me, her expression blank for a moment, as if she'd forgotten I was there. "I'm fine," she said with a touch of irritation in her voice. She ran her hand through her tousled blond hair and reached for a cheerful mug hand-painted with bright red peonies. "I just need some time to wake up. I'm always like this first thing in the morning." She picked up the coffeepot, sniffed at it, wrinkled her nose, and put it down. "I think I'll start with some chamomile tea. It's easier on the stomach than caffeine. I'll switch to coffee later, if I really need it." She seemed to be avoiding looking at me directly, and I noticed her eyes were red and puffy as if she'd been crying.

"I can make that for you," I said quickly. "Maybe you should just sit down and relax, Ali. This has been a trying time for all of us." I opened a cabinet and started rummaging through the shelves when she put her hand on my arm.

"Taylor, I wish you wouldn't fuss like this." She blew out a little sigh. "You're hovering over me night and day, and it makes me feel like I'm eight years old. I've lived on my own for quite a while, you know, while you were off in Chicago doing the corporate thing." *Doing the corporate thing?* Could it be that she was jealous of my success? We'd taken two completely different career paths, and I never thought she envied my choice. She looked at me directly then, pursed her lips, and reached past me for a box of tea tucked away on the top shelf.

"Oh, sorry," I said, immediately chastened. "I didn't mean to hover and interrupt your morning routine." I mustered a smile. "I'm impossible without coffee, and I tend to forget that not everyone is like me."

"Yes, you do tend to forget that," she said flatly, filling the kettle with water. "I like to take my time waking up, that's all. You're fired up on all cylinders and ready to go when your feet hit the floor," she said in a softer tone. "That's good for you, but it doesn't work for me." She padded downstairs and I heard her open the front door. A moment later, she appeared back upstairs with the morning paper in hand. From the expression on her face, it didn't look like her mood had improved.

Ali settled herself at the table, absorbed in the paper, and I stood awkwardly by the kitchen counter, wondering what to do next. The silence stretched out between us, and the kitchen was deathly still except for the ticking of the retro Kit-Cat Klock above the sink. The cat's revolving eyes and pendulum tail moved in time to the seconds ticking by, and

I watched it blankly for a moment, my thoughts on my sister. Ali was clearly upset, but there seemed to be nothing I could say or do to comfort her.

Was it just Chico's death, or was something else going on? Was she worried about the success of the shop, and had yesterday's sad news pushed her into a bout of depression? She'd had such a take-charge attitude last night, calling for the emergency meeting of the Dream Club, and now she appeared listless, almost lethargic. What had happened to cause the downward spiral? I wondered if she'd tried to dream about Chico, as Persia had instructed us. I didn't dare ask her because it was painfully obvious that she was not in a chatty mood this morning.

I poured myself another cup of coffee and debated what to do next. When Ali steadfastly refused to look up from the paper, I gathered up my notepad, intending to head to my bedroom to regroup.

"Taylor," Ali said in a tiny voice. I turned and she offered me a tremulous, fleeting smile. "I didn't mean to be such a grouch. This whole thing with Chico—it's just been a shock to me, you know?"

"Yes, of course I do," I said, patting her awkwardly on the shoulder. "It was an enormous shock to everyone."

"I shouldn't have taken it out on you, though," she said with a sad, hopeless look in her eyes. "I know you're just trying to be helpful."

"Things always seem a million times worse when you don't sleep," I offered.

"Oh, but I did sleep," she replied, her voice wobbly. "But I dreamed about Chico all night long."

# 12

I was sorting out the luscious collection of gummy bears a few hours later when the Harper sisters stopped in to buy some horehound drops. I have to admit, I'm not a big fan of the root beer–colored hard candies. Perhaps they're an acquired taste. Horehound drops definitely fall into the "retro" category of confections, and I think Ali stocks them just for Minerva and Rose. I suspect they're not technically a candy at all, as people use them during cold and flu season as throat lozenges.

You either love them or hate them, and I happen to fall into the latter category. I much prefer lemon, sassafras, or wild cherry drops if I'm trying to ward off a scratchy throat.

"Would you like to try a sample of the gummy bears? We just got them in, all new flavors." I reached for a scoop, ready to offer them tiny paper cups filled with candy.

"They look lovely," Minerva said, her bright eyes scanning the display. "I didn't realize gummies came in so many colors. Did you arrange them? You did a lovely job, Taylor, very artistic." She tapped her sister on the shoulder and urged her to take a peek at the counter. I'd just finished cleaning the glass and had arranged the candy in colorful rows and concentric circles.

"Artistic?" I flushed with pleasure. "Well, I don't know about that, but I never realized how much fun it is to work on a display case." I walked around the front of the counter to take another look at my work. As a lifelong "bean counter," I've always assumed I didn't have an artistic bone in my body. So Minerva's remarks were high praise, indeed.

"There's quite a collection," I said encouragingly. "Almost every flavor you can think of: wild cherry, cinnamon, blue raspberry, and green apple. There's even a sugar-free version; those are popular with some folks."

"Oh, we absolutely have to bring home some gummies," Minerva said. "We don't need to sample them, dear. Just wrap up a pound and a half, Taylor. Not the sugar-free kind, the regular ones."

"Any particular flavor?"

"No, just mix them all up, dear." She paused and looked at the neat rows of pastel disks on the bottom shelf. "And add a pound of Necco Wafers, will you? My godson, Trevor, loves those."

"And he likes the chocolate coins that come in the little mesh bags," Rose reminded her.

"Yes, he does, glad you said that," Minerva said. "Add a couple of those, please."

The two sisters helped themselves to some fresh lemonade, and while I wrapped up their purchases, they chatted about a neighbor who was hospitalized. "She was a Porter," Minerva said idly, "and they've never had strong constitutions. Weak stomachs and nervous disorders. Of course, she was a Hooper by birth, but I think she had ties to the Campbells back in the sixties."

"Yes, her second cousin twice removed was a Campbell," Rose agreed. "And her great-aunt was a Guthrie. The Guthries had a few black sheep in the family, as I recall."

"Oh Lordie, yes, I remember back in the day . . ." I tuned

out while Minerva took a trip down memory lane, recalling people and events from half a century ago.

The Harpers seem to know everyone in Savannah, and it occurred to me that they might be privy to some interesting facts about Chico's background. I had the feeling that they hadn't revealed everything they knew last night at the Dream Club meeting. Could they deliberately be holding back some key information? The thought crossed my mind that they might be protecting someone. But who? Chico was fairly new to the area, and I couldn't picture him having any strong family ties or social connections. As Lucinda said, "He was an outsider."

I tuned back into the Harper sisters' conversation and had to bite back a smile. The sisters had moved on to more recent scandalous events in Savannah high society and had strong opinions on what was acceptable and what was out of bounds.

"So the children from his first marriage attended his wedding on the yacht?" Minerva was asking in an incredulous tone. "Wasn't that a bit awkward?"

"Very. And actually, it was the children from his first *two* marriages who attended the wedding and reception on board," Rose said, lifting her eyebrows. She held up two fingers for emphasis. "Two former marriages. Six children total, and one of them is older than his new bride." She gave a disdainful little sniff. "The third Mrs. Aldrich. She's named Tiffany or maybe it's Tawny. In any case, she looked younger than the flower girl. People couldn't stop staring at her."

"Absolutely shocking," Minerva harrumphed. "His grandmother would be spinning in her grave. Some things just aren't done. At least they weren't in my day. People stayed married whether they were happy or not."

"Well, these are different times," Rose offered. "Edward said he wanted his children there, and he didn't care who was offended. I suppose blood is thicker than water."

"Yes, you're probably right," Minerva agreed. "In the end, it all comes down to family."

I laid the bags on the counter and delicately cleared my throat.

"Did you have a restful night, Taylor?" Rose asked, suddenly shifting her attention to me. She gave me a searching look while I brushed a stray lock of hair out of my face. I knew I looked bedraggled, and I was frustrated that the ancient air conditioner couldn't seem to keep pace with the scorching Savannah heat. I've been meaning to talk to Ali about replacing it, but money is tight and I don't think she has the budget for improvements. I could feel a thin layer of perspiration forming on the back of my neck and wished I'd pulled my hair back in a scrunchie.

"Not really," I admitted. "I'm hoping that staying busy will keep me on my feet." I smiled. "I think I'll be fine as long as I don't stop to take a breather."

"It's all right to take a break now and then," Ali said, walking down the spiral staircase. "I meant to open the shop myself this morning," she said apologetically. "I decided to lie down for a few minutes after breakfast, and the next thing you know, I was out like a light."

She looked better than she had earlier, with a touch of color in her cheeks and a spring in her step. Maybe she was putting the horrendous events of yesterday behind her. I hadn't had a chance to ask her about her dreams of Chico, and I knew she wouldn't want to say anything with the Harper sisters there.

"That's all right," I said quickly. "I've had fun arranging some of the displays." I pointed to the dazzling collection of gummy bears. "We can change everything back if you don't like it this way."

"Well, let me take a look." Ali let her gaze drift over the assorted candies for a long moment, her face expressionless. She bit her lower lip and shook her head slightly from side to side. I wondered if I'd overstepped my bounds and was all set to apologize when she broke into a big smile.

"I love it. You have a real knack for this, Taylor. I think we should revamp all the displays. My arrangement was functional, but yours is much more attractive. It's a work of art."

"That's just what I told her!" Minerva exclaimed. "Artistic!"

Ali laughed and gave me a high five. "I'm learning new things about you every day," she said, her sunny mood seemingly restored. She poured herself a glass of lemonade and nibbled on a sugar cookie while I waited on Lucinda Macavy, who'd come in for some Burnt Sugar peanuts.

"I'm addicted to these," she said with a girlish giggle. "I suppose everyone has a guilty pleasure, don't they?"

"Probably," I agreed, smiling at her. Lucinda is so prim and straitlaced, it was amusing to think of her admitting to any pleasures, guilty or otherwise. I filled a large bag for her while she checked out the new gummy bear display.

"I think I dreamt about poor Chico last night," she confided. "Do you remember how Persia said we could will ourselves to dream about him? I tried it, and to my amazement, I believe it worked." She lowered her voice to a conspiratorial whisper. "It was a very odd dream." She seemed to be waiting for some reaction from me, so I nodded for her to continue.

"You dreamt about Chico? Oh, do tell us about the dream, dear," Minerva said, and turned toward us, all ears. For an octogenarian, she certainly had an acute sense of hearing. Rose learned forward, her elbow planted on the counter, hoping to catch every word.

"It was all very odd. I'm not even completely sure it was Chico. I was watching a man dancing in the ballroom of a lovely mansion with a very attractive woman. She was wearing a flowing white gown, and he was swirling her around and around in a waltz."

"A waltz?" Ali piped up. "That's odd. Chico taught Latin dancing. I don't think he ever did ballroom dancing."

"I know, Ali, but remember Sybil told us that details get all mixed up in dreams," Minerva said pointedly. "Sometimes one person stands in for another and one thing is substituted for another. It's all about symbolism. You can't interpret them too literally."

"I do recall her saying that," I said, inwardly wincing. I hoped we weren't going to get into a long spiel on dream analysis. Ali's dark mood had dissipated, and I didn't want to dredge up the tragic events of yesterday.

"Tell us more about the dream, dear," Minerva said encouragingly. She settled herself on a black leather stool next to the counter, and Rose moved to a pale lavender antique side chair that Ali had picked up at a garage sale. It was obvious that they were settling in for a good long chat, and I shot a nervous glance at Ali. Her features looked serene; either she really wasn't upset by the conversation or she was managing to hide her discomfort.

"It was the most beautiful ballroom I've ever seen," Lucinda went on. "Every detail is so vivid. I can see it in my mind. It was the most gorgeous room, like a painting."

"It was like a painting?" Rose asked eagerly. "So you mean it was strictly a representation of a scene, not an actual scene?"

Lucinda gave a dismissive little wave of her hand. "No, wait, I think I'm getting confused." She bit her lip and scrunched up her face. "It *was* a real scene, but there were beautiful murals on the walls and on the ceilings. That's what made me think about paintings."

"What sort of paintings?" Ali looked intrigued.

"Angels and cherubs. They reminded me of something . . ." Her voice trailed off as she pursed her lips and then snapped her fingers. "I know what it was! They looked like paintings I saw on the ceiling of the Sistine Chapel. I was a chaperone for a senior class trip to Rome a few years ago."

"Really?" Minerva and Rose exchanged a look. "So all the murals had a religious theme. That's very interesting, indeed." She stopped to take a sip of lemonade. "Were there French doors leading onto a patio and gardens? A whole wall of doors with gauzy white curtains?"

"Why, yes," Lucinda said, a look of astonishment crossing her face. "That's exactly what the room looked like. The doors were open, the curtains were blowing in the breeze, and I could see the gardens. They were spectacular." She clasped her hands together. "They were tiered, all different levels, with slate steps—"

"Slate steps leading down to a pond," Rose cut in. "With a fountain in the middle. A statute of Cupid, with a bow and arrow. And there were lovely trees lining the pond, I expect."

Lucinda's mouth formed an O of astonishment. "Yes, you described it perfectly. There was a fountain with the Cupid statue and the weeping willow trees, but how in the world could you know that? Did you have the same dream? Or are you a dream-hopper?"

I looked up, interested. Sybil Powers always maintains that people who are tuned into this sort of thing can become dream-hoppers, visiting another person's dreams. They can insert themselves into the dream, or just observe the dream for a few minutes and then move on to someone else's dream.

Minerva laughed. "Rose is no dream-hopper. The reason she recognizes the ballroom, dear, is that we've been there many times. Years ago, I mean. In our youth." She exchanged a rueful look with her sister. "We had some lovely waltzes in that very room, didn't we, Rose?" She gave a happy sigh, her blue eyes focused on a distant memory. "Our dance cards were always full, back in the day. We'd dance the night away with our handsome beaus and have cocktails on the white stone patio."

"You've been to this place—the place in Lucinda's dream?" I asked. My pulse jumped and I wondered if there really was something to dream work. How could Lucinda have dreamt about a place she had never seen? Ali would say it was all part of the collective unconscious and we all have certain images deep within our psyches. This was all a little too woo-woo for me, but I must admit I was intrigued by Lucinda's story.

"Of course, dear. Half of Savannah has been there. It's the old Collier mansion outside of town. It's on the historical register. When the Colliers made a grand tour of Italy, they fell in love with some frescoes in Florence. The moment they came back to Savannah, they commissioned an artist to duplicate them in their ballroom. Back in those days, it was quite a showplace."

"That is was," Rose agreed.

"Then after the original Colliers passed away, it went to seed," Minerva continued. "The younger generation of Colliers couldn't afford to keep it up in the grand style, and there wasn't enough money left in the estate to maintain it. Luckily a developer saw the possibilities and bought it and remodeled it, restoring it to its former glory. They had someone from the Historical Society oversee every step of the process. We take the past seriously here in Savannah, Taylor," she said, lifting her eyebrow.

"So it sounds like quite a lovely dream," Ali cut in. She'd been listening quietly, her expression unreadable. "And you say you saw Chico in the dream?"

"Well, that's just the thing," Lucinda said apologetically. "I really can't be sure about the man who was dancing. He was tall and had dark hair; that's the only thing I know for certain. And the woman, his partner, was blond and very thin."

*That leaves out Gina*, I thought to myself. Gina was a voluptuous redhead.

"So you're not sure of his identity? But you saw everything else so clearly," I said. "The cherubs, the curtains, the fountains, and gardens."

"I know," Lucinda said, her eyes clouding. "But the man is a different story completely."

"You said he was tall and dark-haired," Ali said encouragingly. "Can you remember anything else? Try to picture him dancing and tell us exactly what you see. Close your eyes and concentrate."

"He was spinning his partner around and around," Lucinda said dreamily. "And there were flames leaping up in the background, but he didn't seem to notice them. I could see that part of the scene very clearly. And when the song ended, they embraced, and that's when I finally had a good look at him. His head was tilted to the side and I was standing just a few feet away."

"And—" I interjected. I felt a wave of impatience bubbling up inside me; I wanted Lucinda to cut to the chase.

"And," Lucinda said, her voice low and hoarse, "I had quite a shock. Because that's when I realized he had no face."

# 13

A little chill went through me, and I set down my glass carefully on the counter. I felt the hairs rise on my forearm, and my heart hammered in my chest.

"Good Lord," Minerva gasped and turned to her sister. "Did she just say what I think she said?"

"Yes, she did." Rose nodded grimly. "She saw a man with no face. That's a recurring image in dreams. Or I should say, in *nightmares*," she added pointedly. "You must have been terrified," she said to Lucinda, her voice soft with sympathy.

"I was," Lucinda whispered her reply. "It was so awful. I shook my head from side to side and forced myself to wake up. But what does it mean?"

Ali raised her eyebrows and shot Lucinda a thoughtful look. "A faceless figure can mean a lot of things," she began hesitantly, and something about her tone made me wonder if she was trying to be diplomatic. Ali has always been forthright and direct, but now she seemed to be choosing her words carefully.

"So it's a common theme?" Minerva asked.

"Oh, yes. I've run into it before, in dream workshops I've taken. When you dream about someone faceless, or a person wearing a mask or a hood, it can be a self-protective measure." Ali poured herself a glass of tea, and I noticed her hand was shaking a little.

"How so?" Minerva asked.

"Well, it could be the mind's way of protecting you from an image you're not ready to deal with. Maybe you can't face seeing the identity of the person behind the mask. So you obliterate the face entirely. But in this case"—she waved her hand in the air—"that doesn't really make sense, because we already know who the victim is. It was Chico," she said sadly. We were silent for a moment.

"I hope I don't have that dream again," Lucinda said fervently. She gave a little shudder and folded her arms across her chest as if a cold wind had swept through the room. "I never should have listened to Persia. Telling myself to dream about Chico didn't accomplish a thing except get me really upset." I remember Lucinda telling the group that she liked to dream about kittens and babies, things that made her smile and lifted her spirits.

"Something positive may still come out of this, Lucinda. You've given us a lot to think about," Minerva said, slowly getting to her feet. She handed me her credit card and waited while I rang up the candy. "But I'm afraid at the moment, we're as much in the dark as ever. It's odd that you described the old Collier mansion in such detail, my dear. Are you sure you've never been there? The Waltons hold an open house at Christmas to benefit one of the local charities. And of course, the estate is one of the stops on the garden tour. Their gardens are fabulous. Among the finest in Savannah, I'd say."

Lucinda shook her head. "I don't get out much," she said, "especially since I've retired."

It was hard to imagine Lucinda, who was quiet as a church mouse, attending any social events. She picked up a lace doily and ran her finger over the fine workmanship. Ali had scattered a few handmade vintage doilies here and there to tie in with the shabby chic décor. "Who are the Waltons? I thought you said the Colliers owned the estate."

"The Colliers were the original owners, several generations ago. But Thomas Walton, the city councilman, bought the estate from a developer, and he and his wife, Jennifer, live there. She's a lovely person, very involved in children's welfare." She carefully omitted saying anything about Councilman Thomas Walton, and it seemed this was deliberate.

"I think I saw a political ad for a Walton down by Forsythe Square the other day," I said slowly. "I think the name was Thomas Walton. Middle-aged, dark hair, strong jaw?"

"Yes, that's him," Rose said. "Being city councilman is just a stepping-stone. He has high aspirations. He's making a run for the United States Senate." She raised her eyebrows. "Of course, people in Savannah have long memories, and who knows if he'll be successful?"

"Do you mean he has a few skeletons in his closet?" I asked, puzzled.

Rose laughed. "Oh heavens, Taylor, everyone in this town has a few skeletons rattling around. He won't be the first Savannah politician with a few surprises tucked away, and I daresay he won't be the last. Boys will be boys, and men will be men, you know." Minerva gave her a warning look, and Rose looked slightly abashed. "I suppose I shouldn't gossip like this," she said demurely. "You always tell me that, Minerva."

"You know what Mama always taught us, Rose. If you can't say something good about someone, don't say anything at all." She frowned at her sister, her face radiating disapproval.

I thought of Alice Roosevelt Longworth's quote: "If you can't say anything good about someone, sit right here by me." She loved that saying so much, she even had it embroidered on a silk-screened throw pillow in her elegant Washington home.

Lucinda and the Harper sisters left a few minutes later, and Ali and I decided to have a late lunch upstairs before tackling the inventory. Dana had arrived to handle the shop, and her cheerful, energetic demeanor was in sharp contrast to my sister's listlessness. Although Ali's dark mood seemed to have lifted, she still seemed out of sorts and preoccupied, brewing a cup of her favorite mint tea and sipping it as she stared idly out the living room window.

"You must be starving," I said. "You missed breakfast." I tried to keep my tone light; the last thing I wanted was to face another lecture on my tendency to "hover."

"That's okay, I'm not really that hungry. I just can't seem to concentrate today." Barney and Scout were sleeping on the window bench and she ran her hand over Barney's silky fur. He gave a soft meow and turned over in his sleep, raising a paw over his eyes to block out the light. Scout was sleeping in a tight ball, nose to tail, snoring lightly, his ears twitching a little.

"Well, let me make your favorite lunch, and then we can get busy," I said, putting as much enthusiasm into my voice as I could.

"My favorite lunch?" Ali looked confused.

"Don't you remember? Tomato soup and a grilled cheese sandwich? You've loved that ever since you were in grade school."

"That was a classic, I do remember that." She laughed. "You always made it for me when I got sick. You said that it would cure anything."

"It's classic comfort food; of course it will."

"I have a better idea," she said, reaching for her purse. "I think I'd feel better if we got out of here for a while. Let me give Dana a few instructions and then I'll take you out to lunch. I found a place that makes the best grilled cheese sandwiches in the world."

"In the entire world, or in Savannah?" I asked teasingly.

Ali grinned. "Same thing, sis. Same thing."

Business was slow at Sweet Caroline's on Bay Street, and we grabbed a table near the window. The lunch crowd had wound down, and people were dropping in for drinks and pastries. It had a friendly laid-back atmosphere, and everyone seemed to know each other. The café was located in a great spot near Franklin Square, and Ali told me it was written up in a travel guidebook. A few people were seated at outdoor umbrella tables, but the Savannah sun was still high in the sky and the heat was oppressive. I was glad to duck inside and feel the comforting blast of the AC cranked up on high.

"Everything here is homemade," Ali said, glancing up at the specials on the chalkboard. "Caroline does three or four different soups every day, and she bakes her rolls right here on the premises. All fresh ingredients." She looked over the menu while the server poured us tall glasses of sweet tea served in mason jars. "If I ever open a restaurant, I'd like to open a place just like this," she said. She sat back, happily munching on a selection of mini muffins the server had brought along with the iced tea.

I could see that I was going to have to watch my calories here in Savannah. Temptations abounded and I wasn't getting much exercise. It seemed silly to invest in a gym membership since I didn't know how long I'd be staying here. I vowed to start a daily one-hour walking tour of the city. It would be good for the mind, body, and spirit. Ali's soft voice cut into my thoughts. "I think it would be such fun to be a restaurateur, Taylor, don't you?"

*A restaurateur?* I blinked. As always, Ali was dreaming of something bigger, something better, and not concentrating on what was right in front of her. I didn't want to ruin the fragile relationship we'd established so I decided to say something positive.

"Well, I think it might be a little too much to take on right now, since you already handle a candy shop." A little frown crossed Ali's face and I quickly added, "A nice compromise might be to add the snacks and light lunch menu we talked about. We could capitalize on your location and the tourist trade," I said hopefully. "And you'd have fun trying out different recipes and deciding which ones to add to the menu. You have a flair for that; you're really creative."

I didn't want to mention that I'd already come up with some notes and cost projections. Ali has always had trouble taking suggestions. I've learned that it's better not to be too direct with her and to take a more subtle approach.

"It's not a bad idea," she said thoughtfully. "Everything would have to be organic, of course, and homemade. I guess we could offer a few soups and salads to start. And maybe add a roasted veggie panini down the road."

"That's a terrific idea," I said warmly. "What shall we try today?" I asked as the server returned to the table.

"I'm going to have that grilled cheese sandwich and tomato soup we talked about," Ali said. "They make it with soy cheese and you'd swear it was cheddar." Her tone was light and cheerful, and she had a blush of color back in her face. She was right—getting out of the house was just what the doctor ordered. "Why don't you order something different and we can share?"

All the choices looked delicious, but I finally settled on corn chowder with roasted red peppers and a croissant sandwich filled with brie and raspberry preserves. Sheer heaven. Ali had developed an appetite after all, and we happily wolfed down our lunch with refills on the sweet tea.

We were debating on whether or not to have dessert when Liese, the server, appeared with two coffees and two scrumptious servings of chocolate cake. She placed the desserts in front of us with a flourish, and I noticed the cake seemed to be layered with a mocha mixture. It looked sinfully decadent, and I practically salivated just looking at it.

"On the house, from Madame," she said to Ali. "For you and your guest."

"Oh, how sweet of her," Ali exclaimed. "Tell her thank you and to please stop by so I can introduce her to my sister."

When Liese smiled and darted away, Ali said, "Caroline is one of my favorite people in Savannah. She moved here from the south of France a few years ago and opened a much grander restaurant called La Bagatelle in the heart of the city. Then her husband died suddenly and she nearly retired from the business. But she had a change of heart. She didn't want to disappoint her loyal customers so she decided to sell La Bagatelle and open this place. It's less formal and it's really popular with the locals."

"I can see why," I said, biting into the delicious dark chocolate confection. "The food is fantastic."

"I'm so glad you enjoy it, mademoiselle," a sweetly lilting voice said from behind me. I turned to see a stylish woman in her mid-fifties bend down to give Ali a quick hug. She was chic in that way only French women can pull off, and her white pencil skirt and cobalt blue silk blouse complemented her coloring. She had deep blue eyes and shiny black hair that she wore in a stylish cut, quite short, but perfect for her face. She was stunning and I could see the real affection she felt for my sister.

"My dear Ali," she said, "how are you? I heard about the tragedy at the dance studio. You and Chico were close, no? So sad, I was so sorry to hear about his death."

Ali, flushing a little, said, "Yes, it was quite a shock to all of us." She paused. "Can you sit with us for a minute? I'd like you to meet my sister, Taylor. Taylor, this is Caroline LaCroix." I noticed Ali gave her name the French pronunciation, *Karoleen.*

"*Enchantée*," Caroline said formally and shook my hand. She slipped into the empty seat and said, "It's lovely to have you in Savannah, Taylor. I think it's good for Ali to have family around her. I hope you can stay here for a long time."

I shook my head. "Well, that's a bit up in the air at the moment," I said. "Right now, I'm enjoying helping out in the shop and seeing a few of the sights." Ali and I had never really discussed how long I'd be staying, and sister or not, I didn't want to overstay my welcome. But I couldn't forget that my condo, my job, and my friends were back in Chicago. At some point, I'd have to return and pick up my life there. I'd been managing to do a little work from my iPad for the time being, but that situation couldn't continue indefinitely.

"But it would be a great *dommage* to not take the time to really explore this marvelous city," Caroline said in her lovely French accent. I remembered from my high school French that *dommage* meant "shame." She patted my hand. "If you need anyone to show you the sights, I'm here. There are twenty-two squares in the Historic District, did you know that?"

"Yes, I read it in the guidebook. And thank you so much." She was the second person to offer to show me around Savannah, and I realized that Southern hospitality is more than just a myth.

"I really want to catch up with you, my *chère* Ali. But we're catering a little event tonight at the Walton estate, and I have to finish up some desserts."

Ali shot me a look across the table. "The Walton estate? What's going on there?"

"Some political fund-raiser," Caroline said, waving her hand in the air. "Thomas Walton"—she lowered her voice and leaned in close—"is pulling out all the stops. You know he's running for the Senate, right? I think he's falling behind in the polls, so he asked me to put together a series of intimate little dinners for the big donors. I'm doing round tables for eight, close to fifty people total at each dinner. And a cocktail party in the garden to start things off. That way everyone gets a chance to talk with him."

"I'm sure it will be lovely," Ali said. "What a wonderful setting."

Caroline nodded. "Yes, the estate is magnificent. I'm using magnolias for the centerpieces with ivory and pale peach table linens. The ballroom is very large so there will be vanilla candles everywhere, both on the sconces and on the tables. That should banish any shadows; I want the whole effect to be light and airy."

*Banishing shadows.* I thought of what Rose Harper had said about Thomas Walton and the skeletons he had rattling around his closet. Was that just idle talk, or did the octogenarian really know something nefarious about him?

"Do you know the Waltons very well?" I asked Caroline. If she was surprised by the question, she covered it quickly, her expression bland, her smile never faltering.

"Not so well," she said, darting a quick look at Ali. I was sure that the Waltons were the subject of pretty juicy gossip, but Caroline was far too discreet to reveal it. "I know Madame Walton, Jennifer, from the Ladies Auxiliary Guild. She is *charmante, très aimable.* How do you say it? Charming and very nice." She stood then, and clasped my hand in her own delicate one. "Welcome again, Taylor. Think about making Savannah your home. It is indeed *merveilleux.* If I can make your stay more pleasant in any way, just say the word."

# 14

"Caroline is lovely, isn't she?" Ali said when we were back outside in the Savannah sunshine. "She's really taken me under her wing."

"Did you get the feeling Caroline knows more about the Waltons than she's letting on?"

Ali laughed. "Absolutely. You know what French women are like, the soul of discretion. I think there's a lot more to the story, and we'll never hear it from Rose or Caroline. But there are two special people in Savannah who love to dish, and luckily we're very close to their store."

Ali linked her arm through mine and we turned west on River Street and hurried past the square to a posh antique shop. The outside was spectacular with purple clematis and fiery bougainvillea blossoming on a trellis made of twisted branches arching over the doorway. The frame building was painted a pale lemon yellow, and the shutters were cobalt blue. The front stoop was crowded with overflowing pots of ferns and dusty rose hibiscus, giving the whole place the look of an enchanted cottage.

"Welcome to Déjà Vu," Ali said, pushing open the door.

I stepped past a porcelain umbrella stand filled with lush pampas grass and followed her inside. "The owners are friends of mine. And"—she lowered her voice—"two of the most colorful people you're going to meet in Savannah. Andre has a wicked sense of humor and Gideon . . . well, he's a hoot, what can I say."

"It's gorgeous," I said. "Someone has an eye for color and design."

"Gideon studied floral design before he gave his heart and soul to the antique business," Ali said. A bell tinkled softly when we entered the shop. I was immediately struck by the gleaming plank floors, the buttercream-colored walls, and the tin ceiling; the room seemed diffused with a soft golden light.

"Ali!" A tall, wickedly handsome man in his mid-thirties swept Ali into his arms. "It's been way too long. I thought you'd forgotten about us."

"Forget you and Gideon? Never," Ali said, gently disentangling herself from his enthusiastic hug. "I brought my sister, Taylor, in to meet you. She's visiting from Chicago."

"The Windy City!" he said, pumping my hand. "I love the Miracle Mile. Gideon and I went there last Christmas to check out the store window displays."

"Andre used to work as a set designer in Hollywood," Ali said. "Then he gave it all up to move back to Savannah and open this shop with Gideon."

"My roots are here, Ali, and I just couldn't stay away. Plus Gideon's acting career was going through a dry spell, he didn't want to go back to floral design, and we figured this was the time for a change."

"Gideon was an actor?"

"Daytime soaps mostly," Andre said, "before that market dried up. He did have a walk-on part on the new *Dallas*, and there's always a chance he could be called back for a guest shot, but nothing is definite.

"Working as an actor in Hollywood must have been an

amazing experience for him," I said, taking a quick look around the shop. It looked like they sold high-end European antiques with a sophisticated, cosmopolitan feel. A gorgeous Queen Anne settee in pale blue caught my eye, and when I glanced at the price tag, I nearly passed out.

"Oh, that it was," Andre said. "Of course, it was also an emotional roller coaster. The stories he could tell . . ." He motioned us to a rose damask love seat while he packed up a place setting of Limoges china. "You don't mind if I work while we talk, do you? I'm doing the tablescapes for an event at the Walton estate tonight."

"Really," Ali murmured, exchanging a look with me. "The Waltons? How interesting." Our eyes met for a moment. *The perfect opportunity to find out more about the mysterious Thomas Walton.* This was either fate or an incredibly lucky coincidence. She edged into the conversation skillfully, Southern style, taking a meandering approach.

"This is certainly a beautiful place setting, Andre," she said, admiring the delicate floral pattern on the creamy bone china.

"Very old, very precious," Andre said, handling the dishes carefully. It looked like every place setting had half a dozen pieces, at least. "Jennifer has a dozen or so settings in this pattern, but not enough for a big crowd. So I offered to let her borrow mine, and she asked if I'd oversee the china and crystal tonight. They're excellent customers," he said with a conspiratorial grin, "so I figured it was the least I could do. Plus they invited me as a guest, so I figure I might make some good connections for the shop."

"How well do you know the Waltons?" I asked, trying to sound casual.

"Well, Jennifer's a peach, really a sweetheart," he said. He stopped talking abruptly, and I could see he was going to need some persuasion.

"And Thomas?" Ali prodded.

Andre stood back for a moment, hands on his hips, and

let out a short breath. "Well, far be it from me to gossip"—he gave a self-deprecating laugh—"but I don't know how he made it in politics. Somehow he got lucky and picked up some well-heeled supporters. As my granny always says, even a blind hog finds an acorn now and then."

"You don't like him?" I asked.

"Honey, he's a customer, I don't like him or dislike him. Let's just say I don't trust him. I wouldn't want to get on the wrong side of him, that's for sure." He turned and let his gaze sweep over me. "Say, how would you two ladies like to come with me tonight?"

"We'd love to, but we don't have invitations," Ali said quickly.

"No problem." Andre picked up a pale blue card with heavy embossing. "Gideon's in Atlanta for an antique convention, and you can be my 'plus one.' "

" 'Plus one'?" Ali gave a little moue of disappointment. "But there are two of us."

"A minor point. You'll be my 'plus two.' They can always squeeze in another guest."

"Are you sure?" I asked doubtfully. As much as I was interested in seeing the estate, especially after hearing about Lucinda's dream, I didn't feel like being a gate-crasher.

"This is Savannah, honey chile," Andre said with a grin. "We Southerners are used to making adjustments. I can make it happen with one phone call."

"You're a genius, Andre," Ali said, hugging him impulsively.

"Now you two skedaddle and let me get back to work." Andre gave us a wide smile. "I'll meet you on the veranda at seven. They're serving cocktails first and they've hired a string quartet. Don't be late."

"It sounds heavenly," Ali said.

"Oh, it will be, girlfriend, it will be," Andre promised. "A night to remember."

As we left the shop, I found myself mulling over Andre's

last words. *A night to remember . . .* Where had I heard that expression before? And then it came to me. Oh yes. *A Night to Remember.* A classic book about the *Titanic.* Was the evening going to be a total shipwreck?

**"This is dazzling,"** I said, admiring the live oaks lining the long curving driveway to the Waltons' estate. It was a perfect Savannah night, with a touch of softness in the air, and I caught a whiff of late-blooming jasmine.

"I must admit, I've really been looking forward to seeing this place," Ali said. Her eyes shone and she looked beautiful in a navy blue cocktail dress. I was happy to see that her early melancholy had vanished and her sunny nature seemed to be reasserting itself. "It's like something out of a storybook, isn't it?" she asked. "An antebellum mansion, with porticos and balconies, and all these magnificent trees draped in Spanish moss. I can hear violin music coming from inside. It makes me think of Tara, the mansion in *Gone with the Wind.*"

She gave a little sigh as we pulled into a circle paved with oyster shells under the portico. The Waltons had valet parking, and a young man rushed to open the car doors for us and take the keys. Our hosts were clearly pulling out all the stops for this fund-raising event. "I wonder what it would be like to live here," Ali said in a low voice as we made our way to the mansion.

A couple behind us was chatting about their recent trip to "the islands," and debating the various merits of owning oceanfront houses on St. John and St. Barths. This was obviously a well-heeled crowd, and I wished I'd worn something a bit dressier tonight. My Ann Taylor sleeveless black shift was the only cocktail outfit I had in my suitcase. I'd managed to dress it up with some gold jewelry and a silk scarf I'd borrowed from Ali, but I couldn't compete with all the designer fashions swirling around me.

"What would it be like to live here? It would be expensive," I said wryly. "Can you imagine the upkeep on this place? The landscaping probably costs more than I make in a year."

Ali laughed. "Taylor, you are always about the bottom line! Is that all you ever think about?"

"Most of the time, yes. I have the soul of an accountant, remember?" Ali had said that to me once in the heat of an argument, and now it was a running gag between us.

We were ushered into the foyer, and I caught a glimpse of twin stairways that spiraled up to the second story, a gleaming dark wood floor, tastefully faded oriental rugs, crystal chandeliers that sent sparks of light dancing around the room, and fragrant pots of magnolias everywhere. If *Architectural Digest* did a piece on Southern mansions, this would be a great place for a photo shoot.

And then I stopped dead in my tracks and suddenly the beautiful furnishings didn't matter anymore. I was drawn to the sound of sweet violin music and soft laughter coming from the veranda. The French doors were swung wide open, and I could see guests sipping cocktails while waiters in black tuxedos circulated with trays of food. I thought I spotted a familiar face among the elegant guests.

I blinked and looked again. Were my eyes playing tricks on me?

My heart was thudding with excitement; this was a man I never expected to see again. A man who once was everything to me. Bittersweet memories flooded me and I took a deep breath, willing my voice to remain steady.

"Ali," I said urgently, clutching her arm, "look over on the right, out on the veranda. The man in the navy blazer talking to the girl with long blond hair. Is that who I think it is?"

She followed my gaze to the tall, broad-shouldered man with coolly assessing eyes. He was raising a champagne glass to his lips and we saw him in profile, just a quick glance of finely aristocratic chiseled features and artfully tousled black hair.

Then the crowd shifted and he turned in our direction. For one long moment, our gazes locked and he nodded, his lips curving into a sexy, lazy smile that I remembered all too well. He gave me a long, slow, intimate look. I swallowed hard, trying to ignore the tingling feeling that was running up my spine. All my senses seemed to have gone on hyperalert, and I tried to tune out the cacophony of music and conversation so I could concentrate on what my sister was saying.

"Yes, it's Noah," she said softly. "Someone told me he was here in Savannah, but I wasn't sure."

"And you didn't tell me?" My heart jumped again as I watched Noah murmur to the young woman in the low-cut black satin dress with spaghetti straps. He leaned in close to her, and she threw her head back and laughed, her caramel blond hair streaming down her back. My stomach clenched watching them, but I tried to keep my expression neutral.

"I wasn't sure," Ali said. "Someone said they thought he'd moved to Charleston or Hilton Head. He's left the FBI, you know. He didn't tell you?" She paused, watching me closely, her eyes clouded with concern.

Did she think I was going to fall apart because my ex and I happened to turn up at the same event? If he really did live in Savannah, we were bound to run into each other eventually. I would have liked to have had time to mentally prepare myself, but it was too late for that now.

I shook my head. "I have no idea what's going on in his life. We didn't stay in touch, Ali." I took a deep breath as Noah said something to the girl and then turned to move toward us. She placed her hand on his arm in a playful gesture, as if to restrain him, and then grinned and released him. If this was his date for the evening, he was robbing the cradle, I thought sourly. Noah was my age, and the girl looked to be in her early twenties. And drop-dead gorgeous.

She was toying with her glass, staring at me with frank curiosity.

"But what's he doing in Savannah?" I whispered. I wanted to find out as much information as I could before he reached us. Luckily a couple of women tried to engage him in conversation, slowing down his progress, as he made his way across the veranda. Noah was always catnip to women, and judging from the flirtatious smiles tossed his way, I could see that nothing had changed. I was glad I had a few extra seconds to compose myself.

"I'm not sure. I heard he's some sort of private investigator." She grabbed a drink from a tray a waiter was passing and took a big sip. "Uh-oh, here he comes. I think I'll make myself scarce."

"No, Ali, please stay!" I pleaded with her, but she disappeared into the crowd, and suddenly I was face-to-face with Noah Chandler. We had had an intense two-year relationship when we both were working in Atlanta. I was a strategist for a consulting firm, and he was with the Atlanta field office of the FBI. I was away on business most of the time, and he was always flying across the country on assignments.

In hindsight, neither one of us had the time or energy to devote to a relationship. No wonder Noah and I didn't make a go of it. The timing was off and we both were workaholics, too tired and irritable to invest time and attention in each other. After one major blowup, I moved to Chicago and tried to put the past—and Noah—behind me.

I thought I had. Until now.

# 15

"Taylor." The low sexy voice was like a caress as he took both my hands in his and leaned in to kiss my cheek. It was such a polite, chaste kiss that no one would ever guess there had been anything between us. Certainly not a red-hot, sizzling love affair that had ended badly.

"Noah." I drew back from his embrace as gracefully as I could and clasped my hands in front of me. He looked amused. "I didn't know you were here in Savannah."

Noah snared a couple of glasses of champagne from a passing waiter and handed one of them to me. I tried not to notice that his fingers lingered on mine for just a second too long, and I dipped my head to hide the rush of emotion that swept over me. Like they say, old memories die hard.

"I had a bit of a career change," he said, letting his gaze skim over my black sheath. "I always liked you in black," he said thoughtfully. "It suits your coloring."

"Tell me about your new career," I said, determined to draw the conversation back to safer channels. Out of the corner of my eye, I saw Ali standing by the musicians, looking over at us, probably wondering how I was handling the unexpected reunion.

"I'm a private investigator now," he said lightly. "I liked working for the Bureau, but I decided I'd be much happier being my own boss."

"Here in town?"

Noah nodded. "I rented some office space in the Historic District. On Drayton Street, close to Lafayette Square." His dark gaze held mine and then he said, "So what brings you to town? I heard you'd moved to Chicago."

I played with my glass, stalling for time, wondering how much to say. "I came to see Ali for a quick visit and I decided to stay for a while." I'd forgotten how his gray eyes flashed with electricity, and I felt a warm flush creeping up my chest. "I still have my place in Chicago, but I'll be in town for a while to help Ali with her shop."

"She's opened a store?" He smiled. Ali's checkered career history has always been a source of amusement to him. Noah is one of the most focused people I know, and he's always zoomed in on what he wants, with the precision of a heat-seeking missile. He planned his career path carefully. First a bachelor's degree in computer technology, and then a master's in criminal justice, followed by a three-year stint with the Boston PD and then the FBI. The last I heard, he'd been accepted into the elite BAU unit at Quantico. I was surprised to see that he'd gone in a totally new direction. Somehow I never pictured him as a private detective.

"It's a retro candy shop," I told him. "She calls it Oldies but Goodies."

"A retro candy shop." He chuckled. "Ali's always full of surprises." He paused a beat and then said, "Would you like to grab a quick lunch at Oleander someday?" His dark gaze held mine. I must have looked puzzled because he added quickly, "Oleander is a little café on the Riverwalk. All the locals know it. Great food and you're in and out quick. We could catch up—"

He broke off suddenly as a trim woman in a pink lace designer dress interrupted us with a short, bubbling laugh. She laid her hand gently on my arm. "Taylor, I've been looking all over for you! I want to welcome you to town and hear all about that delightful little candy store your sister opened! Andre has been talking nonstop about the two of you. He's singing your praises!" She beamed a Hollywood smile at Noah; it was obvious the two of them knew each other. I felt a little pang of jealousy and tamped it down. "I'm so happy you and your sister could join us tonight. Welcome to Savannah."

Her eyes were glittery, heavily lined with kohl, and she was smiling too much, talking too fast, acting just a little too animated. I suspected she'd been hitting the Cristal pretty hard before the party began. "I declare, if those caterers don't serve dinner soon, I'm not going to tip them a penny. You all must be starving!"

Now it all fit. This trim, slightly tipsy blonde had to be Jennifer Walton, our hostess.

"Thank you so much for inviting us tonight, Mrs. Walton," I said quickly. I still felt a little awkward at tagging along on Andre's invitation. The classic uninvited guest.

"My pleasure," she said, slurring her words a little. "And call me Jennifer." She took a healthy swig of champagne. "How do you two know each other?" she asked, tucking her arm through Noah's. It was a very proprietary gesture.

"We both worked in Atlanta," Noah interjected. "That was a couple of years ago." His tone was completely flat, his expression unreadable. I could have been a coworker, a distant acquaintance, someone of no importance to him. "I was surprised to run into Taylor tonight. I had no idea she was in Savannah with her sister."

"So you two met in Atlanta!" She clapped her hands together. "How lovely—it's one of my favorite cities. Tom and I sneak away to Atlanta for a romantic weekend whenever we can." She narrowed her gaze at me, obviously fishing for information and trying not to show it.

She gave a lascivious wink. "You know what they say. All work and no play makes Tom a dull boy. I keep telling him life is more than politics. He has to have some fun! I know I do." Interesting the way she turned the conversation away from me to herself. I had to admire her skill. "Taylor," she said, suddenly shifting gears, "would you mind if I stole this handsome man away for a while? I need to talk to him about a business proposition." She gave an apologetic smile. "I know it's terribly bad manners to talk business at a social event, but this can't wait."

"Please, go right ahead." I smiled through gritted teeth.

"Enjoy the rest of the evening, Taylor," she said, turning her smile up to full wattage. "I'll be sure to drop by your sister's little store very soon."

*Little store?* So condescending. She may be a spectacular hostess, but there was something off-putting about the woman. A cold kettle of fish, as my granny would say.

"Give my best to Ali," Noah said as he was led away. I nodded, wondering if I would see him again. Did I want to? I wasn't sure. And what was his relationship with Jennifer Walton?

I wandered over to a buffet table and helped myself to some tiny crab puffs. They had an elaborate selection of hot and cold hors d'oeuvres, served on antique silver trays from a pair of mahogany neoclassical sideboards. Savory cheese straws, tiny biscuits filled with goat cheese and chives; mini freshly cut sandwiches filled with smoked salmon, cucumber, tomato, and cheese. Eye-catching and delicious. These were all things that we could serve as part of Ali's "light lunches and snacks" menu.

Savannah is known for its fabulous food, and this would be a good time to start collecting recipes. I stepped back into the drawing room and took in the opulent surroundings. From the creamy ivory curtains to the museum-quality antiques, no expense had been spared in restoring the mansion to its former glory.

"I love the pineapple finials, don't you? Jennifer ordered

them last month from a specialty shop in town. So very Savannah," a middle-aged woman murmured. "And she repeated the motif with the door knocker. She has excellent taste, don't you think?"

"Yes, I do," I said warmly. I wondered what a pineapple finial was, and glanced around for a clue. I couldn't tell if the woman was staring at the pale gray silk wallpaper or the seascape in the ornate gilded frame. If the seascape was a Winslow Homer, it was worth a small fortune. There was a muted floral pattern on the wallpaper, but nothing even vaguely resembling a pineapple. "This is my first time visiting the estate, and I have to say, I'm feeling a bit overwhelmed. I'm Taylor Blake," I said, sticking out my hand.

"Hildy Carter." She shook hands, and I noticed she was wearing a ruby the size of a walnut. "Yes, it's a lot to take in. This is one of the best restorations I've seen, and I'm in the business."

"Really?" I murmured politely.

"I run a decorating business in Savannah." She was stuffed into a black cocktail suit a couple of sizes too small and was wearing a white silk blouse with pearls.

"That must be fun; there seem to be so many grand old homes here."

"Yes, there are, but it's a cutthroat business. And sometimes customers aren't as loyal as you'd like them to be. They latch on to the flavor of the month. Out with the old, in with the new," she said with a trace of bitterness. "Are you visiting family here?"

"I am." I wasn't sure how she'd pegged me as a visitor, not a resident, but maybe it was the Northern accent. When I told her about Ali and the shop, her smile fell right off her face. She was probably disappointed when I mentioned that we lived in a small apartment on the second floor. Ali's little two-bedroom flat above the shop was filled with yard-sale finds and done up in shabby chic décor. We certainly weren't the type of high-end customers she was looking for.

"I just realized your sister's shop is right across the street from Chico's," Hildy said, her hand flying to her mouth. "Good heavens, what a terrible thing that was. Do they know what happened to him?"

I shook my head. "It seems unclear. The police are still investigating."

"Well, far be it from me to speak ill of the dead, but let's just say that I wouldn't be a bit surprised if someone murdered him. You know what they say," she said, nodding grimly, "if you play with fire, you're bound to get burned." For a split second, Lucinda's dream flashed through my mind. Hadn't she seen flames leaping all around the dancing man with no face? I remember being stuck by that image. But what could the connection be between Chico and the Waltons?

"That dance instructor broke a lot of hearts here," Hildy went on, "and you know what they say about karma. It comes right back and smacks you every time." I must have looked distracted because she took a step closer, her tone solicitous. "Is everything all right, dear?" Hildy asked. "You look like you've seen a ghost."

"I'm fine," I assured her. "It's just a bit warm in here, and I need a breath of air. Would you excuse me while I freshen up?"

"Of course, and if you or any of your friends ever need a decorator, here's my card." She pulled out an expensive embossed business card and pressed it into my hand. "Enjoy your stay, dear."

I quickly made my way to the downstairs powder room, which was like something out of a movie. *Architectural Digest* meets antebellum. The pale peach wallpaper was stenciled with delicate ferns, and the crown molding was dripping rosettes and curlicues. The attention to detail meant hand-carved, I decided. A creamy bisque porcelain bowl had been dropped into an antique marble-topped mixing stand, which served as a counter. I quickly splashed some water on my face and dabbed on some lipstick. I was about to reach for the doorknob and paused when I heard voices outside.

"I think someone's in there, we'll have to wait," a female said in a bored, slightly nasal voice. Her accent was decidedly not Southern, and I quickly pegged it as Long Island. She tapped lightly on the door and twisted the knob. "Damn it, what's she doing? Writing her memoirs?" She gave a loud snort.

"We could go upstairs," her friend suggested. "There's a bathroom right at the top of the stairs."

"I wouldn't recommend it," Ms. Long Island said with a sigh. "The last time I tried that, I wandered down the wrong hallway and Jennifer accused me of snooping in her bedroom. Can you believe it?" Her voice rose to an angry spiral. "That woman is paranoid, especially when she's had too much to drink."

"Hah! Which is like all the time. I know, she can be a real be-otch. So is it true what they're saying about Chico?"

A pause and then, "I don't know. But even if it is, so what? What's sauce for the goose is sauce for the gander, as they say."

"What does that mean exactly? I never understood that saying. Hey, I just remembered there's another bathroom out in the pool house. I can't wait another minute."

The voices faded then, and I quickly unlocked the door and stepped into the hallway. I was shaken and confused by what I'd heard. Chico was involved with the Waltons. But how? It seemed unlikely they would move in the same social circles. The dance instructor and the politician and the politician's wife? None of it made sense.

The conversation I'd overheard between the two women was cryptic to say the least. And the quote from the womans's granny buzzed in my brain. *What's sauce for the goose is sauce for the gander.* Did that mean Jennifer Walton was fooling around? And that Thomas Walton was doing the same thing? There seemed to be some murky secrets buried in his past, but I thought they had to do with shady business dealings, not adultery.

But even if Jennifer Walton was "stepping out on her husband," as they say in the South, what did that have to do with Chico? Certainly the two of them weren't lovers. It was impossible to imagine the wealthy socialite being involved with a rough around the edges Lothario like Chico.

I caught up with Ali as she was heading into the dining room.

"I heard we're sitting together at dinner," she said, sounding pleased. "I made sure I thanked Mr. and Mrs. Walton for inviting us, and I told Andre we were having a great time." She reached out and touched a magnolia blossom in a cut glass bowl centerpiece. "We need to tell Caroline how beautiful the flowers are. Let's make sure we catch up with her before we leave." I nodded in agreement. Ali is big on the social niceties. That's one thing our mother drummed into us, even if she wasn't around that much when we were growing up. "This is like something out of a fairy tale, isn't it?" She glanced at the beautifully appointed dining room and gave a happy sigh.

"Yes, it is." *A fairy tale? Maybe. But was there something sinister lurking just beneath the surface?* I found my place and slipped into my chair. We were seated at a round table for eight, and someone had written my place card in elegant-looking calligraphy. That told me Jennifer Walton paid a lot of attention to detail. Or perhaps she employed a secretary for such things? I wondered if Caroline had done the place cards as well as the catering. The table settings were beautiful, and I saw Andre cupping his hands around some candle flames that were flickering, threatening to go out. The French doors were open and a slight breeze, fragrant with honeysuckle, was wafting into the room.

We were forced to sit through a boring welcome speech from Thomas Walton. He looked slightly dissolute with a sizable paunch, a bull neck, and the beginnings of a red-splotched "drinker's nose." It was hard to imagine him being catnip to women, but power and money are known aphrodisiacs. The waiters hovered, eager to serve dinner, but he droned on about what he would do for his constituents if they sent him to Washington. Typical politician, I thought to myself. His wife playfully pulled on his cuff, and he finally raised his hands in an "I surrender" gesture and took his seat.

"Wasn't that inspiring?" A young woman seated on my right immediately began clapping when Walton sat down, and he raised his glass to her in a toast. She was obviously on his payroll, I decided. No one could possibly be that enthralled by Walton's remarks; they were dull, predictable, and full of assurances that he would put those "Beltway politicians" in their place. He didn't seem to have any concrete ideas about how he would change things, just the usual platitudes.

"It was very interesting," I agreed. *For lack of a better word*, I thought to myself. "Are you a volunteer with his Senate campaign?"

She looked about twenty-two, slim as a fairy, with silky blond hair, straight out of a shampoo commercial, and a wide smile. "I'm a staffer," she said with a hint of pride. "Amber Locke." She stuck out her hand, and I shook it a bit awkwardly. We were sitting in such close quarters, it was hard to maneuver.

I had to smile. Her eyes were shining with excitement, and she was staring at me with something akin to worship. I wondered if I had ever felt that young and idealistic. "Have you been with him a long time?"

"Ever since I graduated from Emory with a major in poli-sci. I've always loved politics, and I'd been waiting to find just the right candidate to support. Councilman Walton hired me full-time, and I'll be going with him to Washington." She gave a girlish giggle. "After he wins the election, I mean," she added quickly.

"Of course," Ali murmured. "So it's a sure thing? The election?" I know Ali has no interest in local politics, but she is unfailingly polite, eager to let others direct the conversation.

Amber gave an impromptu little speech, extolling the merits of her employer. She had obviously memorized her talking points well, answering objections before any had even been raised.

The waiters began serving hearts of palm salad on nicely chilled plates, and I let my mind wander, taking a good look at Jennifer Walton, who was chatting with her husband. She was attractive in a rather brittle way, and I wondered what her background was. How had she met Thomas Walton? Had she started out as a staffer like Amber, working on one of his earlier campaigns?

And more important, what did she have to do with Chico? And with Noah, for that matter? I couldn't help noticing that Noah was sitting at one of the "A" tables, close to the front of the room, where the Waltons were holding court. Our table wasn't in Siberia, but it was close to it, nestled near the kitchen, where we heard the whoosh of the swinging doors and the shouts of the line cooks to the servers. Still, it was nice to be included in such an A-list event, and I was happy to see that Ali was coming out of her funk. She was smiling and laughing, seemingly enjoying her chat with the young staffer.

I thought about the girl with the Long Island accent whose conversation I'd overheard. I'd probably never find her in this crowd, and even if I did, how could I ask her to clarify what she meant? It was too embarrassing to admit I'd been eavesdropping, and in any case, it wasn't any of my business. My head was buzzing pleasantly from the chardonnay, and after a few minutes, I decided to forget the thoughts that were whirling in my mind and simply enjoy the evening.

# 16

"Now that I've started dreaming about him, I can't seem to stop," Dorien said irritably. "I wish you had never made that suggestion to us, Persia. I don't feel like having Chico invade my dreams every single night. When I wake up, my head is spinning. I'd like to have some restful sleep again." We'd called an impromptu meeting of the Dream Club to compare notes, and Dorien was being her usual prickly self. There were nine of us this evening; Gina was visiting her sister in Charleston and wouldn't be back until late the next day.

"Well, honestly, Dorien, I was just trying to help." Persia sat back and poured herself another cup of tea. I saw her eyeing the brownies; Ali had made three kinds tonight. Rich, dark, Kahlúa brownies—my personal favorite—along with blond brownies and cheesecake brownies.

Persia's bejeweled hand was hovering over the tray, and Ali said gently, "Why don't you try all of them, Persia? I cut them small, so it would look like a tasting tray."

Sam Stiles gave a wry smile at this polite fiction as Persia swooped down like a hungry seagull and snatched up a handful of the delicious little cakes. The brownies were cut in generous servings but Ali, as always, was being tactful. I felt certain Persia could polish off the whole tray in a heartbeat if no one was looking.

"You know I've been dreaming about him, too," Minerva said thoughtfully. "It was almost like you hypnotized us, dear." She gave Persia a long, direct look, and Persia frowned right back.

"Oh honestly, what is wrong with you people? It's not like I brainwashed you," Persia said sullenly. "I thought the whole idea of the club was to share our dreams and analyze them."

"Yes, but it's gone a bit beyond that if we're being directed what to dream about," Rose Harper said gently. She was sitting next to her sister on the settee, and they were wearing almost identical "housecoats" of peach flowered cotton.

"I'm ready to change the subject," Sybil said brightly. "Last night I dreamt I was on an ocean liner and it was being tossed about in a storm. I felt like Shelley Winters in *The Poseidon Adventure*. Anybody have any clues what that could mean?"

"That's a common dream image," Ali said slowly. "Being surrounded by water, drowning, or being adrift at sea are all classic anxiety dreams. It means you're being buffeted by life's events."

Lucinda nodded eagerly. "That's true. I used to have a dream like that when I was feeling overwhelmed with my job as headmistress at the Academy. I was always in a rowboat, alone at night in a vast ocean, and the rowboat was springing a leak. A big ship was coming toward me in the distance, but I knew it wouldn't reach me in time. I was so alone." Her voice trembled a little, and she suddenly looked older and more vulnerable. I knew she had never married and had no family; perhaps she really did feel alone in life.

"Everyone needs a soft place to fall," Sam said, as if she were reading my mind.

"It must have been terrible for you," Ali said gently.

"Yes, it was dreadful. It was so dark, and I was terrified. I didn't know who to turn to, and I didn't know how to manage the boat." She shook her head helplessly. "I didn't have a clue how to save myself." She paused and said in voice that was almost a whisper. "Sometimes I feel like I can't control my own life."

"Can we get back to my dream about Chico, just for a minute?" Dorien cut in. She has a brusque conversational style, and I'm not sure she realizes that she sometimes comes across as being a tad rude and insensitive. "Not that I *want* to spend my time thinking about this guy, but I want to get it out before I forget it."

"Go ahead," Ali prompted. "Tell us about your dream."

"Well, this is going to be a bit of a surprise," Dorien said, leaning forward as if she enjoyed being the center of attention. "I saw Chico in my dream, and it was so real, I felt like I could reach out and touch him. I had gone to the dance studio, which is certainly odd, because I would never go to a place like that. Not in a million years." She gave a little shudder and continued. "I opened the door and there was Chico standing in the middle of the studio with a woman and child." She paused and said meaningfully, "I had the feeling they were his woman and child, if you get my drift."

"Sometimes a baby or a child in a dream has a symbolic meaning," Persia offered. "It can mean you have a desire to nurture or care for someone."

"Or maybe it's not symbolic at all," Rose offered. "Maybe your subconscious is trying to tell you something important about Chico. That he's married and has a family waiting for him."

Minerva nodded, her eyes bright with interest. "A woman and child. That certainly puts a new twist on things. Does anyone know for sure if Chico was married?" There was dead silence, and it seemed that none of us had any idea. I found myself wondering what Gina's take would be on this.

People seemed to be speaking more freely without her there, but she probably knew more about Chico than anyone in the room. "Well, that's something that's easily checked, right, Sam?"

Sam Stiles hesitated for a moment. I wondered how she would handle her dual role as investigating detective and Dream Club member. So far, all the dreams about Chico had involved imagery and emotions—visions of fire, of jealousy, of a frightening figure with no face. This was the first time anyone had raised a concrete question, and I wondered if she felt she was being put on the spot.

"Are you allowed to tell us anything about the case?" I asked her. "Don't say anything if you're not comfortable talking about it. We understand."

She flashed me a grateful smile. "I suppose it's okay to share this, since it's a matter of public record," Sam began. "In case anyone's wondering, Chico *was* married at one time to a woman named Lisa Ortez"—Lucinda let out a little gasp and then quickly covered her mouth—"but his current marital status is unclear. The records must exist somewhere, but we don't have them in the U.S."

"Do you mean he was married to someone back in South America?" I asked. Funny, but Ali had suspected Chico had a wife and children tucked away somewhere. I remember she'd mentioned it to me the night she introduced me to Chico, but I wasn't sure if she totally believed it. From what she'd told me, her brief relationship with him was already in a downward spiral and she didn't confront him on it. What would be the point? Chico would surely lie to her. He liked to pass himself off as single and available.

"Yes. That's exactly what I mean." Sam's voice was clipped, and it was obvious that was all she was going to say at this time.

"Is there any chance that some of his relatives are in the States?" Minerva asked. She turned to her sister. "Do you remember the shouting we heard that night?"

Rose nodded. "I do. Someone was hollering in Spanish or maybe it was Portuguese. I could only make out a few words here and there, but the tone certainly wasn't friendly. I studied both those languages in school because our father did a lot of business in Latin America. Both Minerva and I used to be fluent, but that was many years ago."

"Did you tell the police about this?" Sam asked.

"I've already told the police all about this, dear. I gave them a full accounting the night of the . . . incident." *The incident*. No one seemed to be calling it a murder. At least not yet.

"Yes, of course you did," Sam said, looking weary. She shook her head as if to clear it and bit back a yawn. "These late nights are getting to me." Sam had dark circles under her eyes, and I thought that being a police detective wasn't nearly as glamorous as they made it out to be in shows like *Major Crimes* and *CSI: Miami*. Sam had come up in the ranks and earned the respect of grizzled veterans on the force, but I think it had taken a toll on her personal life. She never said much about her home life, except everyone knew she was divorced with no children.

"Rose, did Chico have South American friends here in Savannah?" I asked. "Perhaps that was the source of the shouts you heard." I slid a tiny slice of key lime on her plate and she smiled her thanks. Rose eats delicately like a cat, taking her time as she samples tiny portions of every single dessert.

"Not that I know of." She looked at Sam, her blue eyes keen and expectant. "I imagine you're trying to track down everyone who might have known him."

"Yes, of course. Anyone who might . . ." Her voice trailed off, and I wondered if she'd said too much.

"Anyone who might have had a reason to kill him," Dorien said flatly. "That's what all of us should be concentrating on." She directed a level look at Sam. "If we can do anything to help the police, we'd like to, you know."

Sam nodded. "I appreciate that, I really do." She gave a rueful smile. "I don't think my captain is into dream analysis," she said apologetically. "I've heard some amazing things come out of this group, but not everyone feels the way I do. Detectives tend to be sort of a hard-boiled lot." She shrugged, and we locked eyes for a moment. I could see that Sam was softening her earlier stance and was starting to appreciate the work we did in the Dream Club.

"That they do," Sybil agreed. "I've read hundreds of mysteries, and the police always groan when someone wants to bring in a psychic as a consultant. Psychics can be powerful resources," she said earnestly, "and proper dream analysis can be just as helpful."

The meeting broke up an hour or so later, but Gina turned up just as Minerva and Rose were making their way down the steps.

"I got home from Charleston a little early," she said apologetically. "Is there still time to have a cup of coffee?"

"Of course," Ali said, reaching for the pot. "And we have loads of desserts."

"Just coffee, please," Gina said. "My sister made a big family meal, topped off with homemade cheesecake, and I'm absolutely stuffed."

I had the feeling there was something on her mind, and I suspected it involved the investigation into Chico's death. I poured us mugs of hazelnut decaf, and we sat around the cozy kitchen table. Barney purred around my ankles while Scout curled up in the empty chair. I bent down and scooped Barney onto my lap, running my hands over his soft fur.

"I heard an interesting rumor when I was in Charleston," Gina said. She was perched on the edge of her chair, her voice tight with tension. "Apparently there's a story going around town about Chico."

"About his death?" Ali asked quickly.

"No, something else. Something very unexpected, that hits close to home," she said, locking eyes with Ali. "My sister has a friend on the city council here in Savannah. The word on the street is that Chico was planning a big real estate deal when he died. A major deal," she added for emphasis. "A couple of people on the zoning commission knew about it, but it was pretty hush-hush and hadn't made the newspapers. At least, not yet."

"Chico? A real estate deal?" I said incredulously. "I can't believe it." I thought of the cheesy dance instructor in the tight pants and couldn't picture him as the South's answer to Donald Trump. His own studio was sorely in need of repair; there was nothing high-end about the establishment. So why would anyone think he was planning on being a real estate mogul?

Gina gave a ladylike snort. "It was a surprise to me, too. But I think you should know what he was up to." She gave a dismissive little wave of her hands. "I'll tell you what I heard, and you can decide for yourself whether or not to believe it. At least you'll have the facts."

Ali reached for the creamer and paused, her hand in midair. "Now you've got me really curious. What are they saying about this deal?" Her tone was casual, unconcerned, but I saw a telltale red flush begin to creep up her neck.

"Did you know Chico was planning to buy up all four shops on this street?" Gina's tone had a steely edge to it, and Ali drew back. I saw a pulse beating in her throat and wondered what was upsetting her. Chico was dead and her job at the studio was over. So what did any of this have to do with her?

"All four shops? Do you mean Minerva and Rose's flower shop, Luigi's, and the old movie house?" Her eyebrows shot up in surprise.

"And your shop," Gina pressed on. "You have a yearly lease, right? And it's up pretty soon, right?"

"Yes, it is. But how was Chico involved in this? I don't understand." Ali's voice faltered.

"Chico was in negotiations with the two brothers who

own this building. They've been interested in selling for a long time, and Chico jumped on the opportunity." As Gina spoke, I glanced around the tiny kitchen with the outdated appliances and the chipped Formica countertop. It was hard to imagine this being a golden "opportunity" for anyone.

"How did your sister know—" Ali said, and then quickly switched gears. "How would Chico have the money to buy up a building? I thought he was just scraping by with the dance studio." She gave a dismissive wave of her hand. "He worked twelve hours a day, but the studio wasn't a gold mine. I figured Chico just made expenses and maybe a little extra to pay you."

Gina snorted. "Chico had a lot of disposable income, but not from the dance studio. I don't know where he got his money, but I bet the police are looking into it right now." She kept her gaze locked on Ali's face, her own expression serious. "And these buildings would go for a song. They can't be rehabbed. It would cost a fortune to renovate them and you'd never get your money back."

"But why would he buy them up?" Ali asked. "None of them are showing a profit. Who would want to buy a failing business?" She kept her tone light, but her lips had thinned into a straight line and her jaw was clenched. I knew she was keeping something back. But what?

"That's the part I'm not sure about." Gina paused, her gaze bright and intent. She was wearing a wide enameled bracelet on her wrist and kept fiddling with it. It was blood-red with a black snake curled head to tail. An odd image and yet strangely familiar. Had I seen it before? "You had no idea about any of this? You're hearing this for the first time?"

"I had absolutely no idea about any of this," Ali said calmly. She seemed to have gotten herself under control and took a sip of her coffee. "Did Minerva and Rose have a clue this was in the works? I can't imagine them ever being willing to sell that place. They've run it for decades; they have an emotional attachment to it. It's a family business."

"A nice sentiment, but if the price is right, everybody is willing to sell." Gina gave a cynical laugh. "Or maybe Chico had an ace up his sleeve—he might have figured out a way he could pressure them to sell. I'm not sure about the details. All I can tell you is that this information came from a very good source."

"Well, I don't know if it's true or not, but I can tell you that I had no idea about any of his plans." Ali shifted in her seat, twin spots of color popping out in her cheeks. I glanced up, surprised at the note of defensiveness in her tone. "If I lose this building, my whole business would go under. It would mean the end of everything I've worked for." Tears welled in her eyes, and her voice took on a sad little note. "I don't how I could survive losing this shop," she said, looking around the cozy kitchen." I don't think I could bear the idea of starting all over again." She sat back and took a deep breath, straightening her shoulders. "And frankly, I find it a little hard to believe."

Her gaze was cool and direct, and her voice was steady as she folded her hands calmly on the table. I looked at her finely chiseled profile for a long moment. She was sitting as still as a statue. Her back was ramrod straight, but a tiny muscle was jumping in her jaw and her lower lip was trembling, almost imperceptibly. It was the only flaw I could see in her perfectly composed demeanor. My breath caught in my throat and my spirits sank.

I knew she was lying.

# 17

The kitchen was silent except for the monotonous ticking sound of the clock cat's tail swishing back and forth on the wall clock. Gina had finally left, and Ali and I were alone in the kitchen. Ali had her hands wrapped around the mug of coffee, staring into space. She glanced at me briefly, and then looked away. Her eyes were guarded, and I waited for her to explain herself, to confide in me. I studied her face for a full minute, and then I couldn't keep still a second longer.

"Ali," I began, "you need to come clean with me. You knew about Chico and his plan to buy up the buildings, I am absolutely positive about this."

"It was that obvious?" she asked wearily. Her face reddened slightly, and she still refused to look at me directly. "If you picked it up on it, then I guess Gina did, as well."

I reached across the table and laid my hand lightly over hers. "I think it was only apparent to me," I told her. "And that's because we have a history, remember? You and I know things about each other that no one else could possibly figure out. You need to tell me exactly what's going on here, Ali. I want to help you."

"It's complicated," she said, finally meeting my gaze. "I didn't want to talk about it earlier because I was too embarrassed. And maybe I was a little ashamed, I don't know." She gave a hopeless shrug.

"Embarrassed?" I blinked. I hadn't been expecting this. "Why were you embarrassed and ashamed?"

"Because I feel like a complete idiot! I found out about the sale quite by accident; a customer who's on the city planning commission mentioned it. Chico wasn't even going to tell me. Unbelievable, right? When I confronted him that night, he admitted it. I was going to lose everything, and he didn't care. How could he be so heartless? And how could I have been so stupid not to see it?" She paused, leaning back in the chair, rubbing her neck as if she was trying to will away the tension she must have been holding in her shoulders.

I was so focused on her obvious distress that I nearly missed a key word. And then it hit me. *That* night. She'd said *that* night. My heart thudded in my chest. "Ali," I said urgently, "what night? You don't mean to tell me you were over there the night he died, do you?" One look at her crestfallen expression confirmed it. "Oh my God, you *do* mean that!"

A sharp intake of breath. "I know, it looks awful," she said, giving me a wounded look. "But I just went over there to talk to him, and I swear he was fine when I left. I was only there for a few minutes while you were taking a shower. I should have said something at the time and now it's too late."

I felt like shaking her. "Too late? Ali, of course it's not too late, but you have to tell the police right now. You can't wait another minute. Suppose they find out? It makes you look suspicious"—she flinched and I backpedaled—"it makes it look like you're hiding something."

"But I'm not lying!" she said quickly and then amended, "Well, I didn't say that I'd been over there that night, but they didn't ask me." She paused, flushing. "Not in so many words, I mean."

"Ali, you've made a terrible error in judgment." I plunked my elbows on the kitchen table and rubbed my eyes with my hands. I felt a migraine coming on, but this was no time to search for an aspirin.

"What should I do?" she asked in a small voice.

"Come clean," I snapped. "That's all you have to do. It's a no-brainer." I couldn't hide my irritation with my kid sister. Ali's taken the path of least resistance at other times in her life, and it's always ended badly. I knew I had to step in immediately and insist that she do the right thing this time. "Call Sam Stiles right now." I reached behind me, grabbed my cell phone from the kitchen counter, and passed it to her.

"It's late," she protested. "Suppose she's sleeping—"

"It's not that late," I said sharply. "Tell her you need to see her and set up an appointment for tomorrow. You can go down to the station house first thing in the morning or she can come here." I locked eyes with her, and she looked vulnerable, frightened. "Either way, you have to do it!"

Ali's fingers were trembling as she clasped the cell phone. I got up to give Barney and Scout their evening treats. They like a handful of Temptations snacks before going to bed and begin circling around my feet at nine thirty or so to remind me.

Ali stood up and wandered over to gaze out the window, the cell phone clasped to her ear. I refilled their water bowls and heard snatches of conversation. Ali was talking softly, but rapidly, and her voice wobbled a little. It was probably one of the most difficult conversations she had ever had to face. When she finally flipped the lid closed, she turned to me, blowing out a little puff of air.

"Well, it's set for ten o'clock tomorrow morning," she said, licking her lips nervously. "And you were right. They want me to come down to the station house." She stared at me. "That makes it seem more official, doesn't it?"

I nodded. "I think they'll take a statement. You might not be talking to Sam; they may figure she's too close to the case. You'll probably have to speak with one of the other detectives."

"I'd rather talk to Sam," Ali said carefully.

*You could have talked to her the night it happened, or last night.* I bit back my angry retort; it was pointless to argue with her. "It's not up to you at this point," I said, trying to unclench my jaw. "The captain will make the final decision. All you can do is take a deep breath and tell the truth."

"So it's more complicated than I thought," I said hesitantly. "I never thought Ali would be a suspect, and of course the whole idea of her committing a murder is ridiculous but . . ." I let my voice trail off as the waitress set a roasted veggie wrap in front of me and a fish and chips platter at Noah's place.

She scurried away for two sweet teas, and Noah reached over and patted my hand, his eyes locked on mine. "It's going to be okay," he said softly.

I thought it might be awkward, having lunch at Oleander with Noah, but instead I felt like a huge weight had been lifted from my shoulders. Noah always had a way of making me feel secure; that there was no problem too tough to solve. The two years we'd spent apart hadn't changed anything. When I'd phoned him last night, suggesting a quick lunch today, he'd immediately agreed.

I filled him in on Chico's death and brought him up to speed on the investigation. Ali had insisted on going down to the police station by herself, and I glanced nervously at my watch, wondering how the interview was going. Ali had seemed upset this morning, and I knew she would be nervous talking to a detective.

"It's insane that they think she could be a suspect, right? Anyone who knows Ali knows that she wouldn't hurt a fly." I sighed. "She even rescues June bugs and puts them outside on the grass. How many people do you know would do that? Does that sound like a murderer to you?"

"Just because they're interviewing her doesn't mean they think she's a suspect," Noah pointed out. "She could be a material witness in the case. After all, she was one of the last people to see Chico alive. There might be some details of the crime scene that she could share with the detectives; some clue that no one else has picked up on. It's too bad she didn't come forward with this information from the get-go, but that's water under the bridge."

"What kind of things could she have noticed?" I had no appetite, but I dutifully picked up my roasted veggie wrap and took a tiny bite. It was delicious.

Noah spread his hands on the table. "Anything," he said, raising his eyebrows. "Maybe she noticed something out of place, or maybe Chico seemed agitated." He nodded his thanks as the server placed two mason jars of sweet tea on the table. I was beginning to realize that sweet tea is a Savannah staple. "When Ali told you about her visit to Chico, did she mention anything about his state of mind? Did he take any phone calls? Did anyone come to the studio to see Chico while she was there?"

I shook my head. "No, nothing like that. I'm sure they were alone. She didn't say much about meeting with him. She blurted out the truth to me, and then I insisted that she call Sam Stiles and tell her what happened. And then, just as I predicted, Sam told her to come down to the station house today." I paused. "I wanted to go with her, but you know how stubborn Ali can be. She wanted to go on her own. Probably not the smartest move, but I couldn't budge her on this one."

"That sounds just like Ali," Noah agreed. "She's a free

spirit, always striking out on her own. She doesn't like being dependent on anyone."

"I'm so glad she finally told me about it." I tried not to think what would have happened if the police had discovered her late-night meeting with Chico on their own.

Noah nodded. "You're very intuitive, Taylor. There's always been a special connection between you and Ali. Didn't you have a gut feeling all along that she was leaving out part of the story?"

"Yes, I did. There was a nagging feeling that I just couldn't ignore." I stopped to think for a moment. Noah was right. I'd been trying to quell the uneasy feeling in my stomach that Ali was troubled, and I didn't think it was because she was heartbroken over Chico. It had to be something else. I smiled at him. "You always said the gut never lies."

"That's one thing they drummed into us at Quantico. Trust your instincts. If you think something is wrong, it probably is." He dipped one of his French fries in ketchup and passed it to me. "You haven't lost your taste for French fries, have you?"

"Never." I found myself grinning, in spite of the seriousness of the situation. Our fingers brushed when he handed me the French fry, and I tried to ignore the little buzz of electricity that went through me. I reminded myself to focus on Ali; this wasn't the time to stroll down memory lane, thinking about what could have been with Noah.

We both tucked into our lunch, and I wondered again about Jennifer Walton and how Noah had happened to be at her party. Maybe it was just a business move? It would be smart to network with some of Savannah's most prominent movers and shakers if he wanted to get his detective agency off the ground. I couldn't imagine him being seriously involved with a woman like Jennifer, and unless I was imagining it, he felt the same spark of attraction between us that I did.

Noah was wearing a navy blue Lacoste shirt with khakis,

and looked tanned, relaxed. The Savannah lifestyle seemed to agree with him, and I wondered if the move here was permanent. I vaguely remembered that he had family in the area, and I asked him about it.

"Two aunts who practically raised me," he said. "They're getting on in years, and when I picked a place to settle, I knew I wanted a warm climate on the East Coast. I figured it would be nice to reconnect with them. Maybe I can help them out a little, just a way of repaying them for everything they did for me. They live right here in Savannah, not far from Ali's shop."

"I'd love to meet them," I said impulsively and then flushed. *What am I doing?* My lunch with Noah was supposed to be devoted to solving Ali's predicament, not rekindling our relationship. I wanted to bite my tongue, but Noah didn't seem the least bit taken aback by my suggestion.

"Oh, you will," he said casually. "I've already told them about you, and they want me to bring you and Ali over for Sunday dinner sometime." He laughed. "Come hungry. They believe in old-fashioned Southern hospitality."

We talked about inconsequential things then, sharing memories and finishing each other's sentences. In some ways, it seemed as though we had never been apart. Noah told me about his decision to leave the Bureau, and I told him about Ali's desperate plea to help her save the shop.

"It's funny," I said as the waitress served coffee. "I thought I was coming here for a few weeks, and now I see that I may be here for a long time."

"That's the best news I've heard all day," he said with a devilish glint in his eyes. "If ever you need a tour guide . . ." He let the words hang tantalizingly in the air between us.

"You're the third person to offer to show me Savannah." I told him about Caroline and the Harper sisters.

"You sound like you're settling right in, making connections and finding friends," he observed. "People are drawn to you, Taylor."

I felt a warm curl of desire in the pit of my stomach, and I decided to rein in the conversation and bring it back to neutral topics. I was curious about what Noah could do to help Ali; he'd seemed so optimistic on the phone.

"Well, officially, I won't be involved in the case," he said slowly. "But there's a lot that can be done behind the scenes, and I have a few connections that will work in our favor. I found out from Aunt Ellie that her son, my cousin Chris, is a detective with the Savannah-Chatham Metro PD.

"That's a good start," I said, relieved. "We can use a contact with the local police." I was pretty sure Sam Stiles wouldn't share any information now that Ali had been interrogated, and I needed an inside source to track the case.

"And there's more. Did you know that Sara Rutledge is working at the local paper?"

I blinked in surprise. "Sara's here in Savannah? I had no idea. What's she covering?" Sara had just graduated from J school at Emory when I knew her in Atlanta, and she was covering strictly rookie reporter stories: the police desk, high school basketball games, and occasionally even writing obits. We'd met at the local dog park one summer evening; she was walking her dog, Remy, and I was walking a neighbor's pooch. We're both big-time animal lovers and immediately hit it off. I knew she had wanted to move up in her career, but I had no idea she had set her sights on Savannah.

"I saw her byline on some society pieces. I think she's freelancing, probably taking any assignments she can get. Times are hard in the newspaper business."

Back in Atlanta, I knew that Sara wanted to be an investigative reporter. I wondered if she'd like to do a little sleuthing for me. Reporters have an uncanny way of ferreting out facts and getting reluctant witnesses to talk. I decided to have a chat with Sara later in the day and rekindle our friendship. But right now, I had a more pressing issue. I needed to talk to Ali and see what had gone down at the station house.

# 18

"It was awful," Ali said piteously. It was a little after three in the afternoon and she was curled up on the sofa, hugging a handmade pale blue afghan to her chest. Barney and Scout had snuggled up next to her, offering her their unique brand of feline comfort.

"Have you been like this since"—I hesitated—"since you got home?" I saw she'd made a pot of tea earlier, and the sweet smell of jasmine permeated the tiny apartment. Her face was pale, and her eyes were red-rimmed as if she'd done some serious crying.

She nodded. "I just came in and collapsed. Dana's handling things downstairs."

I nodded. "She was waiting on a couple of people when I came in. You don't have to worry about the shop; it looks like she has everything under control." I sat down beside her. "How did it go? Are you ready to talk about it?" I was determined not to make my usual mistake and grill Ali for details. In the past, she's accused me of going after information like a pit bull. "If you just want to sit quietly, we can do that. Or I can make you a fresh pot of tea, or fix you something to eat. Whatever you want." I reached out and touched her shoulder awkwardly.

"I think I'm ready to talk," she said softly. "And if you could grab the teapot off the counter, it would be great. It's still hot—I made it a few minutes ago. I just haven't had the energy to drag myself off the sofa to get it." She looked up at me. "Pretty pathetic, isn't it?"

"Not at all," I said, jumping up to get the tea. I grabbed two mugs and a plate of shortbread cookies. "You've had an incredibly rough morning, I can see that." I poured her a steaming cup of tea and she nodded gratefully. "Would you like a sandwich?"

"Thanks, but I couldn't face it." She nibbled at the edge of a tea biscuit. "Well," she said slowly, "you asked me how things went at the police station. On a scale of one to ten, it was a two." She tried to smile but I could see it was an effort.

"That bad?" When we were growing up, Ali and I used to rate everything on a scale from one to ten, whether it was boys or math teachers or prom dresses. Ten was the best, and one was the absolute worst. Rating it a two meant it was a near total disaster.

"What happened? Was Sam there?" I sat beside her, already regretting that I hadn't insisted on going with her. What if she said or did something that made her look like a viable suspect? I might have made a tactical error by insisting she call Sam Stiles. Maybe it would have been more prudent to meet with Noah ahead of time since he was a private investigator and see what he suggested? Or perhaps call a lawyer? I felt a little stab of guilt, thinking that I might have unwittingly made Ali's situation worse.

"I saw her just for a second when I came in. She was heading out to another investigation and walked by me without a word. I felt like I was a criminal. She barely made eye contact with me, and I'm sure the other detectives picked up on that."

"I wouldn't read too much into her keeping her distance,

Ali." I moved the cookies away from Barney, who had decided to sniff them with his wet nose. "I'm sure it seemed awkward to you, but don't forget, she was on duty and you were there on police business. It wasn't the time or place to socialize, and she has to play by the rules. If she'd been overly friendly to you, it might have been misinterpreted. I think she was trying to be protective of you. Did you ever think of it that way?"

"You're probably right," Ali admitted. "Still, it was a nerve-wracking experience. They kept me waiting for twenty minutes, and then I was interviewed by a Detective Scott Sanderson. The guy had a face like Mount Rushmore, absolutely no expression." I made a mental note to quiz Sam Stiles about her colleague.

"Was he confrontational? Or just cool and businesslike?"

"He was cold, almost like a robot. He asked me to tell him everything I remembered about seeing Chico that night. What I said to Chico, what Chico said to me." She reached down and pulled Barney into her lap. "He asked me if Chico seemed nervous or on edge, and then he wanted to know if I thought Chico was expecting any guests that night."

"What did you say?"

"I told him Chico wasn't too pleased to see me." Her mouth twisted in a smile. "I told him I was only going to stay a minute, and he didn't even ask me to sit down." She looked at me searchingly. "That's how eager he was to get rid of me!"

I thought for a moment. "Did the detective ask anything else?"

Ali frowned. "He asked if I'd be willing to take a lie detector test." She gave a little shudder. "I don't know if he was saying that to intimidate me or if the police are really planning on giving me one."

*A lie detector test?* Now I really regretted my decision not to involve a lawyer. Things were moving way too fast, and I felt a stabbing pain in the pit of my stomach. Was Sanderson just trying to muscle her, or did he really think they had enough evidence to charge her with Chico's murder? "Anything else?"

"He asked me if I was involved with Chico." She flushed. "You know, romantically involved. I told him no," she said firmly. "I said we were friends and neighbors and that's all."

"And that's the truth, right?"

"It's true," she said, her eyes flashing a little. "When I first moved here, I guess I was sort of lonely and Chico was available. We had a few dinners together, and then I realized he was 'available' to everyone, and I broke it off with him. I think I wised up just in time."

"Anything else?"

"Isn't that enough?" She gave a wry smile. "He asked if I was planning on leaving town anytime soon and said it wouldn't be a good idea."

"Because?" I prompted.

"Because he wants to talk to me again." I didn't like the sound of that, but decided to keep my misgivings to myself.

When Ali decided to take a long nap before dinner, I made a quick call to Sara Rutledge. She lived just a few blocks east of the shop, and we agreed to meet at a wine bar on Bay Street for a quick drink.

"You look amazing," I told her as I slipped into a booth at Chablis half an hour later. Sara is a blond beauty with green eyes and finely chiseled features. She was wearing a sleeveless black-and-white Michael Kors top over a pair of skinny jeans and could have passed for a model. "I can't believe you're in Savannah. I was so happy when Noah told me you'd moved here."

"And we're practically neighbors," she said, reaching across the table to squeeze my hand. "What could be better?" She'd already ordered two Pinot Grigios and pushed one toward me.

Sara and I quickly caught up on the past two years, and then I told her about Chico and Ali. I tried not to let on how worried I felt and just stuck to the facts in the case.

"Did the detective say she was a suspect?" she asked, all business, reaching in her oversized tote for a pad and pen.

"No, not at all. Well, at least not yet. I don't know what their theory of the case is, and I can't imagine what they think her motive would be. She should have come clean about seeing Chico that night. I guess she was too nervous and upset to think straight."

"Hindsight is always twenty-twenty, Taylor," Sara said firmly. "That's rule number one. She's probably just a person of interest to the cops. But I hope they're turning their attention elsewhere. Who looks good for the murder?"

I quickly ran down the list of suspects. No one person stood out from the pack. I thought Jennifer Walton might have something to do with Chico's death, but I didn't have any concrete evidence. Just a gut instinct. A woman at the Walton's dinner party had hinted that both the Waltons were having affairs. *What's sauce for the goose is sauce for the gander*, she'd said. Could Jennifer really have been romantically involved with Chico and then killed him in a jealous rage? Surely anyone who dated Chico would know that he wasn't "exclusive" and liked to play the field. It hardly seemed a motive for murder. Plus from the way she was hanging over Noah at the party, it looked like she had set her sights elsewhere. But I still had the nagging feeling that she might be involved in his murder.

Of course, if Jennifer really had been seeing Chico, it's possible her husband, Thomas, found out and decided to seek revenge. But it was hard to imagine the portly politician turning to murder. Unless he hired someone to do the deed? I was guessing that poison was the most likely cause of death, based on Persia's dream account of the man suddenly keeling over. And if the police did suspect poison, wouldn't it be more likely that the killer was a woman?

I wondered if Gina could have given Chico some slow-acting poison and then left the studio and returned later that evening. Maybe just in time to discover the body and come screaming across the street to Ali's shop? She had certainly seemed stunned and upset, but maybe she was a good actress. Hadn't Ali told me that she once performed in dinner theaters in Charleston?

I saw Sara stop writing, with her pen poised over the paper. She had put a question mark next to all three possible suspects. "These are pretty weak," she said, rubbing her eyes. "We're going to have to dig deeper if we want to clear Ali's name."

I glanced at my watch. It was nearly six and I didn't want Ali to wake up and find me gone. "Can we work on this tomorrow?" I asked apologetically. "I need to get home to Ali; she's had a rough day."

"And that's where you should be right now," Sara said, standing up to give me a hug. "I'm going to get cracking on this right away. I'll look into Chico's financials. If he really was going to buy up those buildings, that might open the door to other suspects. And I think I should check out this Gina Santiago a little more. Something smells fishy here. She just happens to forget her key and then discovers the body?" She wrinkled her nose. "It doesn't pass the smell test."

"You'll let me know what you find?" I asked, slinging my messenger bag over my shoulder.

"Of course. And I'll call Noah, too. The three of us should get together in the next day or so. We might as well share whatever we've got and plan a strategy."

"What should I do in the meantime?" I felt skittish and uneasy, off my game. I like being in control, and I had the unhappy sensation of being mired in quicksand. Everything was slipping away from me, and I knew I had to act fast to recover my sense of balance.

"Don't worry. And please, do your best to reassure Ali,

if you can. That should be your focus right now." She paused. "You've got to trust me, okay? I'm on it and Noah's on it. We've got your back." She gave me a warm smile. "Got it?"

"Got it." I didn't realize I'd been holding my breath and blew out a little puff of air.

I headed back home, trying to stay positive, but a famous quote from Gilda Radner flitted across my mind. "Things tend to get worse, before they get worse." That saying used to bring a smile to my face, but this time it didn't.

# 19

"Does the name Kevin Moore mean anything to you?" Noah's voice sounded ragged with fatigue, and I glanced at my watch. I'd dozed off watching *Letterman* and woke with a start when my phone chirped. I rubbed my eyes, feeling dazed and disoriented.

"Kevin Moore?" I searched my mind and came up with zilch. "Nothing, I'm afraid. But I can check it out with Ali and her friends tomorrow." I shifted Barney off my lap to reach for a pen and notepad. "Can you tell me anything about him?" It was nearly midnight, and I was alone in the den. Ali, looking pale and exhausted, had turned in hours earlier. Noah knew I was a night owl so he didn't hesitate to call me late in the evening.

"He was spotted on a traffic camera, making a few slow passes at the dance studio a couple of days before Chico died. Luckily for us, he ran a red light, so we have a good shot of his tags."

"How much do we know about him?"

"Not a lot, but maybe we'll get lucky. He drives a gray Lexus with California plates, and they traced him to an address in Los Angeles. A nice section of town, Los Feliz. Not much to go on, but it could be significant."

"What was he doing that looked suspicious?" It occurred to me that a lot of people run red lights, and normally that's the end of the story.

"They spotted him on the tapes from the security cameras outside the dance studio. The cameras picked him up three times. He kept circling the block, slowing down in front of the building and then speeding up. I think he was checking out the side of the building." I remembered that there was an alleyway next to the dance studio. "Not enough to charge him with anything except the traffic violation, but it certainly got some attention down at the station house." He gave a weary laugh. "And my cousin Chris really came through for me. He spent hours going over the security tapes."

"It pays to have a friend on the force." I thought about Sam Stiles, our Dream Club member who was a police detective. I figured she was in a difficult spot. She wouldn't be allowed to comment on the case, and everyone knew Chico's death would be the major topic of conversation. "Any description of the driver?" My pulse jumped, and I could feel a little buzz of adrenaline dispelling the cobwebs in my brain.

"The image on the traffic footage is pretty fuzzy, really bad resolution. But he's a white male, maybe mid-thirties, with brown hair and a beard." He paused, and I think he was stifling a yawn. "I have the photo from his driver's license. Assuming, of course, it really was Kevin Moore driving the car. The image is pretty grainy, but I can send it to you. Are you online?"

I touched my tablet and it came to life. "Now I am." Two seconds later, Kevin Moore popped up on the screen. He didn't have a particularly memorable face, but at least we had a possible lead. "Do you know anything about him? What does he do for a living?"

"Nothing on that score," Noah said. "All we have is the picture and the address. How did things go for Ali down at the station house?"

I lowered my voice and quickly filled him in on Ali's interview with Detective Sanderson. "She's pretty shattered by all this," I said quietly. "Of course, we don't even know if Chico was murdered, do we? I thought we were waiting for the results of the tox screen?" Persia had called me earlier that day and told me her boss said the coroner couldn't release the body until the tox results were in. A moment's hesitation and then my stomach clenched.

"Actually, the police have it right now," Noah said softly. "It's definitely been ruled a homicide. Chico was poisoned by an unknown substance. No needle marks on his body so they suspect that he ingested it. There was money in the safe and some valuable watches lying around—"

"So they've ruled out robbery as a motive, and it wasn't a crime of opportunity," I cut in. "That means it was personal. And premeditated. You wouldn't poison someone on the spur of the moment."

"Exactly. They pinpointed the time of death so it should be easier to narrow down the suspects." He paused. "Anyone who visited the studio in the late afternoon or evening is going to be on the detectives' radar screen."

"This is bad news for Ali," I said, thinking quickly. I had the horrible feeling the police might be focusing in on her with a laser-like intensity. At the moment, she was a "person of interest," but all that could change in a heartbeat.

"Not necessarily." Noah's tone was gentle, and I suspected he was trying to reassure me. "The more information they have, the better. I think they're widening the circle of suspects. There's no reason for them to zero in on Ali. There probably were a dozen people who saw Chico on the day he died, and she was just one of them."

I heaved a little sigh. "I'll have to do some checking around tomorrow. I'll find out what I can about Kevin Moore and check out some information about a woman named Lisa. She might be involved, but I'm not sure how."

"Lisa?"

"She could be Chico's ex-wife. It's a long shot, but definitely worth pursuing." I hesitated. "Sara said maybe the three of us could compare notes later in the week. Is that okay with you?"

"Absolutely. And I think we should do it sooner rather than later."

On that ominous note, we said good night and I headed to bed with Barney and Scout trailing after me.

**"I had the** oddest dream," Ali said, emerging from her room early the next morning. She looked very young in her T-shirt nightie with her hair tousled from sleep. It was barely seven, and she slipped into a chair at the kitchen table, rubbing her forehead. The apartment was quiet, and I'd opened the windows facing the street so Barney and Scout could sniff the soft morning air. Later in the day, the plantation shutters would be closed against the white-hot Savannah sun, but right now, I was enjoying the delicate fragrance of the magnolia tree in the front yard.

"A nightmare?" I poured coffee for both of us and took a seat across from her. Barney and Scout jumped down from the windowsill and gave Ali a long, slow blink, which is a sign of affection in the cat world. They'd spent the entire night snuggled under the covers of my bed, and after a quick breakfast, they'd decided it was time for another nap. It astounds me how much they can sleep, but the vet assured Ali it's completely normal.

"No, not a nightmare, just a strange dream. You know how sometimes you have dreams that are just a series of disjointed images that don't seem to be connected? The dream feels like a collection of snapshots from your everyday life?"

"Yes, I know exactly what you mean." I suffered from night terrors and don't dream the way most people do. But I remember what it was like to have dreams that were so vivid and terrifying, I was afraid to go to sleep at night. I'm glad that's all behind me now. My heart went out to Ali, and I hoped that this dream hadn't upset her. "You feel like someone is riffling through a giant file drawer in your head," I went on, "scattering thoughts and pictures everywhere. Everything is random and chaotic. Important items are mixed together with trivial things, and it's hard to make sense of any of it. It's like a rummage sale inside your head."

"That's exactly what this dream was like." Ali paused to sip her coffee. "I was going about my morning routine in the shop when a man with a beard wandered in. He seemed to know who I was, but I didn't know who he was."

"Was there something threatening about him?"

"No, not really. I didn't feel like I was in danger. He didn't say a word, just smiled at me and looked over the inventory. It was unsettling, maybe even a little creepy. He wandered around the shop for a while, taking his time, looking at everything. Finally, he bought some licorice and paid with a credit card. I remember the credit card because it had palm trees and a big yellow sun on it."

An odd dream, indeed. A man with a beard. Palm trees, sunlight. Had Ali somehow tuned into the bearded man who'd been driving past Chico's in a car with California plates? It seemed impossible. Probably just one of those strange coincidences that we all experience. Still, it might be interesting to bring it up at the Dream Club.

"What emotion were you feeling?" From the little I've read about dream analysis, I know the emotional aspect is always more important than the specific details.

"Well, let me think," Ali said, pursing her lips. "I know that I was calm, but I was definitely a little puzzled. At the end of the dream, he handed me a box and gestured for me to open it. When I lifted the lid, I realized it was empty. I had no idea what was going on, but he still didn't say a single word. He just shook his head and looked really sad." She reached for a buttery croissant from Back in the Day bakery and munched away thoughtfully. "Sometimes dreams are baffling." She bit back a little sigh. "I don't have a clue how to interpret this one."

"Neither do it, but I bet I know where to start. We need another set of eyes on this. Gina's stopping by later this morning and we can run it by her."

Gina Santiago rang the bell downstairs an hour later. The shop doesn't open till ten, but she'd ordered a selection of candies for her niece's birthday party, and I had everything packed up for her. I greeted her in the shop and invited her upstairs.

"I threw in some party favors," I told her as she looked over the selection of candy I'd assembled. "A vendor gave me some girly-looking goodie bags, and I thought you could give one to each guest."

"They're perfect," she said, examining the glittery pink bags. She reached for her purse, and Ali laid her hand on Gina's arm.

"Don't go yet," she said. "I need to run something by you."

"Okay," Gina looked surprised as I pulled out a ladder-back chair for her. "What's up?"

"Ali wants to tell you about a dream she had," I said, reaching for the coffeepot. "And I want to show you a photo."

"Now you've really got my curiosity up," Gina said. She looked slim and attractive in her navy yoga pants and blue-and-white-striped sailor sweater. While Ali recounted the dream, Gina stared at her intently, her chin cupped in her hand.

"So that's it. What do you think?" Ali sat back, her expression calm and expectant.

"The empty box is a classic dream image," Gina said. "It

can signify a lot of things, usually loss or disappointment. It goes along with the empty hand phenomenon."

"Empty hand?"

"Do you ever dream that you're holding something precious, and then when you open your fingers, your palm is empty? Whatever you're holding has vanished. One minute it's there, and then poof, it's gone."

"I've had that dream," Ali said excitedly. "I never knew what it meant, but it was always troubling and I felt incredibly sad when I woke up. The feeling stayed with me for hours."

"Here's the photo I wanted to show you," I said to Gina. I put my laptop on the kitchen table and angled the screen toward her. "Does he look familiar?"

Gina stared and her eyes widened. "That's Kevin," she said quickly. "He looks older than I remembered and he's gained some weight, but I'm sure that's Kevin Moore."

"You know him?" I couldn't believe we'd hit pay dirt so fast.

"He's Chico's partner in the studio. I mean, he *used* to be his partner," she amended. "I guess you'd call him a silent partner. They had a falling-out when he realized Chico was swindling him. Chico had a dark side, you know." She glanced at Ali and I wondered if she knew Ali had been briefly involved with Chico. This wasn't the time to spare Ali's feelings, and I wanted to make sure Gina told us everything she knew.

"Please, Gina, tell us as much as you can. Do you know what happened?"

"I don't know all the details," she said, shaking her head. "I know that Kevin fronted a lot of the money for the start-up costs of the studio. He figured all he had to do was put up the money and get his share of the profits. But somehow Chico cooked the books to make it look there never *were* any profits. He hired a shady accountant and paid him extra to fiddle with the accounts—that's my theory."

"But couldn't Kevin just confront Chico and make him pay up? Or take him to court, demand an audit?" I asked. My business training was kicking in, and I know there are plenty of ways to fight "creative accounting."

"It's not that simple. Kevin has a history, and he wouldn't want anyone scrutinizing him too carefully. He and Chico were alike in a lot of ways, always looking for a way to make easy money, a quick score." She tossed an apologetic look at Ali. "I'm sorry to say this, Ali, I don't know how much you really knew about him. Chico was a chameleon; he could be whatever you wanted him to be. He fooled a lot of people." Gina gave a wistful smile, and I found myself wondering if she and Chico had been lovers at some point.

"I probably was naïve when it came to Chico, especially when I first moved to Savannah," Ali admitted with a sad little smile. "He was always so charming"—she closed her eyes for a moment—"that it was easy to overlook the evidence that was right in front of me." She sat up straighter and tightened her jaw. "But all that's in the past. Nothing you can tell me about Chico will hurt me, Gina, so please tell us everything you know."

As I listened to Gina, I realized Chico was more manipulative and cunning than I'd realized. He wasn't just a rat with women; he scammed business partners, cheated investors, hid taxable income, and generally ran a shady operation. I'd originally thought a scorned lover (or an angry spouse) had been responsible for Chico's death. But now I realized that the pool of potential suspects had widened.

It sounded like anyone who'd ever had business dealings with Chico might be out for revenge, and I hoped the police would home in on them. But would they? The department was short staffed, and Ali and I would have to do whatever sleuthing we could—with Sara and Noah's help—to solve the case.

"Do we know for sure this was Kevin driving the car in

the surveillance tape?" Gina asked as she gathered up her things to leave.

She made a good point. The image from the traffic camera showed a bearded man, but it was too grainy to prove that it was Kevin. I suppose it was possible that he loaned his car to someone or had even sold the car. I'd have to ask Noah to look into that.

"We don't know for sure," I conceded. I was considering what our next move should be when Gina jumped in.

"You know what we should do?" She tapped the computer screen with her long blood-red fingernail. "We could show this photo around town. Savannah's a small place. If Kevin was back, it's likely someone saw him. He must have booked a hotel room, eaten out, had a few drinks at a bar, made his way around town. If you really want to find out more about Kevin, I'd do some legwork." She smiled and headed for the stairs. "Keep me posted," she said solemnly. "I want to see Chico's killer caught. He had his faults, but he didn't deserve to die." Her voice wobbled a little on the last word, and I was convinced that she was genuinely mourning him.

"She's right, you know," Ali said, the minute Gina left. "I have some errands to do, and Dana's handling the store. Do you want to come with me? We can print out a few copies of the photo and bring it with us."

"Good thinking." She looked pensive, and I knew something was bothering her. She drained the last of the coffee from her cup and rinsed it at the sink, with her back to me. Her shoulders looked tense and her head was bowed. "Ali, is something wrong?"

She turned slowly to face me, twisting the dish towel in her hand. "This sounds really crazy"—she gave an abashed little smile—"but I've think I've seen Kevin Moore before."

"You have?" I was so startled, I stood up too quickly,

nearly catapulting Barney out of my lap. He gave an indignant squawk and I grabbed him just in time, cuddling him next to me as I slid back into my seat. "Do you mean he's here in Savannah?"

"Not exactly," she hedged, licking her lips nervously "But I'm pretty sure I saw him right here in the shop." She gestured to the stairs leading to the store.

"When was this?" I wondered why she hadn't mentioned recognizing Kevin Moore when Gina was here.

"Last night."

My hand froze on my coffee cup, and a cold ball formed in the pit of my stomach.

"You mean—"

"I mean I saw him in the dream I told you about," she said in a rush. "He was the bearded man who walked into the shop." The cold ball in my stomach squeezed tighter. "I'm sure of it."

"Let's head out," I said, grabbing my purse and the photo. I told myself that it was impossible, it had to be a coincidence. But I couldn't shake the feeling of dread that overtook me or the goose bumps that sprang up on my arms. "It's probably nothing, you know," I said lightly. "One bearded man looks like another."

"Do you really think so?" Ali asked, her tone serious.

My mouth was dry and I swallowed hard. "Yes, I do, but let's go into town and show this picture around. The sooner we get to the bottom of this, the better."

# 20

Before heading into town, we made a quick visit to Lucinda's house to drop off a tray of assorted chocolates for her weekly bridge game. Lucinda lives in an adorable cottage south of the Historic District, and she welcomed us with fresh-from-the-oven cinnamon buns and iced tea. I was eager to start showing Kevin's picture around the local haunts, but Southerners take their hospitality seriously and I didn't want to offend her. Plus the delicious smells wafting from the kitchen were so tantalizing, I was practically salivating. I had skipped out without breakfast, and my stomach gave a low growl of anticipation.

"Why don't we sit in the sunroom," Lucinda said, indicating a lovely octagonal room filled with tropical plants.

"This is gorgeous," Ali murmured. "It used to be screened in, didn't it?"

"Yes, and then I had it glassed in, and added heat and air-conditioning last year when I retired from the Academy. But on a day like this, I prefer to use the screens and enjoy the warm air. I find it so relaxing to sit out here, my own little oasis. It's good for the soul to be surrounded by plants and flowers."

She glanced out at her well-tended garden, filled with trailing bougainvillea, delicate pink and white roses, sunny daylilies, snowy daisies, and lush beds of impatiens. A small fountain bubbled in the shade of a magnolia tree, and the air was rich with the smell of honeysuckle.

"That it is," Ali agreed.

"Is there anything new about Chico and how he died?" Lucinda asked after a moment. I was wondering how to broach the subject, and I was relieved she brought it up first.

Ali took Kevin's photo out of her purse and passed it to her. "There might be a suspect in the case. Does he look familiar to you? He was spotted on security tapes."

Lucinda looked at the photo and gave a delicate shudder. "No, I've never seen him before," she said quietly. "He looks like a thug." She started to pass the photo back to Ali but I stopped her. I noticed her hand was trembling.

"Take another look," I said quickly. "Please," I urged her. "It could be important. His name is Kevin Moore. Have you ever seen him around town? Or anywhere?"

"I'm afraid not," Lucinda said with a thin smile. She pushed the photo away from her as if it were radioactive. One side of her mouth twitched in a nervous spasm, and I noticed she was clasping her hands a little too tightly in her lap. "You said he's a suspect. Is he local?"

Ali told her what we had learned from Gina. I had the feeling Lucinda knew more than she was letting on, but she kept her expression bland, maintaining her composure. She was hiding something, but what?

"So how was the dinner at the Waltons?" Lucinda asked, deftly changing the subject.

"It was wonderful," Ali gushed. "What a place. Did you ever go back to that same dream, Lucinda? The one about dancing in a ballroom with a man with no face?"

"I've never had that dream again," Lucinda said slowly,

"and maybe it's just as well." She raised her eyebrows meaningfully. "Some things are better left unexplored," she said quietly.

"The mansion in your dream sounded a lot like the Waltons' place," I piped up. "Did you ever investigate that further?" I remembered that Lucinda had mentioned she was going to look for some old photos of the mansion, when it was the Collier estate, and see if it resembled the ballroom in her dream.

"I did," she said, brightening. "I found some wonderful photos from the Historical Society and copied them. It's quite amazing. The frescoes and the French doors are exactly like I pictured them in my dream. And the fountain, too. It was remarkable—everything was identical, down to the tiniest detail. I'll have to remember to share that at the next meeting of the Dream Club."

"These rolls are delicious," I said after a moment. I smiled at Lucinda. She was leaning back on the settee and seemed more relaxed now that we weren't talking about the photo. "I bet they're made from scratch."

"Why, yes, they are," she said, beaming. "Sour cream is the secret ingredient. It's one of my great-aunt's favorites; it's been in the family for years. Would you like the recipe?"

"I'd love it!" Ali said, enthused. "Taylor and I were talking about expanding the shop and offering coffee and desserts. This would be a wonderful addition to the menu. If you'd allow it, of course."

"Why, I'd be honored." Lucinda said. "I'm putting all my recipes in a computer file, and I just printed out some copies of the cinnamon roll recipe for the bridge club." A bell dinged from inside the house, and Lucinda glanced at her watch and jumped up. "I need to check on my blueberry muffins." She gestured to a glass-topped table in the far corner of the sunroom. "You'll find some copies of the cinnamon roll recipe right there next to the computer. Just help yourself; I made plenty."

Lucinda bustled off to the kitchen, and I crossed to the glass-topped table for the recipe. The laptop was open and I accidentally jostled it. The screen sprang to life, and what I saw made my heart skip a beat. Lucinda had logged in to a members-only section of an online dating service called Find Your Mate, and it was open to her home page. Horrified, I glanced at her online profile and winced at a rather unflattering headshot and quickly closed the screen. Lucinda and an online dating service? As Ali would say, who knew? The wren-like woman with the quick nervous mannerisms was full of surprises. I could hardly wait to tell Ali.

"You look like the cat that swallowed the canary," Ali said as soon we got outside. We headed north toward Forsythe Square, and the noonday sun was filtering through the banyan trees lining the sidewalk. We'd decided to have an early lunch at a little family-run place on Henry Street that has some of the best crab bisque in town.

"I have something to tell you," I began. "And you're going to find it a little shocking."

"The cinnamon rolls weren't really homemade and they came out of a can?" Ali joked.

"No, the cinnamon rolls are the real deal. But back at Lucinda's, I saw something on the computer screen that rattled me a little." Ali raised her eyebrows and shot me a questioning glance. "Shy little Lucinda is looking for a man—online."

"No! Lucinda? I can't believe it," Ali said and started to giggle. "Please tell me you're kidding." I told her about the dating site I'd discovered on the computer. "There has to be some other explanation. Maybe she was checking it out for someone else."

"'Fraid not," I said. "I saw her profile page with her photo. She was wearing a navy blazer with a crisp white blouse and looked rather stern. Exactly like a headmistress. I don't think she's going to have many takers with that picture."

"Oh dear, that's probably the same photo in the Academy yearbook. It's dreadful. I wish she had confided in me. I could have helped her with hair and makeup, you know, made her look a little more approachable. And maybe I could have introduced her to someone, so she didn't have to go on one of those awful dating sites."

I shook my head. "Lucinda would be horrified if she thought you knew about this. Please don't mention it to her, Ali. You mustn't breathe a word."

Ali's lips twitched and then she snapped them shut like a turtle and turned an imaginary key. "My lips are sealed," she said with a grin.

We settled in a booth at the Back Burner Grille just in time to see Persia coming in the front door. I remembered that Persia worked as a paralegal at a real estate office nearby, and the restaurant was popular with Savannah lawyers. I felt like I'd stepped into a *Matlock* episode when I saw a group of men at the neighboring table. They all had silver hair and were wearing seersucker suits, talking animatedly over their mason jars of sweet tea and generous platters of chicken potpie.

"Can I join you?" Persia asked, giving a wide smile. "I'm taking a quick lunch break, so I'm just going to have a bowl of soup and run." She slid into the booth next to Ali. "Have you been out shopping?"

"Something like that." I smiled. *Shopping for a suspect*, I thought to myself. I dug Kevin Moore's photo out of my purse. "You haven't seen this guy around town, have you?"

Persia wore red-framed cat glasses, which dangled elegantly from a chain around her neck. She perched her glasses on her nose and squinted at the photo. "Nope, never. But if he's in Savannah, Marlene will know."

"Marlene?"

"One of the best waitresses in town. She's got such a

following, they mention her in the local guide books. Show her the picture when she takes our order. I bet she can help you out." Persia glanced briefly at the menu and then looked at us, brimming with excitement. "Have I got some news for you!" she said.

"Good or bad news?" A frown flitted across Ali's face.

"That depends on who you are," Persia said mysteriously. She had our complete attention and was enjoying every second of it. "I learned something very interesting. It has to do with our friend Chico, and it came as a huge surprise to me. In fact, it's something of a shock."

"You learned something from a dream?" Ali asked.

Persia waved her hand in the air as if she were swatting a fly. "Not in a dream, honey. This is the real thing. I learned it from the law office." She leaned forward across the table. "I was researching some real estate records, and I discovered that Chico was planning on buying up practically an entire block of buildings. On *your* block," she said, nodding at Ali. "You would have been out in the cold if he'd stayed alive, sweetie, and that's the truth."

"Yes, I know," Ali said sadly.

"You've already heard?" Persia looked astounded. "Hardly anyone knows about this. I'm curious—how did you ladies find out?" She looked disappointed, as if someone had stolen her thunder.

"We heard a rumor," I said quickly. There was no need to tell Persia what we knew or didn't know; my main interest was ferreting out as much information as I could from her. "How did you discover this, Persia?"

"It was just plain dumb luck." Persia tapped a manicured nail on the tablecloth. "I picked up a wrong file by mistake. That's when I discovered that Chico planned on buying up the whole block and selling all the buildings to some real estate developer."

"But they wouldn't be worth much," Ali objected. "Most

of the buildings are really run down. Chico's studio was probably one of the nicest places, and the outside wasn't much to look at."

"But Chico had a plan. The developer was going to get some money from the state for 'gentrification.' That way, he could receive funding to rehab the buildings, turn them into B and B's, and attract tourists who were looking for a little charm in a downtown location. Close to all the sights with all the comforts of home. Southern charm at a reasonable price. It was genius, sheer genius."

"But you say Chico was going to buy them up? Where would he get the money?"

Persia bit her lips, her eyes thoughtful. "Now that's the part I can't figure out. I don't see how he could have had that kind of money to invest. Do you suppose he was doing something illegal? Or had some source of income that nobody knew about?"

"Like what?" Ali asked.

"I don't know, I'm stumped. That's the part of the story that doesn't make sense." Persia gave a little sigh. "Where's Marlene? She always covers this table." She glanced worriedly at her watch. "I hate to eat and run, ladies, but duty calls. If she doesn't show up soon—"

"Hold your horses, Persia, I'm right here." A large woman in a crisp pink uniform appeared at the table like a genie out of a bottle. She grinned at Persia and whipped out a pad. "Can I get you the usual, hon?"

"Just the crab bisque today, please," Persia said. "No time for a panini."

"What about the lemon pie?" Marlene winked at us. "It sells out real quick, but I always hold back a few pieces for my favorite customers."

"Well, in that case, you tempted me. But please make the pie to go, Marlene. I'll eat the soup here and save the pie for back at the office."

We quickly gave our orders, and before Marlene darted away, I whipped out Kevin's photo. "Any chance you've seen this guy before?"

"She never forgets a face," Persia offered. "Take a real good look, Marlene."

"Sure, I do remember him," Marlene said, tapping her pencil on the order pad. "He was in here for dinner the other night. It was Saturday."

"You're sure about that?" My pulse jumped with excitement. Now we could prove that Kevin was in town the day before Chico was killed.

"I'm positive. I know it was a Saturday because he ordered the chicken and dumplings; that was the special that night. I remember he asked me how it was fixed. Obviously a Northerner," she snorted, rolling her eyes. "I don't think he'd ever heard of chicken and dumplings. Anything else?"

"No, that's fantastic, you've really helped us." I tucked the photo back in my tote bag and sighed. "Well, that's a step in the right direction," I said as she hustled back to the kitchen.

"How does this Kevin person fit into the picture?" Persia asked.

"We're not sure, but Gina thinks Chico swindled him in a business deal. It had something to do with the dance studio. But maybe Kevin's involved in this new real estate deal, too. He could have loaned Chico the money, and maybe Chico cut him out of the deal? Chico's probably into Kevin for a lot of cash."

Persia raised her eyebrows. "But how's that a motive for murder? If Kevin killed Chico, he'd never see a dime of that money." I thought of Noah always telling me to follow the money trail. It was one of his favorite expressions. We did, but the trail was getting cold.

"True," Ali agreed, biting her lip. "It had to be something else. Maybe Chico was blackmailing Kevin."

"Over what?"

"I have no idea," Ali said. "We need more information. There are a lot of missing pieces, and I feel like we're attacking an iceberg with a toothpick."

"Persia," I said, "do you have any idea what's going to happen to the real estate deal, now that Chico's dead? Is someone else going to step in and take his place?"

"Well, it wouldn't surprise me if they did; it's a real good opportunity if someone has that kind of cash lying around." She turned to Ali. "Do you happen to know Hildy Carter? One of the lawyers told me she had her eye on that block of buildings earlier this year. From what I heard, she was scrambling to get together the money and Chico beat her to it."

"Hildy Carter, the decorator?" I remembered the woman who was talking about "finials" at the Walton dinner party. I had never gotten around to Googling the term.

"That's the one," Persia said, reaching for a biscuit. A tempting array of biscuits, muffins, and corn bread squares were nestled in a small wicker basket in the center of the table. I had been doing my best to resist temptation, but now that Persia had a biscuit in hand, I felt my own hand creeping toward a blueberry muffin.

"I remember she said times were tough in the decorating business. I had the feeling she was hard up for money." I also recalled that when she mentioned Chico's death, she had said something about karma.

Persia laughed. "Oh, don't let that pauper act fool you. She inherited a ton of money from her daddy and she's a sharp one, always looking for a good investment. You have to move fast on these deals, and I think Chico beat her out by a few hours. Or at least he would have, if someone hadn't knocked him off. At least, that's the word around the office. I'll tell you one thing about Hildy—she doesn't like to lose. She's sweet as pie, until you cross her."

I raised my eyebrows, not sure what to do with these new pieces of information. "Chico's death could be a lot more complicated than anyone realized," I said, putting my napkin on my lap. "It's like trying to put a jigsaw puzzle together when you don't have all the pieces."

"That's a darn good analogy and I feel the same way," Persia said. She sat back, catching the eye of the plump waitress, who was headed for our table. "But for the moment, let's put Chico out of our minds and enjoy our lunch. Marlene just came out of the kitchen with our order, and that soup smells heavenly." After Marlene had served us, Persia reached for a sour cream muffin when she suddenly paused with her hand in midair. She had a Cheshire cat smile on her face, and Ali and I exchanged puzzled looks

"Is something wrong, Persia?" I asked.

"Oh no, nothing's wrong, but I just remembered something," she said, casting a thoughtful look at Ali. "I had the strangest dream last night. One of those out-of-the-blue, it-could-never-happen dreams. The kind where you wake up and think, 'Wow! What was all that about?' "

"Really?" Ali leaned forward, eager to do an interpretation. "We all have those dreams from time to time, I'd love to hear about yours."

"And I'd love to tell you about it," Persia said, shaking her head. She gave a throaty chuckle, her eyes bright with merriment. "But I think I'll save it for the Dream Club. It's about one of the members, and it's a doozy! If I talk about it right now, I'm going to collapse in a fit of giggles. That's how outrageous it is."

"You can't even give us a hint?" Ali's tone was plaintive.

"Just remember, still waters run deep," Persia said mysteriously. "Very deep."

# 21

"I have no idea what she was talking about, do you?" I said as we stepped into the bright Savannah sunshine. It was nearly two o'clock, and tourists were sitting in Lafayette Square eating mint chocolate chip ice cream and poring over travel guidebooks.

"Not a clue." Ali laughed as she pulled her sunglasses out of her purse and hoisted her bulging tote bag a little higher on her shoulder. "Persia certainly was being secretive. My mind is still reeling from our visit to Lucinda. Who would have suspected she'd signed up for an online dating service? It was very sweet of her to share her recipe with us, though."

"So you really *are* making plans to offer dessert at the shop? I was so happy when you asked Lucinda for that cinnamon roll recipe, but then I thought that maybe you wanted to flatter her."

"Oh no, I wasn't just being polite. Those rolls were awesome. I've been thinking about what you said. I think we should start off small, bring in a few tables and chairs, and offer desserts and coffee. It could lead to bigger things for us down the road. A whole new revenue stream and some new customers as well."

"Absolutely," I said, enthused. I didn't want to push Ali too fast, but I could already picture making Oldies but Goodies a fun gathering place. We could hold regular events, maybe have some book signings, or even offer cooking lessons from local chefs. And if we could get a magazine like *Savannah Styles* to feature us in an article, it would be a huge draw. My mind was racing with possibilities, and I heard Ali give a low chuckle.

"Calm down, Taylor," Ali said, sending me a knowing smile. "I can see the wheels churning in that fast-track mind of yours, and I want to take this slow."

"Slow," I said hesitantly. "Okay, I get it, Ali, I think you're right. Slow can be good. One step at a time." What was I saying? Slow isn't my style. Full speed ahead is my style. As General Patton said, "Lead me, follow me, or get out of the way."

"I mean it, Taylor." Ali's voice was firm, her eyes serious. "It's a wonderful idea, but I want to do this my own way. Oldies but Goodies is a nice little candy shop, and I don't want to change it too fast. I've seen what happens when people expand too quickly. The shop could lose its whole character as a vintage candy store, and we could end up with a hybrid that no one wants."

"Got it," I assured her. "We'll do it your way," I promised. Secretly, my thoughts were racing like a gerbil on an exercise wheel, but there was no need to rock the boat just now. We had a murder to solve.

"I hear Chico's wife is back in town. She's going to be handling all the funeral arrangements. I suppose we should check the obits column in the *Savannah Tribune* for details."

Sybil Powers sat back on the chintz-covered settee with

a satisfied look on her face. "I'm assuming we all want to go, don't we?"

If she'd hoped to deliver a bombshell, her wish had come true. There was a stunned silence, and then the Harper sisters tittered nervously.

"A wife?" Minerva said in loud whisper. "I had no idea he was married. He was such a"—she paused delicately—"man about town."

"For heaven's sake, Minerva," Rose said impatiently. "No one says 'man about town' anymore. You make him sound like Cary Grant. He was a player, I believe that's the term they use nowadays. A real skirt chaser."

I was pretty sure no one said "skirt chaser" anymore, either, but I was enjoying the conversation too much to interrupt.

"Oh, did I say his *wife*? Silly me, I meant his *ex*-wife," Persia purred. She grabbed a Madeleine and took a tiny nibble, glancing around the circle. The Dream Club had just started, and we had a full group this evening, including Sam Stiles and Gina Santiago.

Sam was preoccupied stirring lemon into her jasmine tea and didn't look up at Persia's pronouncement. I had the feeling she was determined to maintain a low profile whenever the talk turned to Chico's death. As a police detective, she really didn't have much of a choice; if she discussed the case, it would be unethical and unprofessional.

Ali froze, the tray of assorted marrons wobbling dangerously in midair until Sybil reached out and steadied it. Ali was a bundle of nerves tonight and seemed upset anytime Chico's name was mentioned. I took the tray from her and placed it in the center of the table.

"Are you sure about this?" Dorien, jaw jutting forward, asked bluntly. "The guy was married?"

A little frown appeared on Persia's lips, but she quickly dabbed her mouth with the edge of her napkin. "I'm positive," Persia said flatly. It was clear she didn't like being challenged.

"Oh, everyone knew he had a wife or two stashed away someplace," Gina said. "I'm just surprised she showed up here in Savannah."

Ali sank into a seat next to me. "Change of subject, everyone. Let's get into dreams, okay?" I thought I heard a note of pleading in her voice.

Persia nodded. "I'd like to go first, if I may." She glanced quickly around the room to make sure no one was going to object. "I had a very odd dream last night," she said. She looked at me and winked. "I've just been bursting to tell someone."

"Well, go ahead," Dorien said irritably. "You've got the floor." She made a sweeping gesture with her hand that was meant to encompass the room. The little sneer on her lips made it clear she hadn't intended it as a gracious gesture.

Persia clasped her hands together dramatically. "Lucinda, my dream was about . . . you."

Lucinda flushed and put her hand to her throat. A worried look flitted across her face but she said gamely, "Really, Persia, I was in your dream? How very odd." She forced a thin smile.

"What was I up to?"

"Let's hope you weren't strolling naked down the freezer aisle in Publix again," Dorien said churlishly. "I haven't been able to get that image out of my mind." I glanced at her, perplexed. Dorien has never been known for her tact, but she was being particularly abrasive tonight.

"You were dancing, Lucinda," Persia said, drawing the words out. "With Chico. And the two of you were drinking white wine out of lovely cut-glass goblets." She gave a little sigh and lifted her eyes to the ceiling.

I exchanged a look with Ali, who shrugged and raised her eyebrows. *White wine and cut-glass goblets?* Persia certainly had an eye for detail. And a taste for the dramatic. It seemed overly descriptive to me, but she loves bold colors and designs, so maybe it wasn't too much of a stretch. I'd have to ask Ali if artistic people have more detailed dreams than ordinary folks.

"What!" Lucinda paled. "Is this some sort of joke, Persia? Because I don't think it's the least bit funny." A deep flush worked its way up Lucinda's collarbone and was settling under her chin.

"Of course it's not a joke." Persia looked flummoxed. "Why would I joke about a dream? This is the one place where all our dreams are taken seriously. I thought we were free to say anything we wanted. Honestly, Lucinda, I had no idea this would upset you." She folded her hands in her lap and struck a pious pose. She looked up at Ali. "Would you like me to continue?"

"I think we should leave it up to Lucinda," Ali said diplomatically. Ali hates any kind of confrontation, and I wondered how she'd work her way out of this one. Was Lucinda being overly sensitive, or was Persia out for blood?

Lucinda heaved a sigh. "Yes, of course, please continue, Persia," she cut in. "Say whatever it is you have to say." Ali and I exchanged a look. Lucinda's reaction was baffling.

I couldn't recall her ever being upset by someone recounting a dream before. Did she think Persia was mocking her? A more sinister thought flitted through my mind. Was she reacting so strongly because she had something to feel guilty about?

"You were alone in the dance studio with him," Persia continued. "The lights were low and music was playing. He'd lit some candles. I remember they smelled like cranberries."

*Uh-oh, wine and music and candlelight. I could see where this was headed.*

"Really, Persia," Lucinda rasped. She put her hand to her throat as if she were losing her voice. "Are you suggesting that we were indulging in some sort of romantic interlude?"

"Indulging in what?" Minerva said. Minerva is notoriously hard of hearing, and Lucinda's voice was barely above a whisper. "What did Lucinda say? I missed it." Minerva nudged Rose and scowled.

"She thinks Persia is accusing her of having a romantic interlude," Rose said patiently, drawing the words out like taffy.

"Romantic interlude?" Minerva cackled. "In my time, they called it hanky-panky. Why can't people just speak their mind these days?"

"Oh, my goodness, it wasn't anything like that, dear," Persia continued. "You were taking dance lessons from Chico. It was all on the up-and-up. You looked very graceful, and he was like a prince, spinning you around the floor. It was a Latin number, and I was impressed at how you followed the steps so well. Almost as if the two of you had danced together for years."

I had never heard anyone refer to Chico as a "prince" before, but I kept my opinions to myself. I was curious how this would all play itself out.

"What happened next?" Gina prompted. Her voice had a hard edge to it. Either she knew something about Chico and Lucinda, or she was tired of Persia taking so long to tell the story.

"Nothing, that was the end of the dream," Persia said with a little smile.

Ali frowned. "Why are you so sure Chico was giving her dance lessons? Maybe it was a"—she paused—"a social evening."

Persia shook her head. "I don't think so. I forgot one little detail. Lucinda wrote him a check when the dance was over," she said triumphantly. "That's how I know he was giving her dance lessons."

"Interesting," Gina said coldly. "She wrote him a check. Quite a telling detail."

"But what does the dream mean?" Sybil said. "I don't have a clue how to interpret it."

"This is going to be a tough one," Minerva said. "Maybe we should all think about it and come up with some interpretations for next week."

"Good idea," Rose seconded. "I don't mean to change the subject, but I do have to say, these lemon bars are exquisite, Ali."

Ali flushed with pleasure. "Thank you so much," she said, looking relieved. I think she was happy to move on to a new subject. "Taylor and I have a little announcement to make. We're going to add a dessert menu to the shop, and I'll be trying out lots of different recipes on you. You'll be my beta tasters, and we'll keep the ones you like."

"I think that's a wonderful idea," Minerva said heartily. "You could bring in some bistro tables and scatter them around. The shop is easily big enough to accommodate them."

"And umbrella tables for the sidewalk," Rose said. "Everyone likes to sit outside in nice weather. And it's almost always nice weather here," she said, looking directly at me. She knew I lived in Chicago, the "Windy City."

"You're right," Ali agreed. "We already have a couple of tables in the back, but we need to have some in front of the shop. It would draw people inside."

We spent the next few minutes talking about the expansion planned for the shop, and Sybil treated us to one of her famous "dream-hopping" experiences. This time, she traveled back to sixteenth-century France and managed to insert herself in one of Marie Antoinette's dreams. I thought this was a stretch, but everyone else seemed to accept Sybil's theory that time and space are fluid and don't pose any barriers to dream work.

"Marie Antoinette! How exciting," Dorien said. "I hope she wasn't in prison, dreaming about the guillotine."

"No, she certainly wasn't," Sybil huffed. "She was a young girl, just arrived from Austria, and was dreaming about the man she was destined to marry, the Dauphin. She felt like a prisoner at the French Court of Louis XVI, and she was dreaming about running through a field of wildflowers. I think the flowers represented freedom; that would be my interpretation."

"Flowers can also symbolize new beginnings, new life," Sam Stiles offered. This was the first interpretation she had offered tonight. I noticed she hadn't said a word when Persia had described her dream about Lucinda and Chico.

"Yes, that's a very popular dream symbol," Ali agreed. "I've had those dreams myself, especially during stressful times in my life. I'm running barefoot in a field of flowers, and the colors are so vivid, really vibrant. It's a very comforting dream."

"Was Marie Antoinette speaking French in her dream, or were there subtitles?" Dorien asked wickedly.

"Of course there were no subtitles," Sybil bristled. "This wasn't a foreign film, it was a dream. I had complete access to her inner thoughts and emotions, and I saw everything through her eyes. There was no need for dialogue."

"Well, that's certainly convenient because I expect you've forgotten your high school French by now," Dorien sniped. "Now, may I tell everyone about my dream?"

As always, Dorien was itching to hog the floor. Dorien described a pretty mundane dream about climbing a cliff and admiring a beautiful vista and a spectacular sunset. The reddish brown colors of the rocks and hills seemed to suggest the Southwest, and Dorien confided that she was planning to visit her sister in Albuquerque.

"This seems pretty straightforward," Persia offered. "You didn't feel any anxiety about being at the top of the cliff, did you, Dorien?"

"Not a bit. I was as happy as a clam."

"Then I'd say it's a wish fulfillment dream, wouldn't you,

Ali?" When Ali nodded her consent, Persia asked if anyone had a different interpretation, but no one had any new ideas.

Ali had taught me that dream content can simply reflect "residual material" from the day and not have any particular significance. Dorien admitted that she'd spent an hour at the computer before bedtime, checking out flights to New Mexico, so it wasn't surprising that her mind created a scenario that placed her in a desert setting.

The brain needs time to process information so dreaming is a way of sorting new material and putting it in the context of a series of images. Sometimes the thread has a strong emotion attached to it and sometimes not. The meeting ended shortly afterward, and I was heading to the sink with a pile of dishes when the phone rang. I caught myself wishing it was Noah. I was surprised by how much I was looking forward to our next meeting with Sara.

"I'll get it," Ali said cheerfully. A moment later, her faced hardened and her voice grew chilly.

"Detective Sanderson," she said in a flat voice, "what can I do for you?" She turned her back to me, pacing around the kitchen, listening for a full thirty seconds. "Okay, I'll be there," she said. Her tone was leaden, defeated.

"What did he want?" My pulse was pounding and I tried to read her expression when she turned to face me.

"Another interview," she said, sounding hopeless. "Down at the station house . . . first thing tomorrow morning."

"It will be all right," I said, rushing to her side to give her a hug.

"Do you think so?" She shook her head, her eyes blank. "I'm not so sure, Taylor. Not this time."

# 22

"What did Sanderson say exactly?" Noah picked at his lobster salad, and I could tell he wasn't enjoying it. He's strictly a meat-and-potatoes kind of guy, but he'd gamely ordered the lobster salad because it was the house special at Andrea's on Broughton Street. I used to tease him about expanding his gastronomic borders. I thought wistfully about all the good times we'd enjoyed together back in Atlanta. Those were carefree days, without the threat of a murder investigation looming over us.

"Very little," I said crisply. "He asked for another meeting with Ali this morning, and naturally, she refused to let me go with her." I glanced at my watch. Ali was probably being grilled by Sanderson right this minute, and I felt my breath catch in my throat. Ali had looked pale but calm when she left the house, and I hoped she'd managed to keep her composure.

"Ali can be stubborn at times," Sara said with a smile. "She knows her own mind, that's for sure. Do you suppose Sanderson has new information about the case?" The three of us had met for an early lunch to compare notes, and even though my stomach was roiling with worry over Ali, I felt comforted being in the company of good friends.

"I have no idea, but the thought crossed my mind." I bit back a sigh and speared a chunk of sweet potato off my roasted veggie platter. "I wonder what he could have come up with?"

Noah shook his head, and Sara shot me a sympathetic look. "I think it's time for a status report," she said, pulling out a notebook. She pushed aside the remains of her margarita pizza and reached for her reading glasses. "Shall I go first?" Noah and I nodded and she said, "Do either of you know someone named Lucinda Macavy?"

"Of course. She's a member of the Dream Club. Ali and I both know her very well." I couldn't imagine where Sara was going with this, and Noah had lifted his eyebrows at the name.

"The word on the street is that Chico might have been involved with her."

"Involved? You've got to be kidding." I immediately thought of Persia's dream about Chico and Lucinda wrapped in each other's arms, dancing around the studio to Latin music. "That's impossible."

"Nothing's impossible," Sara said archly. "That's the first rule of reporting." She smiled at Noah. "I bet it goes for detective work, as well."

"That it does," Noah said, pushing his salad away. He glanced around for the waitress, and I knew he was going to order dessert. Southern desserts are to die for, and Savannah has some mouthwatering classics.

"Well then, far-fetched," I said, gulping down some sweet tea. Persia's dream couldn't be true, could it? A sudden thought hit me. "Wait a minute. You meant romantically involved, right?"

"Oh no," Sara said firmly. "I meant financially." She shrugged. "I suppose they could have had a little something going on in the bedroom department, but"—she allowed herself a little giggle—"she doesn't really seem like the type to hook up, does she?"

I had to bite my tongue to keep from laughing. It was doubtful that Lucinda had ever heard the expression "hooking up" and she would be appalled to think it was being applied to her. Lucinda, with her white gloves and gardening awards, was every inch a Savannah lady.

"No, she doesn't." I remembered her profile photo on the dating site—she'd been dressed like a prim schoolmarm. Then I recalled Persia's comment: *Still waters run deep.* "What was the financial connection between them?"

"One of my pals is an investigative reporter, and she said Chico had a history of scamming women out of their life savings. I should say 'women of a certain age' who were lonely and vulnerable. It's the kind of thing that's tough to prove, but Chico's name came up in an FBI investigation on Ponzi schemes. There was never enough evidence to formally charge him, but it looked like he was cheating women out of their life savings."

"I wouldn't think Chico was clever enough to set up a Ponzi scheme." I took a big gulp of sweet tea. The restaurant suddenly seemed stifling to me even though a Casablanca fan was whirring slowly above us.

"It's not that hard to do," Sara said. "You just have to pay off the early investors, the people at the top, and then you keep everything that comes in after that. If you buy in early, you come out okay, and if you're at the bottom of the pyramid, you lose your shirt. Of course, you've got to find people gullible enough to agree to the idea."

*Pretty clever*, I thought, *and completely illegal.*

"Chico might have been smarter than you think," Noah offered. "He was the first one to recognize that buying up the buildings on your block was a smart move, remember. He spotted it as a golden opportunity, not just a bunch of run-down buildings."

"The guy could smell money a mile away," Sara cut in.

"And he managed to swindle Kevin out of his share of the dance studio," Noah continued. "Plus he seemed to have a pretty significant income stream on the side."

"We still don't know anything else about that angle, do we?" The more I learned about Chico, the more I disliked him.

"He has a history of robbing business partners and scamming investors. Chico might have pocketed large sums of money and stashed them in secret accounts. It would take a team of forensic accountants to sift through all his records and make sense out of them."

"So maybe this is all about money?" I said thoughtfully. "If that's true, why are the police looking at Ali as a suspect?" As soon as I asked the question, the answer lit up in my mind like a neon sign.

"Because she was over there shortly before he was killed." Sara looked sympathetic.

*And because they had a history*, I added silently. Sara didn't know that part of the story, and I wasn't about to get into it with her.

"Your turn," Sara said to Noah.

Noah opened a manila envelope and pulled out a grainy black-and-white photograph.

"You didn't get this from me," he cautioned. "I'm going to show it to you, and then I have to take it back."

"What is it?" I said eagerly. I was hoping against hope that it was evidence that would clear Ali or at least point the finger of suspicion at someone else.

"It's a screen shot from a surveillance video of Chico's dance studio," he said, lowering his voice. "Tell me if you can identify the woman entering the studio."

The image was poor quality, the lighting was terrible, and the resolution was far from optimal. But the figure on the screen was immediately recognizable. My heart stopped in my throat.

"That's Dorien Myers," I said softly. "She's a member of

the Dream Club." I frowned, baffled, as my mind tried to make sense of the inexplicable. "She has no connection with Chico."

Noah shrugged. "Apparently she does. Look at the time stamp on the screen shot."

"Six o'clock," I said, my voice wobbly with shock. "The night he died. There was no reason for her to be there that night." *Or any other night.* First Lucinda and now Dorien? Chico was starting to resemble a giant spider, extending his web further and further, ensnaring more prey. And like Ali, Dorien hadn't volunteered any information about visiting the studio. I wondered if Detective Sanderson would grill Dorien as he had my sister.

"And she's carrying something," Sara said, leaning across the table to see the photo. She looked at Noah. "What is that? It looks like a picnic basket. Weird." She glanced at me. "Unless she's bringing him dinner." She flicked me a glance. "Does that seem likely to you?"

"It's the last thing I would expect," I said, shaking my head. I felt like one of those restaurant owners on a reality show, watching their employees on hidden camera. The employees usually behave in a way that was completely unexpected and the owners are predictably shocked.

"This doesn't make sense," I said quickly. "Dorien despises Chico. She showed absolutely no reaction to his death. She couldn't have been emotionally involved with him."

"Who said anything about her being emotionally involved?" Sara asked, her tone cynical.

"Oh," I said quietly. "You mean—"

"I mean Chico was poisoned and this chick was bringing him dinner. Or delivering a gift basket with food in it. You do the math."

"Dorien wouldn't have any reason to kill Chico," I said. I was still having trouble believing Dorien even knew him or had visited the studio. She knew who he was, of course, because Gina is a member of the Dream Club.

A dead silence descended on us. "You're sure this is Dorien?" Noah pulled out a pad and scribbled down her name. "And she lives here in Savannah?"

I rattled off her address and phone number, and he grinned. "You've just saved the police a lot of work. She was in and out of the studio in five minutes. I didn't bother bringing the second screen shot because it was even grainier than this one."

"I still can't believe it," I said slowly. "There has to be some other explanation." I licked my lips. I felt vaguely guilty that I had somehow betrayed Dorien by identifying her.

"Pictures don't lie," Noah said, stuffing it back in the envelope. "And don't worry, your name won't come into this. The cops can interview Dorien and see how she explains her presence at the studio. The timing fits in with the estimated time of death." He must have seen the shocked expression on my face. "Look, Taylor, you may be right. Maybe there's some perfectly innocent explanation. But you have to ask yourself, why didn't she tell the police that she was there that night?" *Why indeed?*

"Could she have been delivering the basket for someone else?" Sara asked. "Does she do deliveries for a local shop? Maybe it was a gift basket, filled with wine and cheese. Or maybe she works for a restaurant, delivering dinners." She chewed on the end of her straw, squinting in thought.

I shook my head. "No, that's not possible. I'd know if she did. We talk about everything in the Dream Club." A stray thought pinged in my brain. Ali had said that it looked as though Chico was expecting someone to visit him that evening. Why did she say that? Maybe he'd lit some candles? Or had put out wine and cheese? I struggled to remember exactly what she'd told me, but my mind stalled and I drew a blank. Why wouldn't Dorien admit to being there? What could she possibly be hiding?

I tried to recall exactly what the studio looked like when we'd hurried over there that day. All I could remember seeing was the crumpled body of Chico lying on the floor, and my mind recoiled at the image.

"Tell me more about Dorien," Sara said, interrupting my morbid thoughts and drawing me back to the present. "Is she single or married? What does she do for a living?"

"She's single. She has a little shop in the district and does tarot readings."

"Hardly a lucrative enterprise," Sara sniffed. "Chico doesn't sound like the type who'd ask for a reading, does he? And that still doesn't explain why she was carrying a basket."

"Not at all," I admitted. An idea wriggled in the corner of my mind. Had someone mentioned that Dorien wanted to expand her business? I struggled to remember the conversation and gave up. My thoughts were whirling like colors in a kaleidoscope, and I needed time to reflect quietly on everything I'd heard. Dorien as Chico's killer? It seemed impossible. But the notion that my sister had anything to do with his death was equally impossible. Everywhere I turned, I met a solid brick wall of resistance. I remembered Dorien's dream about a "woman and child" in Chico's life. Had she invented that dream, to draw suspicion away from herself?

"What do you do when all your leads dry up?" I asked Noah. I tried to keep a note of defeat out of my voice, but my neck was throbbing and I felt like a boulder was settling on my shoulder blades.

"That's easy, you look for new ones!" Sara said brightly. Like Ali, Sara has always been a "glass is half full" sort of person, and nothing can dim her sunny personality.

"Not a bad idea but there's another possibility," Noah said, picking up the dessert menu and giving it a quick scan. "You go back and look at your leads again very closely. Go over everything with a fine-tooth comb. See what you missed. Look at the witness statements very carefully. Go over every word in the interviews. Try to read between the lines. If you have video, look at the body language. And watch for pauses or hesitations. Sometimes what *isn't* said is just as important as what *is* said. I learned that as a rookie agent at the FBI."

He reached across the table and rested his hand on mine, just for a moment. It wasn't a romantic gesture, more of a friendly one, but I felt a little buzz go through me. "I know you're worried about your sister, Taylor, but this is no time to give up. We're just getting started. I promise you, this is all going to work out okay." He smiled, a familiar grin that reached his eyes and shook me down to my toes. "Now," he said, gently withdrawing his hand from mine. "Who wants dessert?"

Sara beamed. "I thought you'd never ask."

# 23

"We're here today to remember Chico," Gina Santiago said later that week. Lisa Ortez, Chico's ex-wife, had finally come forward and posted a small notice in the *Savannah Herald* about a memorial service for Chico. She'd asked Gina to organize the event and to contact as many friends and clients as she could. Gina had told us that the actual funeral would take place in Colombia and Chico would be buried in his family's plot. This was just a small gathering with coffee and cookies to share memories of the flamboyant dance instructor.

It was late afternoon and the studio was lit with dozens of candles. The crime scene tape was gone and no trace of the earlier tragedy remained. A soft, rose-colored light bathed the room, bouncing off the gleaming wood floors and silver candlesticks.

Rose and Minerva had brought a large wicker basket of artfully arranged lilies and hydrangeas, even though Lisa had stipulated "no flowers." She'd requested that mourners make a donation to a Latin-American children's charity instead.

Lisa had told Gina that she and Chico had a ten-year-old son but she had never seen a penny of child support. *Would that make her angry enough to kill him?* I wondered how long she'd been in town. It seemed odd that Lisa and Chico had been out of touch for years, and then she suddenly turned up during the week he was murdered.

I remembered Minerva and Rose claiming they'd overheard Chico shouting at someone in Spanish on the night he was murdered. Could his argument have been with Lisa?

"This ex-wife, she's not at all what I expected," I heard Minerva whisper to Rose as Ali and I slipped into folding chairs behind them. I glanced at the wooden podium that had been set up at the far end of the studio.

Gina introduced Lisa Ortez, who took her spot at the podium, looking composed. A drop-dead gorgeous Latina with glossy back hair that reached to her waist, she began speaking in a soft, heavily accented voice. "I'm going to play some of Chico's favorite music," she said after a short speech. The room filled with a familiar Latin beat while Gina and Lisa looked thoughtful.

"She's glamorous, that's for sure," Rose sniffed. "Pretty enough to be a model, I'd say."

"And she doesn't look like she's grieving," Minerva said archly. "Or if she is, she's certainly hiding it well."

"Look, here's Persia," Rose said. "I didn't know if she'd show up."

"Hush, Rose, the ceremony is about to start."

Sybil Powers and Lucinda Macavy were already seated in the front row, and Dorien and Persia were just arriving. A dozen rows of folding chairs had been arranged, and they were quickly filling up with mourners. My mind was still reeling with the knowledge that Dorien had appeared at Chico's studio the night of the murder. She hadn't said a word about it, and I was hoping to get an update soon from Noah and Sara. Surely the Savannah PD would interview her, wouldn't they? I felt a tiny bit guilty over my part in naming her but told myself the police would have quickly discovered her identity anyway.

And what in the world had she been doing at Chico's that night? Ali, ever the optimist, insisted there was some perfectly innocent explanation for Dorien's visit, although she couldn't come up with one when I pressed her for an answer.

I idly speculated if Jennifer Walton would appear. I wondered about her relationship with Chico and if there was any way to discover if she was having an affair with him. It seemed unlikely, but at this point, I didn't want to rule anything out. I scanned the rows of guests and didn't spot her. Maybe she wanted to disavow any relationship with Chico.

Ali sat next to me, and appeared calm, her gaze focused on Lisa Ortez. "Are you okay?" I asked, ever the big sister.

She turned to me, her eyes clouded. "I think so," she said. "Seeing Lisa standing up there"—her voice faltered a little—"makes me wonder if I ever knew Chico at all."

"Maybe none of us did," Hildy Carter said, squeezing past me to take an empty seat. I remembered Hildy from the dinner at the Waltons'. "This was a guy with plenty of secrets." The plump little decorator was dressed in black from head to toe. She caught me staring at her outfit and winked. "I've been waiting for an occasion to wear this. It's Armani and it was a fantastic buy, but the only place you can wear it is to a funeral," she said wryly.

Ali and I exchanged a look. Hildy appeared downright cheerful and her tone was flippant. I wanted to ask her if she was going to try to buy up the block of buildings, as Chico had intended, but couldn't think of a diplomatic way to do it. He had snatched the deal away from her, and his death might have given her a financial windfall. I remembered that Hildy had plenty of money to invest in real estate, and now that her chief competitor had just died, there was nothing holding her back. I also recalled that Hildy "didn't like to lose." Chico's death was nothing less than a win-win for her.

"Did you take dance lessons from Chico?" I finally asked. Hildy was busily scrolling through her messages, chuckling to herself. She clearly wasn't grief-stricken, but then, who was?

"Do I look like the rumba type?" She grinned. "Not with these hips, honey." She snapped her cell phone shut. "Chico and I were in a bidding war for some property, and he beat me to it." I nodded, trying to look surprised. "That was our only connection." I was amazed she was willing to admit it. Money is always a good motive for murder.

"That must have been disappointing to you," Ali said.

"Not really. It all worked out for the best," Hildy said, beaming. "That was my business partner texting me," she said, tapping her cell phone. "It seems I've got an even bigger fish to fry, and now I can make an all-cash offer. I would have tied up too much equity in that deal that Chico and I were competing for. This is a much better prospect and the payoff could be huge. So it all works out well in the end, doesn't it?"

*Except for Chico.*

**"Taylor, I need** to talk to you, it's urgent." Dorien, her voice tight, grabbed my arm as I unlocked the door to the shop. We'd just returned from the service for Chico, and both Ali and I felt surprisingly tired. I think there's always an emotional strain connected with memorial events even if you're not close to the deceased. "Want to come up for a cup of tea? Or would you prefer lemonade?"

"Lemonade would be perfect," she said gratefully. The shop was closed but I always kept a pitcher of fresh lemonade or iced tea in the fridge behind the counter. Ali quickly excused herself, saying she hadn't slept well and headed upstairs for a short nap. She shot me a curious look over her shoulder as she scooped up Barney for a quick hug. If she wondered what was up with Dorien, she was too tired to pursue it and probably knew that I'd give her all the details later that afternoon.

"So what's up?" I said carefully. We were sitting at a small table in the middle of the shop, and I put out a plate of shortbread cookies. I wondered if she could possibly have discovered that I'd recognized her on the surveillance tape and had given the police her name. It seemed unlikely, but she was clearly in a state over something. She was tapping her foot impatiently and practically wringing her hands in her lap.

"I need to talk to you," she said, her voice tight with tension. "I think I've done something really stupid and I need your advice." She glanced at the stairway leading up to our private quarters. "I'm glad Ali decided to take a nap, because I'd hoped to catch you alone. What I tell you has to be kept in strict confidence. Do you agree to that?"

"I'll certainly try," I said, nodding vigorously. *Strict confidence?* That horse was already out of the barn, as my granny would say. I braced myself for what came next.

"Chico," she said in a strangled voice. "I saw him."

For one crazy moment, I thought she meant in a vision, or a dream. She must have read my mind because she quickly added, "I mean I saw him when he was *alive*. On the night he died." She paused dramatically to let the words sink in, and I did my best to look astounded.

"You saw Chico?" I said, stalling for time. "Do you mean in his studio?"

She swallowed hard. "Yes. I was bringing him dinner for two." Her mouth twisted in a sneer. "It looked like he was planning quite a romantic evening. He had the candles lit, and there was a bottle of wine already opened."

I kept up the pretense and put on my most innocent expression. "Why were you bringing him dinner for two?" I said, shaking my head in mock puzzlement. I was probably overdoing the surprised act, but I didn't want Dorien to realize I was the one who'd spotted her on the surveillance tape. "I didn't know you were close friends. I didn't even realize you knew him."

"I don't!" she said, raising her voice. "Or I didn't," she said, quickly taking it down an octave. "Look, this is rather embarrassing, but you know I'm not doing very well with my tarot shop." *Embarrassing? Owning a failing business is nothing compared to being a suspect in a murder investigation.* I longed to say this, but I restrained myself. I decided to sit back and let her tell the story in her own way.

"So I started a little catering business on the side. I thought I'd do a few events for friends, maybe people in the district. I didn't say anything about it in the Dream Club because I didn't want people to think I was a failure."

"I'm sure no one would think that," I said soothingly.

"You'd be surprised," Dorien said with a sudden flash of temper. "We've got some strange personalities in that group. You may not have noticed, but there's a lot of jealousy and backbiting beneath the surface," she said in a self-righteous tone. "It's too bad people aren't a little nicer to each other and realize that everyone has troubles." She stared at the floor with a woebegone expression on her face, her anger melting into sadness.

"You were telling me about your catering business?" I poured some more lemonade, and gave her a smile, hoping to bring her back on track.

"Yes," she said morosely. "It shows just how something innocent can go terribly wrong."

"What happened?" I asked. This time I cupped my chin in my hand, all bright-eyed eagerness, determined to get the truth out of her.

"Chico saw an ad I took out in one of those supermarket weeklies. I'd included a two-for-the-price-of-one dinner coupon, and he called me and ordered veal scallopini."

"Veal scallopini, an expensive choice," I murmured. I was glad Ali had gone upstairs because she would have lectured Dorien on the cruelty inherent in veal crates and reminded her that they were outlawed in Europe. I absolutely agree with her, but there was no way I was going to interrupt the thread of Dorien's conversation now that I had her on a roll.

"Yes, he said it was a special occasion. He told me to be sure to drop it off at six sharp because he was expecting a guest a few minutes later. He planned on reheating the dinner in the oven; I told him the microwave could ruin the taste. I learned that from watching one of Gordon Ramsey's shows," she said confidently. "I wanted to make a good impression so I was there exactly at six."

"What happened next?"

"Nothing," she said, letting her hands flop to her side. "He opened the door, took the basket, and paid me. In cash. I was there less than five minutes. He had already preheated the oven, and I gave him a couple of last-minute instructions for the roasted potatoes and vegetables."

Five minutes. She was telling the truth, according to the surveillance tape.

"Why haven't you told anyone about this?"

"Because everyone will think I killed him!" she said in an anguished voice. "I didn't even know the guy, and he could ruin my business before it gets off the ground. Who'd want to order from a caterer who poisons her clients?"

*Good point!* "Dorien," I said gently, "I think you've made a huge mistake here. You should have said something about it right away. This is information the police need to have. And you can't assume they would point the finger at you. As far as anyone knows, the poison might not have been present in the food. It could have been ingested another way." Although for the life of me, I couldn't think how.

She nodded. "Maybe you're right." She heaved a deep sigh. "I almost said something at the last Dream Club meeting and then I saw Sam sitting there and I wimped out. I could just picture her arresting me on the spot. Can you imagine how awful that would be?" She gave a nervous little laugh. "I guess I've been watching too many TV shows; that's not the way it would happen, is it?"

"Of course not," I said, reaching over and patting her arm. I thought of Ali's experience at the station house with Detective Sanderson. She'd told me the second interview hadn't been as stressful as the first, but she hadn't wanted to talk about it. I didn't push her for details and decided to give her some time and space to deal with it.

"It might be a bit awkward, because Sam is a detective, but you know she'd be on your side, Dorien. She could have advised you on the best thing to do and smoothed the way for you. She'd probably suggest that you come down to the station house and give a statement."

"Do you think it's too late?" Dorien's eyes had welled with tears, and now she brushed at them with a tissue.

"I know it isn't," I said warmly. "It's never too late. If I were you, I'd call Sam right now. Tell her exactly what you told me and do whatever she suggests. And call me or drop by if you need some moral support."

Dorien stood up and surprised me by giving me a hug. "Thanks so much, Taylor, you're a good friend." She paused for a moment, her mouth taking a downward cast. "Sometimes I feel like I don't have any real friends in the club. I guess I'm too much of a loner. People don't take to me. It's easy for women like you and Ali," she said bitterly. "People are drawn to you, right from the start. They want to know you and spend time with you." It occurred to me that maybe Dorien was more isolated and lonely than I'd realized.

"Nonsense," I said firmly, secretly thinking she was spot-on in her self-assessment. She came across as brash and abrasive, not at all open to making new friends. "You're a very important part of the club, and you always have such interesting insights. Really, Dorien, you'll feel much better after you talk to Sam and come up with a plan."

"I hope you're right," she said, reaching for her cardigan on the back of the chair. "I've been so stressed out, carrying this secret around with me. There's nothing worse than uncertainty, is there? I should have told the truth from the beginning and faced the consequences."

"Exactly." I nodded solemnly, thinking of my sister. Ali had hidden the truth about visiting Chico the night of the murder, and her lie was coming back to haunt her. And me.

# 24

"I feel like getting out for a while, don't you?" Ali looked refreshed after her nap. Her skin was glowing and her eyes had lost that tense, haunted look. It was late afternoon, a golden time of day in Savannah.

"What do you feel like doing?" I finished brushing Scout and deposited him on the windowsill next to Barney, who was snoozing contentedly. Barney slept like he didn't have a care in the world, and as Ali was fond of reminding me, he doesn't. Unlike most stray cats, Barney and Scout were lucky to have landed in a loving "forever" home with Ali. Only one in ten cats live their whole life in their original home, and Barney and Scout had hit the jackpot. I was pleased that they seemed to be bonding with me and often rubbed themselves against my legs, hoping for some grooming or a belly scratch.

"Maybe a bit of shopping, or just strolling through the district? And we could grab a bite to eat later? We could even try to look for some bistro tables and chairs if we feel up to it." Ali pulled a brush through her thick hair. She had the ability to look terrific even after tumbling out of bed, her face bare of makeup.

"Sounds like a plan." I pointed to an ad in the free flyer I'd picked up in the supermarket. "There's a tag sale down on River Street, and it says they're selling furniture from a B and B that's being remodeled. Maybe we can find some bargains." That was the accountant in me talking. We really didn't have money to furnish the shop, but I was hoping that some attractive bistro sets would lure tourists in for our coffee and dessert menu. If we really wanted to go ahead with our expansion, the customers needed someplace to sit.

A few minutes later, we took a leisurely stroll toward the Riverwalk. The streets were crowded, and Ali and I were talking over possible dessert items when I saw something that made my pulse jump. "Ali," I gasped, grabbing her arm. "Is that Persia sitting under the green umbrella table over there?"

Ali craned her neck, trying to see past a huge potted palm surrounded by impatiens. "Yes, I think so," she said slowly. "Not too many people wear caftans like that." She giggled. "And I recognize that one. It's one of her favorites. It has goldfish all over it." She was right. Persia's caftan was deep blue dotted with bright lemon yellow goldfish. An unusual look, but somehow Persia managed to pull it off.

She shrugged and started to move on, but I stopped her. "Look at the man with her. I think it's Kevin. How could those two possibly be connected?"

"Kevin from—"

"Kevin from the surveillance tape and your dream," I said, pulling her with me as we ducked behind a pillar. "Kevin Moore."

Persia had pretended she'd never seen Kevin before, the man on the tapes. She'd even played along and asked Marlene, the waitress, if she could identify him. So Persia was determined to keep their relationship hidden. Interesting. But what did it mean?

Ali gasped. "If that's really Kevin, he might have been the last person to see Chico alive." She shuddered. "Aren't the police looking for him?"

"I think they figured he went back to California. They probably don't know he's right here in Savannah."

"You could call Noah," Ali suggested.

I hesitated. "I could," I said finally, "but I don't think they have enough evidence to bring Kevin in for questioning. The only thing he's really guilty of is running a red light. Who knows, he might have already paid the fine."

A reasonable excuse, but it sounded hollow to my ears. The truth is, I'm not sure why I was hesitant to call Noah. Maybe I was feeling a bit hurt that he'd never contacted me after our lunch with Sara? Maybe I had set my expectations too high? I'd let myself imagine that seeing Noah here in Savannah meant our romance would be rekindled. The fact that he hadn't called me told me he had a different view of things. For all I knew, he was already involved with someone and keeping quiet about it. Noah has always been a man with secrets. Back in Atlanta, Noah was always on the move for the Bureau, always silent about his investigations. It's not surprising we broke up: both of us were engrossed in our careers with little time or energy to invest in a relationship.

"But what's Kevin doing here now?" Ali asked.

"And why is he meeting with Persia?" I raised my eyebrows. "What's the connection between those two?"

"It doesn't look like a friendly conversation," Ali said, allowing herself another quick peek. "Persia has her chin stuck out like a bulldog's and look at her waving her hands in the air. She usually only does that when she's angry at someone in the Dream Club. Like Lucinda," she added.

*Lucinda!* I suddenly remembered that Persia had revealed a dream about Lucinda twirling around the dance floor with Chico. Maybe she'd made up the dream. Was Persia trying to point the finger at Lucinda, in the hopes of drawing suspicion away from herself?

It was easy to see why Kevin Moore had a motive to kill Chico. Chico had swindled him out of his share of the dance studio. But what was Persia's link to Kevin Moore? And to Chico?

Maybe Ali was right. The smart thing would be to put my personal feelings aside and keep Noah in the loop. I pulled out my cell phone and left him a brief message. Maybe nothing could be done, but at least he'd know that Kevin was back in town and he could alert the police if he wanted to.

I was still puzzled over Persia and her involvement in all this. It was Persia who'd shocked the Dream Club by describing a "murder right here in Savannah." We'd listened spellbound as she'd shared some telling details about the crime scene: the Latin music, the dark-haired man, the open door leading to the street. Her dream was so spot-on that I remembered wondering if she could have had intimate knowledge of the crime scene. But if she did, wouldn't that make her the killer? Or at least an accomplice? And why would she want to kill Chico?

Judging by the body language, Kevin and Persia loathed each other. How were they connected? Any why did Persia deny knowing him? That was a missing piece of the puzzle, and I was determined to find it.

Persia and Kevin suddenly stood up and pushed back their chairs. I could hear raised voices but I couldn't make out what they were saying. Kevin made an "I give up" gesture, with his hands raised chest-high, palms out, facing Persia. She was jabbing the air with her forefinger and her face was bright red. Was she accusing him of something? And what about the classic palms-out gesture Kevin was making? Was he admitting guilt or telling her he'd had enough of the conversation? I couldn't decide.

I watched them for a full thirty seconds, more confused than ever. I didn't want to alert Persia to the fact that we'd spotted her, so I linked my arm through Ali's and we headed quickly down the street.

"That was weird," Ali said as we turned the corner and found ourselves at another beautiful square.

"Very weird," I agreed.

The sunlight was filtering through the leaves of a banyan tree, making interesting shapes on the sidewalk. I'd only been here a short time, but I already felt like Savannah was my home. *How will I ever leave?* The thought of going back to chilly Chicago wasn't the least bit attractive, and I found myself increasingly drawn to the slow-paced life in the historic town. I'd loved Atlanta, but Savannah was even more relaxed, less "big-city," and seemed to offer a sense of peace and solace that I was craving. Two blocks later, we arrived at the outdoor flea market.

"Look, there's Lucinda," Ali said, waving to the birdlike woman in the beige shift dress.

"Flea markets seem to bring everyone out, don't they?" She hurried over to greet Lucinda, who was looking over a pile of crockery on a display table.

"I like this, but I don't need it," Lucinda was saying to a vendor, holding up a soup tureen with rabbits on the lid. It was a little bit kitschy, but I knew it would fit right in with Lucinda's style.

"But it's so colorful, I think you should buy it anyway," Ali said, touching her gently on her arm.

"I do love chickens and rabbits," Lucinda said, "and the colors are exactly right for my kitchen."

"Is it terribly expensive?" Ali lifted up the tag and winced. "Oh dear, I think it is."

"It's actually a bargain," the vendor piped up. She was a young girl in her early twenties with copper-colored hair and a wide smile. She looked pleased at the sudden interest and took off the lid so we could examine it more carefully. "Just look at the fine craftsmanship," she said. "You won't find that level of intricacy nowadays."

"Is this vintage?" a male voice asked. I turned to see Andre from the antique shop talking to a tall, very tanned man standing next to him. They were inspecting a set of Limoges china and Andre was holding up a dinner plate to the bright sunlight. "If the price is right, it might be worth it to buy an extra set. This kind of thing can only go up in value. And who knows, we might be doing a lot more events."

Ali spotted the pair and rushed over to them. "Gideon!" she squealed, leaning forward to kiss his cheek. "I'm so glad you're back. You were in California when we stopped by your shop the other day. I want you to meet my sister."

"I heard all about it, sweetie," Gideon said. "I can't believe I missed you. And you must be Taylor," he said, leaning forward and kissing me on the cheek. "Welcome to Savannah. I hope Andre has been taking good care of you."

Ali beamed. "Andre managed to get us invitations to a big dinner party at the Waltons," she said. "What a night, everything was perfect. Andre, you did an amazing job."

"They hired us for two more gigs," Andre said, looking pleased. "The Waltons have money to burn, and the sky's the limit when it comes to his campaign. He's pulling out all the stops, and I think it may pay off. Plus they're referring a couple of their friends to us. So things are looking up."

"Come over and help our friend decide on a soup tureen," Ali said. She dragged Andre and Gideon over and introduced Lucinda to them. "Andre and Gideon have one of the nicest antique stores in Savannah," Ali said warmly. She lowered her voice. "They can tell you whether or not this is a good deal," she said. "They're antique experts."

"Oh my goodness, that's exciting." Lucinda looked impressed. "I know it's silly, but this particular piece just speaks to me," she said. "I suppose you think I'm being foolish," she said in her self-deprecating way.

"Not at all," Andre told her. "If it's a genuine Chelsea rabbit, it could be quite valuable. Of course, if it's an imitation, then it's just a cheap piece of crockery."

"What in the world is a Chelsea rabbit?" Lucinda asked.

"Back in the eighteenth century, the Chelsea Porcelain

Factory in England made china sets with rabbits on them. Very distinctive, and nowadays, they're a hot item. Chelsea soup tureens are valuable, definitely worth collecting." Andre leaned down to peer at the lid and ran his finger around the edge. "But is this the real thing? I'm just not sure." He looked back at the vendor, who was standing by anxiously, hoping for a sale. "Do you have the provenance on this piece? Or could we at least look at the mark?"

"I don't have any paperwork to prove it's authentic, but I can show you the mark." She deftly turned the tureen upside down and pointed to a small mark on the bottom. Andre examined it and shot Lucinda a disappointed look.

"I'm afraid it's not a Chelsea," Andre said, shaking his head. "A nice piece, but don't buy it as an investment, Lucinda."

"But it if you love it," Ali urged, "why not go for it?"

"I'm sorry but I think I'll pass," Lucinda said apologetically to the girl with the copper hair. "I have too many knickknacks as it is."

The five of us edged away then, continuing down the aisle, and Lucinda tossed a grateful smile at Andre. Andre and Gideon had decided against buying the Limoges, and we wanted to check out a few more stalls.

"I think you just saved me from making a big mistake," Lucinda said candidly. "I tend to get carried away at flea markets. I should never be allowed to go by myself."

"Well, tag along with us," Andre said. "We go to estate sales all the time. Stick with us and we won't let you get ripped off. I still think you should have bought it if you really liked it."

"I did like the cute little rabbit munching on the leaves," she admitted. "I know it's probably not to everyone's taste, but I adore things like that. But as you say, it wasn't a genuine Chelsea. Andre, how did you figure that out so quickly? You seemed to know even before you looked at the mark on the bottom of the bowl."

"The pieces from the Chelsea factory have more detail," Gideon said. "The one back there was close, but not close enough. With a genuine Chelsea, you might expect to see more figures on the piece and the colors are a bit muted. Once you see a real Chelsea rabbit, you'll be able to spot the fakes more easily the next time."

"That's good to know," Lucinda said. "I happened to see a soup tureen with snails *and* rabbits on the lid, so I bet that was a genuine Chelsea. The style and the colors were very similar to this one."

"Then it probably was." Andre smiled at her. "It's always good to ask for proof, though. Any reputable dealer will be happy to provide you with the provenance. We always do that at our shop." He handed Lucinda a card. "Stop by sometime," he said. "Any friend of Ali's gets a dealers' discount. That's twenty percent off anything you buy."

Lucinda laughed. "Oh, Ali, you have the nicest friends!"

# 25

"What's up?" Noah's voice raced over the line. "I got your message about spotting Kevin Moore in town. Did you find out any more about him?"

We'd just gotten back from the flea market, and Ali had surprised me by heading straight out to play tennis. She was happier than I'd seen her in days, but I was at loose ends, wandering aimlessly around the apartment, when I finally called Noah again.

"Not yet. He was sitting at an outdoor café with Persia, and that's all I know. But there's something else I want to run by you . . ." I paused to fill Barney's bowl with his favorite crunchies. Scout was on special vet food for overweight cats and was chowing down on the opposite side of the tiny kitchen. "You have some crime scene photos, don't you?"

Noah laughed, a soft, sexy sound. "Yes, I have a few shots of the dance studio. But it's not public knowledge." I figured he'd snared copies because of his connection with his cousin Chris on the police force.

"I can keep a secret," I prompted. "I just need a quick

peek at them. Two seconds, really. That's not a problem, is it?"

"No, of course not." He waited a beat. "It's almost six o'clock. What are you doing about dinner?"

"Dinner?" I pretended to think. "Well, I've just fed the cats, and I was going to make myself a salad." As soon as the words left my mouth, I regretted them. It sounded like I was angling for a date. Why didn't I just tell him I had plans or that I was going out?

"I think we can do better than that. How about dinner at Marcelo's? He makes the best lasagna in town. It's still your favorite, isn't it?"

"I'm surprised you remember." I was secretly touched that he remembered my taste in Italian food. I love all kinds of pasta, but lasagna is at the top of the list.

"Shall we meet there at seven? It's right off Franklin Square."

"Sounds good." I tried to inject a casual note into my voice, but the truth was, my heart thumped with anticipation. I had to remind myself that dinner with Noah was going to be all business.

**Marcelo's was packed** but the gorgeous brunette hostess gave Noah a warm smile and ushered us to a window table. I saw her give me a quick once-over, and a little frown flitted across her perfect features. Did she see me as competition? Did she think she had a chance with him? Maybe. To his credit, he ignored her and locked eyes with me as we sat down. He ordered two Pinot Grigios and said, "Something's up. I recognize that look, Taylor."

"You do?"

"Yeah, it's the 'I know something and you don't' look. You must be following a lead you haven't told me about, some new development with the case."

"Am I really that transparent?" I asked teasingly.

"Only with people who know you very well." He grinned. "Did you find out any more about Persia and why she was meeting with Kevin Moore?"

"Not yet." I paused. "I'm waiting for her to say something about it, but if she doesn't, I'll have to confront her."

I nibbled on a dinner roll, hoping the wine would arrive soon. I felt a little uncomfortable dining with Noah tonight. There was a yuppie crowd in Marcelo's, and the soft lighting and candles practically screamed "date night." But I knew we weren't really a couple; we were old friends and nothing more. At least that's what the rational side of my brain told me. The emotional side—the little devil on my shoulder—told me that we might pick things up right where we'd left off.

Electricity was in the air. He picked up my left hand and twined his fingers through mine. "I know you spend every waking moment thinking about the case, and that makes sense to me. You're devoted to your sister. You're not going to rest until Chico's murder is solved and she's not a suspect anymore. I get it."

I nodded. "You're right about that. Until an arrest is made, Ali *will* be a suspect and I'm going to be a wreck." I managed to keep my voice steady, but my heart was thumping at the touch of his warm fingers and I let myself remember what it had been like back in Atlanta. Noah and Taylor. Taylor and Noah. All our friends said we were perfect for each other, and no one suspected we would follow different paths. "It's completely unfair. It's not like she was the only person at Chico's that night."

*Uh-oh.* Noah raised his eyebrows, and I realized I may have let the cat out of the bag. Luckily the waitress arrived just then with our wine, and I untangled my fingers from Noah's and took a hefty gulp.

"Now I *know* something is up," he said, shooting me a shrewd look. "You never drink on an empty stomach. You're way too controlled for that."

I smiled weakly and pointed to the half-eaten dinner roll. "Half a dinner roll—"

"Doesn't count," he cut in. "What's going on, Taylor? Who else was at Chico's that night? This is no time to hold back, and if you think you're protecting someone, I can tell you right now that you're making a huge mistake." His tone had taken on a hard edge; the playful banter had vanished.

The server reappeared with dinner menus but Noah waved her away. "Talk, Taylor. What do you know?"

"Okay, the thing is"—I paused, wondering if I was doing the right thing—"someone from the Dream Club told me something in confidence." I sat back and wrapped my fingers around my wineglass.

Noah immediately went into detective mode, his eyes laser-locked on mine, and his jaw tightened as he leaned slightly toward me. I could see why he'd been so successful at interrogations. It was impossible to hold anything back with those dark eyes boring right into me.

"Go on," he said. His voice had a steely edge to it. "Who was it and what did she say?"

"It was Dorien." I hadn't realized I was holding my breath, and the words came out in a rush.

"Dorien?" he asked, his dark eyes intent. "The woman who reads tarot cards," he said wryly. "What did she tell you in confidence?"

"She finally admitted what she was doing at Chico's the night he died. It turns out it wasn't a date; it was strictly a business transaction. She's opened a catering business on the side, and Chico was her first customer."

"A customer?" Noah shook his head in disbelief. "And no one else knows about this?"

"Afraid not," I said, feeling unhappy at having to rat out Dorien. But did I really have a choice? The sooner the police solved the crime, the sooner Ali could get back to her life. Chico's unsolved murder was like a sword hanging over all of us.

"What kind of food?"

"She brought dinner. For two." I hesitated. "Veal scallopini, not that it matters." I gave a little shrug. "She said she only stayed for a few minutes. She dropped off the dinners and gave him some quick instructions about how to reheat the food."

"Dinner for two," Noah said. "Interesting." He ran his hand over his jaw in a gesture that was so familiar to me, it tugged at my heart. "It sounds like Chico had planned a romantic evening for himself and a lady friend."

"I know," I said softly. "The candles were a giveaway." I thought of Persia's dream. The candles, the soft lights, the Latin music. How could she have nailed it so perfectly if she hadn't been there? But picturing Persia as Chico's lover was too much of a stretch. There's no way those two would ever be a romantic duo.

It had to be someone else. Maybe Jennifer Walton, the politician's wife? If she was really having an affair with him, they couldn't be seen together publicly, so what better place than the dance studio? Or had Chico invited Lisa, the ex-wife, over for a possible seduction scene? And then maybe something went wrong, an argument ensued, and that explained the shouting in Spanish that the Harper sisters had heard?

"And it never occurred to Dorien to go to the police with this information? She delivers dinner to a guy who's later found poisoned? Then she decides to keep quiet about it? Are you kidding me?" He raised his eyebrows.

"I know it sounds crazy," I said, "but I understand where she's coming from. She wanted to protect her new business. Who would order meals from her if word got out?"

Noah laughed and signaled the server for two more glasses of wine. "Do you think she's telling the truth? That all she did was deliver dinner and she had no desire to hurt Chico?"

"I believe her. I know it sounds odd, but Dorien is a pretty quirky, eccentric person. I don't think she worries too much about consequences."

"What's the next step?"

"I encouraged her to tell the police. I think I persuaded her because she finally realized the truth will come out anyway. Now that they know she was at Chico's that night, it's only a matter of time before they turn up at her door."

"So we can place three people who visited Chico in the studio that night," Noah said thoughtfully. "Dorien, who brought dinner, and his mystery guest. And Ali, who went over for five minutes to confront him about the real estate deal."

"And Ali isn't guilty," I insisted.

"Of course not. This certainly puts a different spin on things, though." He reached for a manila envelope on the seat next to him. "Do you want to take a quick look at a few of the crime scene photos before we order? They're not too grisly but—"

"But you know that I have a weak stomach." I finished the sentence for him. "Yes, let's take a look." The server placed our wine in front of us, and I sipped it absently while Noah pulled out a sheaf of photos and handed them to me.

"Can you tell me what you're looking for?" Noah asked, as I riffled through them.

"I'll know it when I see it." I didn't want to tell Noah my suspicions until I was absolutely sure. I skipped past the photos of Chico, lying prone next to the sofa. And the low coffee table, set with candles and serving pieces. The plates half full of food, the wineglasses, and the chiller for the wine bottle.

And then I saw it. It was right where I remembered. Sitting on a lovely mahogany sideboard between the kitchen and the studio.

A large soup tureen, with rabbits and snails. Exactly like the one Lucinda had described.

"I found it," I said, my voice hoarse with excitement. I

pointed out the soup tureen to Noah, and of course, it didn't mean anything to him.

"What does this tell me?" he asked, his dark eyes intent.

"I think it means there were four people who visited the studio that night," I said slowly.

"Is the fourth person Kevin, the drive-by guy with the California plates? Because there's no evidence he actually went inside the studio even though he's still in Savannah."

"No, it's someone much closer to home." I fell silent, my thoughts whirring. It didn't seem possible but Lucinda must have been in the studio at some time. What could prim and proper Lucinda want with the hot-blooded Chico? I remembered that she must be lonely because she'd joined an online dating service. Was she capable of falling for a man like Chico? It seemed improbable, but I knew from personal experience not to rule anything out.

"I think we better order dinner, the place is filling up—" Noah broke off, giving me a long, penetrating look. "Are you all right, Taylor? You look worried."

"I'm all right," I told him. "Not worried, just surprised. I'm trying to get my mind around some new information, that's all." I summoned a reassuring smile. My mind was racing, trying to absorb the photo with the soup tureen. Maybe it was a coincidence? Maybe Lucinda had seen the tureen someplace else? But Andre had said they were unusual and very hard to find.

Had the soup tureen been visible at the memorial service? I struggled to remember, to picture the scene in my mind. No, I decided. It wasn't there. All the kitchen items had been cleared away and the sideboard was bare, except for a couple of floral arrangements. I blinked, wondering how to make sense of all this. I suppose it was possible that Lucinda had visited the studio at some time, for an innocent reason, and that's when she spotted the soup tureen. It was possible, but was it likely?

Noah leaned back and looked relaxed, with his arm

resting on the top of the red leather banquette. "So it's all good, right?"

"Not really." I thought of Lucinda. What would she do if people found out she'd had a relationship with Chico and that Persia's dream was spot-on? "There's one person whose reputation is going to be damaged by this, I'm afraid." *Whether she's guilty or innocent*, I thought sadly.

"A damaged reputation isn't as bad as being charged with murder," Noah said mildly.

"I'm not so sure. Here in Savannah, appearance is everything."

And then I told him about Lucinda and the Chelsea rabbits.

Noah listened quietly, not interrupting. When the server appeared again, looking a bit frazzled, he ordered two lasagnas and then said quietly, "This is a game changer."

"It could be a coincidence, right?" I desperately wanted to believe that there was a logical explanation for Lucinda's comment.

"Not very likely, Taylor. If Lucinda was in the studio that night, she should have come forward with this information immediately. Her fingerprints might still be there," he said thoughtfully.

"Nobody's picked up on that yet, I guess."

"Nobody will pick up on it. I'm sure she's never been convicted of anything so her prints won't be in the system."

I nodded, remembering that Sam Stiles had told me that it was going to take a long time to process all the crime scene fingerprints. There were hundreds of fingerprints, and apparently dozens of clients visited the studio every day.

"Do you think Lucinda could be part of the real estate deal Chico was involved in?"

"I'm sure she wasn't. She watches her pennies very carefully; she's a retired schoolteacher and lives off a small pension." I remembered that Lucinda told me she saves all year for a summer trip to Maine. There was no way I could imagine her being a player in a high-stakes real estate scheme.

Noah drained his wineglass and then drummed his fingers on the table. "Both Lucinda and Dorien visited Chico. Dorien visited him the night he died to deliver food he'd purchased, and Lucinda visited him"—he paused—"who knows when or why?"

A beat passed. "There's still the question of motive," I offered. I finished my roll and reached for another, suddenly hungry. "I can't imagine any reason for either one of them to want to kill him, can you?" Noah shot me an enigmatic smile. "What?" I asked, wondering where his thoughts were headed.

"Follow the money, remember?" The server placed two steaming plates of lasagna in front of us; the smell of tomatoes and roasted garlic was enchanting. She offered to bring us another bottle of wine, but I didn't dare indulge; I had to remain clearheaded.

"Follow the money?" I frowned. "But Lucinda and Dorien don't have any."

A sly half smile crossed his face. "Exactly," he said.

"But what—"

He put his finger to his lips and shook his head. "Think about it," he said cryptically.

# 26

"I had a very interesting dream last night," Sybil announced dramatically. "I do hope I can go first tonight, while the details are still fresh in my mind." She folded her hands neatly in her lap, her rings glittering. Sybil doesn't believe in the adage "Less is more," and was sporting opulent stones on every finger. The rings were dazzling in the light of the fat vanilla candles Ali had scattered around the living room. Her fingernails—so long they could do battle with a porcupine—were freshly painted blood-red.

"Well, of course you can go first," Ali said distractedly. She paused with the coffeepot still in her hand. "Just give me a second to get everyone settled."

"Take all the time you need. I can wait, my dear," Sybil said serenely. She'd taken on a regal air as if she were royalty and Ali her loyal subject.

We'd called an impromptu meeting of the Dream Club for seven thirty this evening. It was the day after I'd had dinner with Noah, and my mind was still reeling from our conversation. I found it impossible to believe that either Dorien or Lucinda had killed Chico. At least Dorien had come clean that she'd visited Chico that night. Lucinda was still keeping secrets.

For the life of me, I couldn't imagine why Lucinda had gone to Chico's studio, but I was convinced she'd been there. Sometime. There couldn't be *two* Chelsea soup tureens with rabbits and snails in Savannah; a call to Gina had confirmed that the tureen had been a gift. A grateful client had given it to Chico a week before the murder, so that narrowed the time frame. I was convinced that Lucinda had been in Chico's studio sometime in the seven days before his death. But why? It was baffling.

"I think you'll find my dream quite intriguing, because it involves someone right here in this room." Sybil's tone was playful, but she was clearly champing at the bit. She barely hid a scowl while Ali fiddled with some "handheld desserts" she wanted to offer in the shop. Everyone's attention had been focused on the platter of goodies on the coffee table, but after Sybil's latest pronouncement, all eyes turned to her.

Minerva Harper shot me a glance and winked. She's always taken a dim view of Sybil's theatrics, and I've never been sure if Minerva really believes in the power of dreams. Sometimes I think she and her sister, Rose, only come for the social aspects of the club. Neither of them drives much anymore, and the meetings offer them a way to connect with their friends and neighbors. Plus Ali's desserts are delectable. I was horrified to see that I'd gained five pounds since I'd moved in with my kid sister.

"How fascinating," Persia offered. "Was it your own dream, or were you visiting someone else's?"

"I dropped in on someone else's dream, and I was in for quite a surprise," Sybil said mysteriously.

I heard a sharp intake of breath, and glanced at Lucinda, who was sitting on my right. She had a deer-in-the-headlights look, and I saw the color drain right out of her face. She coughed on a chocolate-covered pretzel and quickly gulped down some sweet tea. Ali had been experimenting early in the day with a recipe for pretzel s'mores and I'd been dying to try one. I knew it involved round pretzels, dark chocolate squares, milk chocolate for dipping, and marshmallows. An unbeatable combination.

Dorien was fiddling over the desserts, taking a long time to make her selection. A slight flush crept up from her collarbone and she bit her lip. I was sure that both Dorien and Lucinda feared they were going to be the star attractions in Sybil's dream account this evening.

"Is everyone ready?" Ali said brightly. The ladies were scarfing down the desserts like they were starving seagulls, and I was glad Ali had more trays ready in the kitchen.

"We're ready!" Minerva sang out. "Let's hear what Sybil has to say." I noticed she'd filled her plate with half a dozen different desserts.

"Ali, everyone is waiting for you to sit down," Sybil said pointedly. Ali—ever the perfect hostess—was scurrying around, making sure everyone had enough tea and goodies.

"I'm sitting down right now," Ali said, scooting into a chair. "Let's hear it, Sybil."

"Well," Sybil said, drawing out the suspense, "my dream involves Chico and a visit someone made to his studio one night." She arched her eyebrows and looked around the circle. We were a small group tonight, because Sam Stiles had to work and Gina was out of town again. Sybil rested her eyes on each one of us, pinning us with her steely gaze. There was tension in the air, and I heard a few nervous giggles.

"I wonder who it could be," she said, her voice low and taunting. I had a sudden image of a cat playing with a mouse. Dead silence as her eyes swept around the circle a second time. "It could be . . . anyone," she said portentously. "Anyone."

"Stop right there! I can't stand this another minute!" Lucinda cried out, leaping to her feet. "I know where you're going with this, Sybil, and I can save you a lot of time and trouble. Just let me tell the story my own way."

"What story?" Sybil huffed. She glanced around the group, eyebrows raised. "Does anyone know what she's talking about?"

"What's wrong, Lucinda?" Rose asked in her raspy voice. "You're white as a ghost, my dear. Perhaps you'd better sit back down." She reached over and patted Lucinda's arm sympathetically. "She must be confused," she said to Sybil in a hoarse stage whisper.

"I'm not confused, but I do have a confession to make," Lucinda said, her eyes welling up with tears. "And I'd like to get it over with, before Sybil drags this out any longer." She sank back into her chair, her eyes glassy, her face deadly pale. "I know you're talking about me, Sybil. And the answer is yes, I did go to Chico's studio. And I danced with him." She flushed. "That's the truth. But it's not what you think!"

Sybil blinked twice, her face as impassive as the Sphinx.

"Well, now I don't know *what* to think," Rose Harper piped up. "I'm thoroughly confused." She turned to her sister. "Lucinda is confessing to dreaming about dancing with Chico? What's the big deal?"

"The big deal might be that you tried to mislead us, Lucinda. Last week you told us about seeing a man with no face who was dancing with a woman in a beautiful ballroom." Persia's tone was sharp. "You even threw in that description of the Collier mansion. Did you make all that up just to trick us?" Persia shot Ali a pointed look, her face hardening. "I thought we insisted on strict honesty in this group. If members are going to make up stories, someone needs to address this."

"No, it really happened," Lucinda said, her face pink with humiliation. "I mean, it happened in real life and then it appeared in my dreams. In a slightly different form. My mind was reeling over Chico's death, trying to make sense of it. I don't know why the Collier mansion popped up in my dream. Somehow it all got mixed up together." She gave a helpless shrug. "I never meant to be dishonest. That's not the kind of person I am. And I had the same dream again last night."

"When a dream is repeated, it usually means the issue is unresolved," Persia said in a softer tone.

Ali leaned forward. "So that was *you* dancing in the earlier dream? Being twirled round and round the floor? You were the woman you described, wearing the flowing gown, dancing with the man with no face?"

"Yes, I suppose I was." She allowed herself a wistful smile. "I guess the dream represented what I longed for in my life."

"A wish fulfillment dream," Sybil said quietly. "We all have them from time to time."

"But Lucinda," Ali said gently, "you said you had a confession to make. In your earlier dream, you said the man had no face. But this time, the man *did* have a face. The man was Chico." She paused delicately. "And you said it happened in real life, so that means—"

"That means I went to the dance studio the night Chico died." Lucinda's voice was flat, devoid of emotion. I had to keep myself from gasping. My suspicions were right on target.

"Whatever for, my dear?" Minerva asked mildly. "Were you and Chico"—she stopped and blinked—"sweethearts?" She turned to Rose. "Is that what they call them these days?"

"We weren't sweethearts," Lucinda said with something approaching a ladylike snort. "I was there as a client."

"A client? Oh my," Minerva said. "That's the last thing I would have guessed."

"Yes, I"—she was turning beet red—"wanted to learn how to dance in case I decided to date someone."

"Date someone? Surely you weren't planning on dating Chico." Sybil shook her head disapprovingly.

"No, of course not." Lucinda leaned forward, her brown

eyes intent. "I know you're going to think this is terribly silly, but I joined one of those online matchmaking sites." She looked at me, flushing, and I pretended to look surprised. "When I set up my profile I realized I had nothing to list under my photo. I don't drink, I don't play tennis or golf. And I don't dance. No one clicked on my profile because I must sound really boring." She looked miserable, hands clenched in her lap.

"Are all those things required?" Rose asked, puzzled.

"No, but it makes you more marketable if you want to put yourself out there. Not that I have any personal knowledge of these things." Sybil sniffed.

"What happened next?" Dorien asked, her eyes gleaming. Her beady-eyed stare and pinched features suddenly reminded me of a ferret.

"Nothing. I had a quick half-hour lesson with Chico, and I discovered I had two left feet. I paid him for the class and never saw him again."

"Do the police know you were there the night he died?" Ali asked.

"Certainly not," Lucinda said, stiffening her spine. "I think the less said about it, the better."

"But you might know something that would help the investigation," Persia pointed out. "It's your duty to go to the police. Isn't it a crime to withhold evidence?"

"I suppose I should tell them," Lucinda admitted. "I'll do it tomorrow," she said with a note of conviction in her voice.

"Well now," Ali said brightly, "since that's settled, I suppose we can move to another dream. Minerva, would you like to go next?"

"Excuse me," Sybil cut in. "I haven't said a word about *my* dream." She gave a small, sly smile, and I wondered what was coming next.

"But we've already heard everything from Lucinda," Ali said puzzled. "What else is there to know?'

Sybil laughed. "Plenty!" She cocked her head to one side. "Because the person who was with Chico in my dream wasn't Lucinda." She waited for the reaction. "It was Dorien."

Dorien gasped and flinched. Minerva and Rose were leaning so far forward, I thought they might tumble right off the low-slung sofa. Everyone stared bug-eyed at Sybil, and Persia froze in her seat. Lucinda let out a little sigh of relief. Ali and I stared at each other in confusion, unprepared for the sudden drama.

Sybil maintained a frightening smile for a full ten seconds.

Dead silence all around and my heart was pounding like I'd run a marathon. If this was an episode of *Law and Order*, there would be an ominous *chuh-CHUNG* right now and we would go straight to commercial.

# 27

"That has got to be one of the strangest meetings ever," Ali said, sinking down into the sofa. Barney and Scout, who'd been eagerly waiting for the Dream Club ladies to leave, came scooting out of the bedroom and jumped into her lap. "Lucinda taking dance lessons from Chico? That's the last thing in the world I would have imagined."

"It was a bombshell, all right. First an online dating service and now this? The woman is full of surprises."

"And Dorien," Ali went on. "Let's just say she was less than truthful tonight." Ali was right. When Sybil said she'd "hopped" into a dream about Chico and Dorien enjoying a picnic lunch together, I'd expected Dorien to come clean and admit that she *had* brought dinner to Chico the night he'd died. Sybil's dream wasn't far-fetched; it contained some elements of truth. Instead Dorien had stonewalled, giggled nervously, and told Sybil that her dream was way off base. After a couple more dream interpretations and a spirited discussion of the baked goods, the meeting broke up early. Ali had packed up some samples for Minerva and

Rose to enjoy at home, and Dorien swiped the last of the pretzel s'mores and wrapped them in a napkin.

"Do you think we should have confronted Dorien about her new catering business and her delivery to Chico's the night he died?" A troubled frown flitted across Ali's face. "Maybe we're legally obliged to report what she told us."

"No, I think we were smart to leave it alone. At least for now. Dorien gave me her word she'd inform the cops, so I think we should let them handle it. Either way, they already know she was there so it's just a matter of time before they question her."

Ali yawned and I found myself suddenly limp with fatigue. Both of us had experienced a major sugar rush—and subsequent crash—after sampling the goody tray. "I never thought they'd like *all* the choices for the Handheld Dessert Menu," Ali said ruefully. "I thought beta tasters were supposed to give you an honest opinion and critique the selections."

"They *were* honest, and they *did* critique them," I told her. "All the desserts were spectacular. I don't know how you're ever going to decide what to put on the menu." Ali had written up a list of "possibles" and posted it in the kitchen; there were no fewer than twenty choices.

"I suppose I could offer a dozen or so at a time and rotate them," she said. "And maybe feature the most popular ones as a 'special' every week." She pulled a throw over her legs, so Barney and Scout could snuggle together and resume their snoozing. "It might be smart to offer one half-price selection, just to get people to try it. And we could give customers a punch card. Buy nine desserts and get one free, something like that. I think it might increase sales and drive some traffic to the shop."

"Ali," I said in surprise, "you're beginning to sound a lot like me. You're looking out for the bottom line."

She grinned, looking even younger than her twenty-six years. "You never think I take your advice to heart, Taylor, but I do, I really do!" She rubbed Barney's belly as he flipped over in his sleep, snoring lightly. "Dana and I have been tossing around some marketing ideas and coming up with a budget for promotion. I want to learn from you, and I want this place to be successful. It means everything to me."

I thought for a moment. I've played "Big Sister" so long to Ali that I tend to overlook the progress she's made. I have an annoying tendency to jump in and take control, and this is something I know I have to watch. "I'm proud of you, Ali. I don't want to change who you are, you know. I just want to share some strategies I learned in business school." *And in the real world*, I added silently.

Ali nodded. "Wouldn't it be funny," she continued, "if I became more like you, and you became a little bit like me?"

I laughed. "You mean like a grown-up version of *Freaky Friday*? I think it might have already happened."

"I do, too," she said. "You seem calmer and more relaxed since you've been here. I think you've finally learned how to chill."

"There's something about the Savannah lifestyle that appeals to me," I said. "The city is so beautiful, it practically forces you to slow down and smell the roses." It was true. The balmy climate, the sunny days, the beautiful public squares with their inviting wrought iron benches had finally won me over. I felt like a different person from the frazzled corporate exec who'd flown in from Chicago. With each passing day, I was finding it harder and harder to imagine returning to the high-pressure lifestyle I used to enjoy.

Ali decided to turn in early to watch a Cary Grant movie on TNT, and I sat on the kitchen window seat, glancing idly at the street. So much had happened in my short time in Savannah. Was this going to be my new home? I'd have to make a decision about my Chicago apartment pretty soon. I couldn't just leave it sitting vacant. I could sell it, or maybe sublet it. But I'd bought it at the top of the market, and now real estate prices had tumbled. Would I take a hit? Was I prepared to do that to move to Savannah?

The house phone rang and as soon as I said hello, a strange voice shook me out of my daydreams.

"Stop asking questions." The voice was low and menacing, and I felt a little chill go down my spine. Was it a man? Was it a woman? The voice was electronically garbled, and I couldn't tell.

"I think you have the wrong number," I said coolly.

"I've got *your* number. You'll be sorry. Mind your own business." Click. My stomach clenched and I quickly slammed the receiver down.

"Was that for me?" Ali said, padding into the kitchen in her pajamas and slippers. She started to make herself cocoa and then stopped and gave me a searching look. "Taylor, is something wrong?"

"I hope not," I said slowly. "That phone call . . . it sounded like a threat." I gave a hollow laugh. "But I'm sure it's nothing."

"A threat? Who would threaten me? Or you?"

I shook my head. "I have no idea. The caller told me to stop asking so many questions and to mind my own business."

"Is it something to do with the Dream Club?"

"I don't see how it could be." I was fibbing, but I didn't want to alarm Ali. There'd been some interesting revelations tonight, and everyone had learned that Lucinda had been one of Chico's clients. And Sybil had pointed the finger at Dorien, even though Dorien denied she ever had anything to do with Chico.

Was someone in the group uncomfortable with the discussion? Had they mentioned it to someone else? Dream Club discussions are supposed to be confidential, but anything could happen. I knew Minerva and Rose loved to gossip, and I wondered if they had said something to the wrong person. Someone who felt like retaliating.

"Well, it seems odd that the meeting broke up an hour

ago and now you get a threatening message. Unless it's just a prank call."

"That must be it," I said smoothly. There was no sense in worrying Ali, and I was sorry I'd mentioned it. I was seeing Noah and Sara for coffee tomorrow, and I'd run it by them.

# 28

"Tell me exactly what was said." Noah's eyes, dark and intent, were focused on mine.

"I've told you as much as I remember." I toyed with a cappuccino, watching as Sara opened the door to Sweet Caroline's, our favorite French bistro and greeted Caroline La Croix, the owner. Caroline pointed to our table, and Sara came rushing down the aisle, dropping her shopping bags in an empty seat next to me. She had her dog with her, a lovely rescue Labrador named Remy. The dog was so well behaved, she immediately scooted under the table after giving us a quick greeting. Most restaurants wouldn't allow dogs, but Caroline said it is very common in France and none of the patrons seemed to mind.

"So sorry. This has been one of those days," she said, looking frazzled. "What did I miss?"

"Someone has threatened Taylor," Noah said, his tone grim. "I'm trying to persuade her to take it seriously."

Sara gasped and took a sip of the sweet tea we'd ordered for her. "Someone threatened you and not Ali? That's strange. When did this happen?" She reached into her oversized tote and pulled out a pen and notebook.

"I received a phone call last night. Shortly after the meeting of the Dream Club."

Sara gave a wry smile. "I'm going to have to infiltrate this club of yours. Dreams, murders, death threats. Who knows, I might write a bestselling book about it someday."

"Sara . . ." Noah said threateningly.

"Oh, honestly, Noah, I'm just teasing." She turned to me. "Sorry, Taylor, you know I didn't mean it." She gave a broad wink. "I'd forgotten how overprotective Noah can be."

"Can we please get back to the telephone threat?" Noah said.

Sara put on her rimless reading glasses and shot me a quizzical look. "Tell me about the call. You have Caller ID, right?"

"Yes, but nothing showed up. It just said 'private number.'"

"Probably a burner phone. We'll never trace it," Noah said.

"And the person who called, male or female?" She opened her notebook and began scribbling.

"I have no idea. It sounded like a robot. I suppose the voice was altered electronically. I'm afraid I don't have much to go on." I anticipated her next question. "Someone told me to stop asking so many questions and to mind my own business. And then they hung up."

"And we don't even know if the message was intended for you or for Ali?"

"No idea. I'm the one who picked up the phone but I didn't even identify myself." I felt my stomach clench, remembering the eerie intensity of the voice. "I'm trying to downplay this with Ali, I don't want to alarm her."

"She needs to know the facts," Noah said gruffly. "Did anything unusual happen at the Dream Club last night?"

I quickly filled him in on Sybil's dream about Dorien and

Lucinda's confession that she'd taken dance lessons from Chico. Noah already knew that Dorien had admitted bringing dinner to Chico that night, but I repeated the information for Sara.

"Wow, this story gets weirder all the time." Sara looked up briefly and ordered a *tarte de pommes*, one of the house specialties. Noah and I opted for buttery croissants, which Caroline makes fresh every day. "So Sybil dreamt that Dorien was having an outdoor picnic with Chico?"

"Close. What actually happened is that Sybil dropped in on a dream that Dorien was having. Dorien was dreaming about sharing a picnic with Chico in an open field."

Sara raised a skeptical eyebrow. "I wish I could say I believe in this stuff, but—"

"I know, I know," I said quickly. "You don't believe in dreams. I'm not trying to convert you."

Sara rolled her eyes. "I'm really having trouble with the idea that someone can just hop into another person's dream. Even if it is true, and I'm not saying that it is," she added quickly, "it seems like an invasion of privacy. How can you just drop into someone's dream like you were watching a Lifetime movie?" She widened her eyes. "You can't tell me that's not intrusive."

"Sara, I'm not trying to convince you of anything, I'm just telling you what happened. Sybil claimed she dropped in on Dorien's dream." I paused. "Why would she lie about that, as strange as it sounds?"

"Not lie exactly, but maybe Sybil is more clever than you think." Her apple tart arrived, and she eyed it hungrily. "What if Sybil knew that Dorien had brought dinner over to Chico that night? And she invented the whole dream sequence, because she figured Dorien would break down and confess or melt in a puddle of tears?"

I had to laugh. Dorien drowning in tears? Sara didn't know that Dorien was one tough cookie. Dorien refused to admit anything at the Dream Club and blew off Sybil's dream, pretending it had no merit. So now we knew that Dorien was capable of lying in a very convincing way.

Sara offered me a bite of her apple tart, and I shook my head. Normally, I wouldn't be able to resist, but I saw the server coming down the aisle with our croissants. "So," Sara continued, "somehow this meeting of the Dream Club led to the threatening phone call last night. Someone wants you to stop investigating Chico's death."

"We don't even know if the phone call was about Chico," I said.

"But it must be!" Sara piped up. "What else would you be investigating? The message was *stop asking questions*. Nothing else dramatic has happened since you've been in town."

She looked at her notes. "Well, this really adds another ingredient to the mix. Dorien delivering dinner and Lucinda taking dance lessons." She blew out a little puff of air. "Anything else to report, or shall I tell you what I've dug up?"

"You have the floor." I smiled at her. Sara looked very young and eager in a blue silk top from Chaps and skinny jeans.

"I don't have a bombshell; it's more of a firecracker." She gave a dramatic pause. "Okay, here goes. I'm pretty sure that Jennifer Walton had something going on with Chico." She gave us a moment to absorb this, and then ducked her head back to her notebook.

"Really? That's interesting." I glanced over at Noah but his face was impassive. I still couldn't make sense of what I'd seen at the Walton dinner that night. Noah and Jennifer had seemed like they were pretty close, unless I was mistaken.

Sara nodded. "I've made friends with a local socialite who wants to start a gossip column, and she passed this tidbit on to me."

"A gossip column? Surely not in the local paper." I raised

my eyebrows. Savannah has its share of eccentrics, but it's basically a conservative town, and people value their privacy and their reputations.

"Oh, she doesn't call it that, of course," Sara quickly amended. "She thinks of it as a social column, Savannah's version of Page Six. She wants to get invited to all the trendy parties, and she hopes the column will be her calling card."

"Interesting. But the column is still in the planning stage, is that what you're saying?"

"That's right. She hasn't gotten a contract from the newspaper yet; she's just putting out feelers," Sara said.

"But getting back to your source . . ." Noah prodded.

"Oh yes, here's the juicy part," she said, flipping the page. "I found out that Jennifer Walton is really jealous of Gina Santiago." She paused and waited for our reaction. I noticed Noah didn't change his expression. I hadn't seen Gina since Chico's memorial service; she hadn't attended any of the Dream Club meetings and was supposedly visiting her sister in Charleston.

"She's jealous because . . ." I said, hoping to hurry her along.

"Because she thinks Chico was cheating on her with Gina! Chico was seen dining out with Gina, and people said they looked very cozy."

"Wait a minute. You said *cheating* on her? So that means that Chico and Jennifer—"

"Had hooked up," Sara said solemnly. "Lots of people in town knew about it. The word on the street is that Jennifer was furious when she found out that Chico had something going on the side with Gina." *So furious she might have killed Chico?*

"Why are people convinced that Gina and Chico were involved?" I asked. I still wasn't sure this was true. Gina and Chico had worked together for years. I had never sensed anything the least bit romantic between them. Maybe it was all just idle gossip? Maybe they had just grabbed a bite to eat after work and were spotted by some busybody? Two friends having a late supper? There was no need to make it into something it wasn't.

"Apparently, Chico was dumb enough to brag about his conquests. Both Gina *and* Jennifer. And word got back to Jennifer. As far as Gina is concerned, if she worked with him every day, she probably knew he was a player." She gave a wry laugh. "Men!"

I was still waiting for Noah to jump into the discussion, but he was silent. He was carefully spreading sweet butter on his croissant as if he wasn't taking in every word we were saying.

"Oh, sorry, Noah, no offense. I didn't mean you," Sara said blithely.

"None taken." He glanced at me and I grinned. "Do you want to hear what I've dug up?"

"Absolutely," Sara and I chorused.

Noah opened a folder. "The tox screen is back, and it seems that Chico died of potassium cyanide. That's the most likely explanation. But here's the interesting part. They tested the remains of his dinner. The veal scallopini was clear. No trace of cyanide. And they tested the wine. Nothing."

"So how was the poison administered?" Sara asked. "If it wasn't in the food or drink, then that means he didn't ingest it during dinner . . . so I'm stumped."

"There's another possibility," Noah said. "The security cameras picked up Chico standing in the alley behind the studio, drinking something out of a bottle."

I felt a rush of excitement. "Wasn't Kevin Moore slowing down and staring at the alley in the early tapes? He could have met up with Chico and handed him something to drink." My heart thumped in my chest. This might be the first solid lead we'd had.

"Except there's no video of Chico and Kevin in the alleyway," Noah pointed out. "The police can't bring him in for questioning unless they find him."

"Is he here in town?" Sara asked. I'd forgotten to tell her I'd spotted Kevin Moore with Persia.

"I think I saw him the other day," I told her. "Sitting and talking to Persia Walker at an outdoor café."

"Kevin Moore was sitting with Persia?" Sara frowned. "How does she fit into all this?"

"I have no idea; she's one of the members of the Dream Club. I can't imagine what her connection with Kevin could be. Or with Chico," I quickly added. "There's no reason she'd want to hurt Chico, I don't think she ever met him. She showed up at the memorial service, but I think that was just because Gina is a member of our club."

"Do you have a close-up shot of the bottle Chico was drinking from?" I asked.

"Not yet but they think it's an energy drink of some sort."

"Didn't they run a screen on the contents of the bottle? That seems like the obvious thing to do." Sara was making short work of her apple tart. It looked so good, I nearly changed my mind and asked her for a bite.

"That's what's odd," Noah went on. "They never found the bottle. It wasn't in the studio and it wasn't in the alley."

"Is it possible that Kevin Moore gave Chico the drink in the alley, stood there and watched him drink it, and then took the bottle away with him?"

"If that's the way it happened, we'll never know," Noah said.

"And wouldn't Chico think it was strange?" Sara offered. "If someone offered him a drink and then took the empty bottle away? That would make anyone suspicious!" she huffed.

"I think you're right," I agreed.

"And don't forget," Noah added. "There's nothing on tape that shows anyone else in the alley. Just that one shot of Chico drinking a sports drink. That's all we have to go on."

"So now what?" I said.

"Someone should track down that rumor about Gina and Chico," Sara suggested. "Taylor, you could do it, couldn't you? You and Ali are friends with Gina; do you suppose she'd confide in you?"

"I'm not so sure. We're not exactly friends, and you know how Ali is—she's nice to everyone. She probably thinks she's closer to Gina than she actually is. I'll do my best, though."

"I'll keep working the case and try to get some more information from the police," Noah said. "At the moment, they don't seem to have any viable suspects. Three people visited Chico that night, but no one had a strong motive to kill him."

"Unless it was the fourth person, Kevin Moore," Sara said. "I can try to track him down, if you want. And I can try to figure out what his relationship was with Persia. That part is baffling."

"The whole case is baffling," I said. "I can't believe I came to town to help my sister and ended up smack in the middle of a murder investigation."

"How's she doing with the shop?"

"Great!" I told them all about the "handheld desserts" idea that we planned, along with a few of Dana's marketing ideas. Noah seemed preoccupied once we stopped talking about the case, and the fragile connection between us seemed to have vanished. I was puzzled by his on-again, off-again interest in me, and I wondered if this was the way it was going to be from now on. We finished up our pastries then and stepped out into the bright Savannah sunshine, ready to do our separate sleuthing.

I'd promised to see what I could find out about Gina's relationship with Chico, but there was one place I wanted to try first. My mind still kept going back to Jennifer Walton. I felt certain there was more to the story than she was letting on. Was she involved with Chico? Were they lovers? And was she somehow connected to his death?

I decided to pay her a visit. I didn't have any reason to barge in on her, but I decided to use an old Southern tradition. A courtesy call with baked goods. How could anyone refuse? All I had to do was catch her at home, and I'd have it made.

# 29

"Why, this is so sweet of you," Jennifer Walton said. "What a lovely basket. Please come in." She opened the massive double doors wider and gave me a dazzling smile. "I've just been catching up on my bills and my e-mail. One of those lazy days at home, you know."

She was dressed in expensive designer duds: a creamy silk blouse and fitted black slacks with Leboutin low heels. She was wearing full makeup, and her streaky blond hair was pulled back in a ponytail. I wondered if this was her idea of "at-home casual," and if all Savannah women lounged around their houses dressed like this. I glanced around the sitting room, filled with museum-quality antiques and priceless oriental rugs. I'd forgotten how impressive the historic mansion was, with its gleaming wood floors and elaborate millwork.

"I hope you enjoy the goodies," I said, trying to sound as shy and innocent as I could. "We're starting a new dessert menu at the candy shop, and I thought you might like to try some samples. All of the pastries are homemade and we only use Southern recipes." I was going to add that they were "passed down from generation to generation," and then decided that I was probably laying it on a little too thick.

Jennifer laughed. "You can't beat Southern cooking," she said. "I have some recipes I swear by; the kitchen is my favorite room in the house."

Jennifer Walton as Rachael Ray? Since Andre told me Jennifer has a live-in chef and a staff of three, I found that hard to believe. I looked at her nails, beautifully buffed with a sophisticated French manicure. I doubted she'd ever done anything more taxing than press the start button on the Keurig.

"Let's sit on the sunporch," she said. A uniformed housekeeper appeared briefly, and Jennifer asked her to serve us tea.

"Unless you'd like something stronger? We have the makings for mimosas." She had a hungry look in her eyes, and I wondered if tippling mimosas during the afternoon was something she normally did.

"Oh no, tea is fine," I said quickly. "I've got a long afternoon ahead of me at the shop."

"Yes." She smiled, and I caught a look of pity. "I don't know how you girls do it these days. Trying to work and have careers and keep up with your social engagements. And of course, finding time to take care of yourself." She glanced at my casual white jeans and striped top. My outfit clearly wasn't up to snuff in her world. "I just couldn't do it," she said, giving a little helpless wave of her hand. "Taking care of Thomas seems to be a full-time job. He's running for office, you know."

I smiled. "I know, I was at that lovely dinner you hosted for your husband and his supporters." Hah, score one for Taylor.

"Silly me," she said flushing. "I've been so frazzled by all the campaign activities, I'd forgotten you were there. And you had your sister with you, a lovely girl." She paused. "That was very thoughtful, writing me that handwritten thank-you note. These days, so many people forget the social niceties." I nodded sagely, as if I spent a lot of time pondering the demise of etiquette in America.

"Tell me, Taylor, would you like to get involved in the campaign? We have plenty of fun volunteer openings."

*Fun volunteer openings?* I knew exactly what she had in mind: licking envelopes, manning the phone banks, plus assorted copying, faxing, and filing. I've volunteered with election campaigns before and I know the drill. It's grunt work, with very little "fun" at the lower levels.

"It certainly sounds tempting," I said, "but I'm so involved with Ali and the shop, I don't think I could manage it right now." I decided it was time to try another topic. "I can see that your husband has attracted some very dedicated people to his team. I sat next to Amber Locke at dinner."

Jennifer stiffened when I mentioned the young campaign worker and quickly plastered a bright, false smile on her face. "Isn't she just the sweetest thing?" she purred. "I simply love her to death." I'd been in Savannah long enough to know that "loving someone to death" is code for "I wish she'd take a bath with a toaster." Jennifer paused, as if she wanted me to say more, but I just looked at her. "Taylor, honey, what all did you and Amber talk about, if I might ask?"

Time to put on what Ali calls my "earnest" look.

"Well, let me see. Amber told me how much she loves Washington and how she hopes to go there, once your husband is elected to the United States Senate. She's very idealistic and I'm sure she believes your husband can make a difference." I figured that was a safe thing to say and would cover almost any situation.

"Well, she's young, isn't she?" Jennifer said with a sneer. "Of course she thinks that." I blinked in surprise, puzzled by the sudden change in tone. It seemed like my gracious hostess was no fan of Amber Locke, and I wondered why. Was she jealous of the bright young political aide? It was difficult to imagine why she would be. Unless Thomas

Walton was fooling around with the young staffer, and somehow Jennifer had gotten wind of it. I remembered overhearing someone say "what's sauce for the goose is sauce for the gander," at the Walton dinner that night. So someone was suggesting that both Jennifer and Thomas Walton were having affairs.

The maid appeared with our tea, and I glanced at my watch. I couldn't overstay my welcome, but I still hadn't learned a thing about Jennifer and Chico. It was going to be tough to turn the discussion to the dearly departed dance instructor. I didn't dare arouse her suspicions, and it wasn't the kind of thing you could just toss into a conversation.

And then I had a lucky break. The French doors were wide open, and I glanced out at the gardens. I could see workers setting up for an "event," probably another political fund-raiser. Someone had laid one of those temporary dance floors over the lush green grass, so Jennifer was obviously planning on having an orchestra.

She followed my gaze and said, "Yes, another event tonight." She rolled her eyes. "They only seem glamorous when you're not the one hosting them," she added.

"You're going to have dancing tonight!" I said as if this were the most exciting thing I'd ever imagined.

She smiled, probably at my naïveté. "Yes, it's an evening called Dancing Under the Stars, and I've hired a local dance band."

"I bet you're a wonderful dancer," I said softly, as if I were in awe of her.

"Me? You've got to be kidding. I've got two left feet." She sneaked a peek at her watch, probably wondering how long this "courtesy call" was going to take.

I knew I had to speed things up. "You could take lessons, you know." I added a bright smile.

She shook her head, not taking the bait. "I did once, when I was eleven. And then one more lesson last year." She laughed.

*Bingo!* Was she going to admit taking dance lessons from Chico?

"How did you do this time?" I said, careful to keep my voice neutral.

"You don't want to know!" she said ruefully. It was one of those practiced laughs that had no warmth behind it. "Never again. It's not for me. I'm happy to sit on the sidelines."

She glanced at her watch again, and this time she didn't bother to hide it. "So . . ." she said, perching on the edge of her chair. In another second, I knew I'd be ushered out the door. I had to move fast.

"Could I . . . uh . . . use your powder room?" I said, jumping to my feet.

"Of course." She clamped down on her jaw as if she was literally biting back her annoyance. Then she reverted to charming-hostess mode. "Take the hallway on the left, then it's the third door on the right."

"Oh, thank you so much, I'll just be a moment."

Her BlackBerry chirped and she said, "Taylor, if you don't mind, I'll take this call. It seems there's been a mix-up with the florist."

"Oh, of course, please take your time," I said as I hotfooted it out the double doors to the main hall.

What was I looking for? Something—anything—that would link Jennifer to Chico. It seemed like an impossible task, and I was going to have to rely on sheer luck. I darted down the wing on the left and zipped past the lavishly decorated powder room on the right. Decision time. Another set of wings, one going right and one going left. The house was enormous, a maze of wings and corridors and reception areas. I stood stock-still, listening for a moment. I could hear the maid, humming along with the radio, on the right, so that must be the kitchen area.

I took the left wing, hoping to find the master suite. I found something better, a room that had to be Jennifer's study. It was too girly to belong to her husband, the politician. The door was half open and I zipped inside. It was tastefully furnished with pale green silk wallpaper and what looked like a Louis XVI mahogany desk. Swag curtains with a cranberry and green motif on the windows. A modern, custom-made wall unit of burnished teak housed a pricey computer and a filing cabinet.

I tapped one of the keys and the computer sprang to life. Would I be able to find something incriminating? And could I do it quickly? An old e-mail from Chico? Would she be careless enough to leave any evidence around?

A flashing screen asked for my password. My spirits plummeted to my feet. I was glancing frantically around the office trying to find something—anything!—that would connect her with Chico.

And then the sound of footsteps in the hall. "Well, where in the world is she?" I heard Jennifer mutter. The maid answered in a low voice. Just as they rounded the corner, I darted out of the office, remembering to pull the door behind me. Almost subliminally, I spotted a framed needlepoint over Jennifer's desk. *El que rie ultimo rie major.* It sounded familiar; where had I heard that expression before?

"Here you are!" Jennifer said, her voice tight with annoyance.

"I must have taken a wrong turn," I said, putting on my ditziest voice. "I used the little girls' room"—I lowered my voice discreetly—"and then somehow I got turned around."

"Well, I'm afraid I'm going to have to walk you out," Jennifer said in an icy tone. "There's a huge problem with the caterers and I have to deal with it immediately."

"Oh, of course, I understand. I'll just slip back to the sunroom to get my purse."

"Lupe brought it for you," Jennifer said flatly. The stone-faced maid passed me my tote bag, and I smiled as I was ushered out a side door. They didn't even bother walking me down the Great Hall to the front door. "This path will take you to the front circle, where you parked," Jennifer said. Her Southern hostess charm had vanished; I could have been peddling Amway products.

"Thank you for the lovely tea," I said graciously as the door thumped shut behind me.

Jennifer didn't bother thanking me again for the gift basket. That was fine with me; I'd accomplished my mission. My mind went back to the saying posted over Jennifer's desk. *He who laughs last laughs best.* Was it significant?

If I consulted a Magic 8 Ball, I knew it would say, SIGNS POINT TO YES.

# 30

"I can't believe you went to Jennifer Walton's," Ali said. "I'm surprised you even got past the front door. I read in the paper she's hosting a big fund-raising event tonight."

"I think it was the element of surprise. She opened the door and there I was. With a pastry basket in hand! She certainly wasn't expecting me." I pulled up a bar stool to the downstairs counter, where Ali was serving fresh lemonade to Persia and Sybil.

"The pastry basket was an inspired choice," Persia offered. Persia and Sybil had dropped by the shop to buy some candy for a neighborhood block party that evening. All the proceeds were going to a women's shelter so Ali and I had decided to donate the candy.

"It certainly was. No Southern lady would turn away a guest with a pastry basket," Sybil added sagely.

"What did you include in the basket?" Sybil continued. "I didn't think the desserts menu was up and running yet." She looked around as if she expected the menu to be posted on the chalkboard we'd just installed.

"It's not," I admitted. "I just scooped up a few things that were left over from last night's Dream Club meeting. And I raided the freezer, Ali." I held up three fingers in the Girl Scout oath. "I cannot tell a lie."

"Oh no!" she wailed. "I hope you made a list of what you took. I had a few wild card desserts stashed in there. They turned out just so-so, and I didn't know if they should make the final cut."

I scrunched up my face. "There were a few that didn't turn me on," I said, "so I put them back." Ali raised a questioning eyebrow. "The cardamom brownies, for example. Maybe they're an acquired taste. They smelled like burnt rubber."

"I know," Ali said, pouring us all glasses of fresh lemonade. "Something went terribly wrong. And the cumin pound cake. I'm afraid that didn't live up to its reputation, either."

"Cumin pound cake and cardamom brownies?" Sybil wrinkled her nose and quickly reached for a magic seven-layer bar. "Good heavens, where did you find these recipes?"

"I found them online. They sounded so interesting and exotic," Ali said, "but they just weren't the classic desserts that people expect here in Savannah." She was right. Savannah residents love their coconut cake, blueberry muffins, peach cobbler, and cinnamon buns. Tradition is very important in Savannah eateries; it's best to stick to the tried-and-true.

"In my defense, I only took items that you had two of," I said. "I needed a few things to fill out the basket." I smiled. "And by the way, I would eighty-six the tofu treats." I shuddered, remembering the odd-tasting white lumps passing themselves off as cookies. They had the same texture as Play-Doh and were dotted with pomegranate seeds.

"Let's hope Jennifer didn't look too closely into the basket," Ali said ruefully. "I don't want her to think that I'm the world's worst cook."

"Not that Jennifer would ever eat a bite of those desserts,"

Persia sniffed. "That woman is as thin as a swizzle stick. I think she lives on lettuce leaves and Tic-Tacs." She paused, sending me a shrewd look. "So did you have a nice visit with the lady of the manor?"

"She was the perfect hostess," I replied. I didn't mention that I'd gotten the bum's rush, and that Jennifer had ushered me out a side door to the driveway. The side door had probably been the tradesmen's entrance in the old days, I realized with some amusement.

Sybil looked thoughtful. "Did you have any particular reason for calling on Jennifer Walton?"

"Not really." I smiled. "I should have brought her a hostess gift the night of the dinner, but we went there on the spur of the moment. Ali's friend, Andre, invited us. We did send a thank-you note, but I thought a hostess gift would be a nice thing to do, even it was a belated one."

Sybil and Persia exchanged a look. "That was very thoughtful of you, my dear," Sybil said. "I can see you've adopted some of our Southern ways."

"The longer you stay here, Taylor, the harder you will find it to leave," Persia said kindly. "I think you have the soul of a Southerner."

"Maybe I do."

I never told Persia that Ali and I had spotted her sitting at an outdoor café with Kevin Moore. I was hoping she'd bring up the topic herself and the minutes were ticking by.

"So there's nothing new on the investigation?" Sybil asked. Before I could answer, she turned to Ali. "And you, my dear. Is everything all right? I hope those dreadful police officers aren't hounding you."

"I'm fine," Ali assured her. "They're just doing their job, and luckily, I seem to have slipped off their radar screen." It was true. Ali was never questioned again after the second interview. Either Noah had worked some magic with his cronies at the Savannah PD, or the detectives had finally come to their senses and realized my dear, sweet sister would never hurt a mosquito.

But who *was* on their radar screen? I went over the list of suspects in my mind while Ali poured more lemonade and served a batch of freshly made shortbread cookies. I grabbed one and started munching while I let my mind drift over the list of suspects.

Dorien and Lucinda had visited Chico the night he died and had either lied about it, or failed to disclose it. I couldn't imagine that either one of them had a motive to kill him, but I suppose anything was possible. It bothered me that neither Dorien nor Lucinda had immediately gone to the police. That certainly looked suspicious.

On the other hand, could I really have sat next to them at the Dream Club meetings and not realized one of them was a killer? I remember that Ann Rule sat side by side with Ted Bundy for months on end, never suspecting he was a mass murderer. They were working the late shift together in a Seattle crisis clinic, answering a crisis hotline. I felt a little chill go through me at the thought. I might have shared cookies and sweet tea with a ruthless killer. The idea was preposterous. Wasn't it?

Who were the other suspects? Lisa Ortez, Chico's ex-wife, might have been so furious with him over missing child support payments that she killed him in the heat of an argument. But Chico was poisoned, and that didn't sound like a crime of passion. There was something cold, calculating, and well planned about his death.

On the other hand, women killers tend to use poison instead of brute force or guns, so maybe I shouldn't take Lisa Ortez off the list just yet. Plus, Minerva and Rose said they heard raised voices—in Spanish—the night of the murder. Lisa Ortez probably conversed with Chico in Spanish, their native language, but who else did? I didn't know where to go with that lead, and I think Lisa had already returned home. She must have been ruled out as a suspect or the police wouldn't have let her leave the country.

Kevin Moore was a wild card in all this. He'd been spotted on the security tapes, driving by the studio, but nothing else was suspicious. As far as I knew, he never entered the studio and he never appeared in the alley with Chico. I was hoping Persia would admit to meeting Kevin for coffee, but so far she was keeping mum on that topic. So now we had three members of the Dream Club with secrets.

Was it a stretch to say that everyone on this street had a possible motive to kill Chico in order to stop his real estate deal? The proposed plan would wipe out a few businesses. The flower shop would certainly go, but realistically, the Harper sisters were too old and frail to kill anyone. Ali's candy shop would be on the block, but I knew Ali was innocent. The run-down movie theater was already closed, so that wasn't an issue. Ali had told me the owner of Luigi's was ready to retire, so he wouldn't mind if someone bought him out. I was stumped.

Hildy Carter, the decorator, lost out to Chico in a financial deal and someone told me Hildy "hates to lose." But would she really kill him over it? I doubted it. Hildy had plenty of money and she had already found another, more lucrative deal. I couldn't imagine her as the murderer. Noah had told me to "follow the money," but where was it getting me? Nowhere. I was running into a dead end.

I had the gut feeling Jennifer Walton was involved with Chico, but could she have been angry enough to kill him? Had she caught him with another woman? Even if she had, this could hardly have come as a surprise to her. Chico was a known philanderer.

"I'm thinking Jennifer Walton knows more than she's telling." I nearly jumped when Sybil's voice roused me from my thoughts. It was almost as though she'd read my mind. She was giving me a keen, penetrating look, and I plastered a polite smile on my face.

"What makes you say that?" Persia asked. There was a predatory gleam in her eye along with an emotion I couldn't identify. *Was it relief?* Was Persia relieved that the spotlight was off her? Persia had no reason to kill Chico, as far as I knew, but why was she being so secretive?

I thought about the morning I'd met Persia at the bakery and she'd zipped in from her job at the real estate office. Persia had told me that she'd learned at work about Chico's plan to buy up the buildings on the block. She hadn't reacted when she'd seen the photo of Kevin Moore. Not a peep out of her.

But why had she never disclosed that she'd met him for coffee at the outdoor café the other day? Something didn't add up. What was her connection with Kevin Moore, and why was she afraid to reveal it to us? A link to Kevin Moore could also mean she had a link to Chico. But that seemed far-fetched. The more I pondered it, the more confused I got. I remember Ali saying it was like trying to put together a complex jigsaw puzzle when you're missing some key pieces. It was impossible.

"I think I need to tell you about a dream I had last night," Sybil said solemnly. All eyes were on her, and she raised her hand to her throat, preening a little. "I know we usually save dream interpretations for our regular meetings but I just can't wait another minute."

"Then go ahead," Ali said politely. "It sounds like it's a significant dream."

"It could be," Sybil agreed. "Maybe one of the most important dreams I've ever had." She pushed her gold bangle bracelets up higher on her arm and rested her elbows on the counter. "What I'm going to tell you will seem very strange"—she paused, looking at all three of us—"but I think it may be the key to Chico's passing."

Persia gave an involuntary gasp and had to steady herself. She was perched precariously on one of the bar stools, and her peach and white caftan was flowing around her.

"Last night," Sybil said in a tone that gave me goose bumps, "I saw Chico and Jennifer Walton. Together."

I drew in my breath sharply and Ali looked stunned. This was the last thing we were expecting. I was curious to see how the dream played itself out.

"What were they doing?" Persia said, regaining her composure.

"Driving," Sybil said, raising her eyebrows. "Driving with the top down in that little red sporty car of his. Driving along a country road, somewhere marshy, lots of Spanish moss, definitely the low country at dusk. They were singing, without a care in the world, and looked very happy."

*The low country.* Didn't someone tell me that Chico and Jennifer used to sneak off to Charleston together? A country road, marshy, certainly sounded like the road that went from Savannah to Charleston.

"This is unbelievable," Ali said, shaking her head. "I don't think Jennifer even knew him."

"But stories have been circulating," I reminded her. "People have been gossiping that Chico and Jennifer were having an affair. Surely you must have heard all the talk about them."

"Yes, I heard all that, but I just chalked it up to the rumor mill," Ali said smoothly. "This is Savannah, Taylor. Everyone loves to gossip, and sometimes the truth takes a backseat to a juicy story. It doesn't matter if it's true or not; all that matters is if it's interesting."

"Can you tell us anything else?" Persia prodded. For once, she wasn't trying to trump Sybil in the dream department. Persia seemed to recognize that Sybil's dream had a meaning that we could only begin to fathom. I could see from her expression that she thought this was "the real deal."

"It was very vivid," Sybil said slowly. "The colors were so vibrant, it was like the whole scene was painted in Technicolor."

"That's usually a sign of happiness," Ali said in a low

voice. "Vivid colors and bright sunlight mean that the dreamer is lighthearted, in a good frame of mind."

"It can also suggest *love*," Sybil said, not missing a beat. "If I'm not mistaken, those two were lovers."

"And the car and the winding road were symbolic, hinting that they were taking a journey through life together?" I asked.

Sybil snorted. "I don't think you need any fancy-pants interpretation for this one, Taylor. I think the dream represented exactly what was going on. Chico and Jennifer were driving off somewhere, heading for a night of illicit passion." She nodded her head and sat back with a satisfied smirk.

*Illicit passion?* I tried not to smile. Who talks like that anymore? It sounded like a phrase out of a pulp romance novel from a hundred years ago.

"Well, this is certainly something that the police should look into," Persia said. We were silent for a moment, and I noticed Persia's mouth was pulled down in a frown. I guessed she was unhappy that Sybil had come up with such a flashy dream, after all.

"Persia, did you have any interesting dreams last night?" Ali asked politely.

"Nothing to match Sybil's," she admitted.

After another round of fresh-squeezed lemonade, Sybil and Persia headed home, loaded down with a collection of vintage candy for the block party that evening.

"Well, what did you think of that?" Ali asked, the minute they were out the door.

I sighed. "I don't know what to think. Sybil was certainly convincing." I hesitated, wondering how to broach the subject. "Ali, I've been meaning to ask you something. Do you think people in the Dream Club ever make up these dreams, just to have a good story?"

"Taylor! That would be completely unethical." She pursed her lips in disapproval. "Our club is based on the study and interpretation of dreams. Honesty is key. If I thought anyone was trying to mislead us, I'd ask her not to come back. We have a strict honor code, and I expect everyone to abide by it. I won't tolerate deception."

"Wait, slow down a minute," I said placatingly. "I wasn't really talking about deception, just someone spicing up a dream to make it sound a bit more intriguing. Would that be so bad?"

"It wouldn't if we regarded dreams as entertainment," she said primly "But we don't. We look at them as messages from our subconscious. Dreams exist to alert us to something or someone in our waking lives that needs our attention. Whether it's a celebration or a warning."

Ali's mouth tightened, and I wished I'd never brought it up. "Well, in that case, I think we should follow up on Sybil's dream," I said, stashing the last of the lemon ice box cake back in the refrigerator. Ali had cut hefty wedges for Persia and Sybil to take home with them. "If there's really some truth in what she uncovered, then there must be a way to test it."

Ali rinsed out the lemonade pitcher and stared at me. "I can't imagine how."

"Let's start with Chico's car. This is the first time I've heard anyone mention it. Does he drive a red sports car like the one in Sybil's dream? And what happened to it?"

"You know, that's a good question," Ali said, staring outside at the street. It was nearly five and there was no traffic. "I can't believe I forgot this, but Chico drove a red Miata, a convertible." Her eyes widened. "Just like the car in the dream."

"Where's the car now?" I asked, feeling a rush of excitement. I felt as though we were finally on the right track.

"I have no idea. He used to park it behind the studio, and when he drove it, he pulled out of the alley and turned onto Howard Street. So I never really saw him coming or going. But I know he had a red convertible because he showed it to me once." She glanced down, embarrassed. "I never drove out of town with him, if that's what you're thinking."

"That's not what I'm thinking at all," I assured her. "I'm thinking we need to find out what happened to the car. Was it part of the estate?"

"I guess it would be, but Chico died without a will, so where does that leave us?"

"Nowhere." I sighed. "I wonder if the police examined the car. It wasn't really part of the crime scene," I mused, "so they might not have looked at it too closely."

"But you think we should?"

I nodded my head. "I know we should. And I think Noah can help us."

# 31

"As far as I know, Chico's car is still at the studio," Noah told me. He'd dropped by the shop to talk about the latest development in the case. This was the first time he'd been in Oldies but Goodies, and I saw the quick look of surprise as he glanced around the shop. It was early evening, and we were open for the after-dinner crowd. Dana was waiting on customers in the front, and Ali was huddled in the back corner, working on the new desserts menu.

"You talked to the cops?"

Noah grinned. "You could say that." I knew from his smile that Noah did what he always did—he figured out what he needed and then he'd worked his way around the system. Noah is a genius at slicing right through layers of red tape; he said he learned that skill when he worked for the Feds.

"So the car hasn't been impounded," I said, watching as a couple with young children ogled the candy selections. It seemed their toddler wanted one of each. She raced down the aisle, putting sticky handprints on the glass covers of all the bins, squealing with delight. Dana smiled tolerantly and winked at me. You'd never guess she'd just spent twenty minutes polishing everything until it gleamed.

"Why haven't I seen it?" I frowned and looked out at the empty parking space in front of Chico's. No car in sight.

"Maybe because you haven't looked in the right place." Ali said. "We need to check the area behind the studio. Chico never parked his car on the street. He liked to save those spaces for customers. And he parked at an angle, taking up two spaces, hoping no one would ding the gleaming paint job."

I jumped up, nearly knocking over my coffee cup. "You're kidding! You mean it could be sitting there right now?"

"Well, Noah just said it hasn't been impounded. Right? So if it's not down at the police station, it could be sitting right across the street. Unless someone has claimed it, of course." What Ali said made perfect sense.

"That means we should take a look." Noah pushed back his chair and stood up.

I told Dana that we were leaving for a little while and hoofed it across the street with Ali and Noah close behind. Could Sybil's dream have been right on target? It seemed to be, unless she'd already known that Chico owned a little red sports car. Then all she had to do was invent the whole dream scenario to impress us. I still wasn't sure if I believed in Sybil's prowess as a dream expert, but either way, this could be a major development in the case.

The red Miata was parked exactly where Ali had indicated, right behind the dance studio. The double metal doors to the back entrance of the studio were firmly locked and chained shut. The little car sat forlornly, tucked away behind a giant Dumpster. It was impossible to see from the street. I doubted many people knew it was there, and I wondered why Gina hadn't mentioned it to us. I wondered if she'd been devastated by Chico's death since we hadn't seen much of her since the funeral. Was it grief? Or was it something else?

I'd never considered Gina a suspect, and I couldn't imagine any motive for her to kill her boss.

"Taylor," Ali said excitedly, "I think it's unlocked!" She reached the car before we did and made a motion to grab the door handle but Noah stopped her.

"Wait," he said, pulling her back. He stared closely at the area around the door handle and I noticed a faint powdery residue. "They dusted it for prints," he said quietly. "But I bet that's all they did. The car didn't seem connected to the murder, so they didn't go any further."

"Can I open it?" When Noah nodded, Ali pulled open the passenger door and slipped inside. The car was clean, but had a stale smell from being closed up for several days. She checked the glove box and it was empty. No registration or insurance policy. The ashtray was clean, but that wasn't a surprise: I remembered Ali telling me that Chico wasn't a smoker. There was a drink holder and a little place for coins, and that was empty, too. Chico was obviously a neat freak; it was the cleanest car I've ever seen.

"Let's check the trunk," I suggested. Noah flipped open the lid and we peered inside. It was spotless. The rug looked brand new, and I suspect that Chico had never stashed anything in there.

Noah walked around the car, lost in thought. "You say someone dreamt that they saw Chico riding around in this car?"

"Sybil from the Dream Club," Ali replied, "one of our most skilled dream analysts."

"A dream analyst?" Noah muttered under his breath. He looked like he was going to say something else, and then thought better of it. Our eyes locked for a moment. I'm sure Noah figured the Dream Club was a bunch of hooey, but he would never do or say anything to hurt Ali's feelings.

"He wasn't alone in the car, he was with a woman," Ali said. "Jennifer Walton."

"Really?" Noah's voice was completely level. If he had

any reaction, he was hiding it well. Once again, I wondered about his relationship with Jennifer.

"So this is a dead end," I said tiredly. I suddenly felt weary and defeated by the whole investigation. The car had been a new lead and one worth checking out, but my spirits sank when I realized it wasn't going to yield any new information.

"Maybe not," Ali said, examining a scrap of paper. "Look what I found hidden between the seat and the passenger door. It looks like a gas receipt."

"A gas receipt? It must have the date and time printed on it." Noah looked up, interested.

Ali nodded, her eyes wide. "Seven ten p.m., two days before Chico's death. Wow, I can't believe this." She passed the receipt to Noah, and I noticed her fingers were trembling.

Noah squinted at the receipt and then smiled at me. "It looks like I underestimated your friend Sybil," he said, his eyes dark and intent.

"Well, she was certainly right about the car," I said, wondering what was going to come next. "But what does that leave us with?"

"Maybe a break in the case," Noah said. "She was also right about the woman. Look who signed the receipt."

I leaned forward and gasped in surprise. "Jennifer Walton?" I couldn't believe it. She'd signed her name to a credit card receipt in a flowing, girlish hand. And the gas was charged at Sandy's on Route 17. I hadn't seen this coming.

"I know exactly where that gas station is," Ali said excitedly. "It's a little mom-and-pop place on the way to Charleston." I must have looked surprised, because she added, "They make the best veggie burritos around. I always stop and get one when I'm out that way. The owner makes them herself."

"Why would Jennifer be buying gas for Chico's car?" I asked, still trying to get my mind around the new discovery.

"Chico never paid for anything," Ali said, her face

flushing. "He was always short of cash, or he forgot his wallet. I'm not surprised he let Jennifer pay for the gas; he probably figured she was a rich socialite and he was a dance instructor, struggling to get by. I never saw him pick up a check in his life, not even for a cup of coffee."

"So he was a cheapskate," Noah said flatly. "Sponging off women."

"Who knows? He might have had a lot of expenses we hadn't heard about. Maybe he was drowning in debt." Ali gave a little sigh. Ali is so tenderhearted, she can't stand the idea of anyone speaking ill of Chico.

"But he hoped to make a killing on the real estate deal," Noah said thoughtfully. "So that means he either had money tucked away somewhere, or he had someone who was going to bankroll the venture."

"If he bilked someone out of a lot of money, that might be a motive to kill him," I said thoughtfully. "What if they lost their life savings or their retirement?" I thought of Lucinda, who was living on a small schoolteacher's pension. Would she have been foolish enough to invest in one of Chico's risky schemes? If so, she might have been wiped out financially.

On the other hand, if he'd bilked Jennifer Walton out of a lot of money, it wouldn't be so significant. She reportedly had a small fortune stashed away and could take the hit of losing a chunk of money to Chico. Unless she had to figure out a way to explain the loss to her husband? That opened up a whole new area to explore. Did Thomas Walton suspect his wife's affair? It would certainly be damaging to his political career. I still had the nagging feeling that I was missing a key piece of information.

"But then they'd never get their money back," Ali objected, pulling me out of my thoughts. "How would that accomplish anything? A dead man can't pay up."

"Revenge could be the motive," Noah said. "Someone

might figure the money was gone forever, and was so furious, he or she killed Chico in a fit of rage."

Except I thought we'd discounted the "fit of rage" motive, since Chico was poisoned. It takes time and effort to research various poisons and learn how to administer them.

"What shall we do now?" I asked, feeling more confused by the moment.

"This is evidence," Noah said, pulling a small plastic bag from his pocket. He held the receipt by the corner and dropped it in. "It has to go straight to the Savannah PD."

Noah left for the station house, and Ali and I headed back to the shop just as a new wave of tourists arrived. Dana had blown up some colorful helium balloons and was handing them out to the children. She'd ordered them from a specialty shop; **OLDIES BUT GOODIES** was splashed across the balloons in bold letters. A nice marketing technique, and I caught her eye to give her a thumbs-up. Dana was proving to be a wonderful asset to the shop, and Ali's head was buzzing with marketing ideas. Business was definitely picking up, and for the next couple of hours, I put the murder investigation out of my mind.

My thoughts turned to the gas receipt later that evening when I was slipping into pajamas. So Chico and Jennifer had been an item. Another piece of the puzzle in place. Just as Sybil had described, they'd driven out in the country in his little red sports car. I tried to imagine the two of them together, the socialite and the dance instructor. What did they have in common? What in the world did they have to talk about? Was Chico just using Jennifer, trying to con her out of some money? Or was he genuinely attracted to her? We would probably never know. At the moment, I had more questions than answers.

I suddenly remembered why that plaque above Jennifer's desk had caught my eye. *El que rie ultimo rie mejor. He who laughs last, laughs best.* That phrase had been bouncing around my head like a Ping-Pong ball for the past few days. Someone had quoted it recently. But who?

"**This adds** a new twist to the case," Sara Rutledge said the next morning. I'd persuaded her to visit the shop for breakfast. Coffee was brewing and Ali had made some of her famous blueberry sour cream muffins. A fruit plate with melons, strawberries, and mangoes was in the middle of the table, and Sara had added a vintage Fiesta pitcher filled with yellow roses. The table setting looked like something out of shabby chic and had a wonderful homey feel.

"This is so cool," Sara said, looking around the cozy apartment. I'd set the antique pine table with some bright red woven placemats I'd bought at an outdoor market in the district. The shutters were open to catch the morning breeze, and sunlight splashed on the heart pine floors. Sara had left Remy downstairs with Dana, because I wasn't sure how Barney and Scout would react to a canine guest. "I'd love to have a place like this; it has a lot of charm."

"And a lot of history." I'd found some old black-and-white photos of the building in its earlier incarnations as a jam factory and a newspaper office and had them framed with identical metal frames. The photos had a very cool, retro look, and guests always commented on them. There's a special vibe from old buildings, and you can almost feel the spirits of the people who lived and worked in them.

"Where are you staying?" Ali asked.

"I'm renting an apartment off Victory Drive," Sara said. "It's nothing special. Very modern, sort of sterile actually. It reminds me of an office building—nice finishes, but no charm, no character. Maybe I'll come to you for decorating tips," she said to Ali.

"You know I'd be glad to help. I love doing stuff like that."

Once Ali had poured the coffee and sat down, the talk

turned to Chico. I told Sara all about the gas receipt Ali had found in Chico's car, and she shook her head in amazement. "I never would have guessed that," she said quietly. "I have a surprise of my own," she said, pulling out a grainy photo. It was a close-up of a sports drink called High Test. "A friend enhanced it after I managed to get that screen shot from the security tape Noah told us about. This is what Chico was drinking in the alley next to the studio."

"This has to be where the poison came from," I said, "but we still don't know who gave him the bottle."

"That's what he was drinking?" Ali gasped. "High Test was his favorite drink; it's a disgusting wheatgrass mixture."

"They didn't find any bottles of it in the studio," Sara said. "I checked with Noah."

"That's because he was always running out. He drank that stuff by the gallon. I used to tease him that he was addicted to it." For a moment, her eyes welled with tears. Whatever their relationship had been, I knew that Ali still missed him.

"But if the police didn't find any bottles lying around—" I began.

"He kept them in an extra fridge in a storeroom in the back. He had to special order them by the case from Atlanta, since none of the local stores carry it." Ali gave a tremulous smile. "He was always trying to get his students to drink it; he said it boosted his energy. No one could stand it. It looked like pea soup, smelled really foul, and had a bitter taste."

"You know, that's interesting," Sara said. "A strong flavor would mask the taste of the poison. It would make it less likely that Chico would even notice it."

"That's true." Ali took a sip of coffee. "He used to chug the stuff down as fast as he could. I think it was the only way he could tolerate it." She paused. "It's sad to think he was killed by a health drink. Sort of ironic, really."

"A *poisoned* health drink," I reminded her. "And come

to think of it, how would the killer even know about High Test unless he knew Chico pretty well?"

"He wouldn't," Ali said, her eyes wide. "So there was nothing random about this, was there?"

"Poison is never random," Sara said. She and I exchanged a look. It seemed that Ali just couldn't accept the idea that Chico's murder was personal. Her feelings for him had gone deeper than any of us had realized.

"Are you keeping Noah in the loop?" Sara asked, breaking into my thoughts. "You don't need an excuse to call him," she said devilishly. I knew she hoped Noah and I would get back together. I think she missed the days when all three of us were friends in Atlanta, and I missed them, too.

I nodded. "I'm touching base with him later today."

# 32

Noah invited me for a quick lunch, and we met at Forsythe Square. It was such a perfect day, we decided to forgo a restaurant meal and buy baguette sandwiches filled with creamy Brie to eat outside. He handed me a bottle of iced tea, and I examined the label carefully.

"Don't worry, it's not poisoned," he said wryly, scooting a little closer to me on the wrought iron bench. The square was filled with tourists admiring the fountain and snapping pictures.

"I have to admit, I'm looking at bottled drinks more carefully these days." I quickly filled him in on my conversation with Sara, and it is turned out he had a surprise of his own.

"I did some checking on the financials," Noah began.

"Follow the money," I said.

Noah grinned. "Always. I see that I've taught you well." He pulled out a tiny notebook and flipped it open. "Ever hear of the Rossiter Foundation?" When I shook my head, he went on, "Neither have I. That's why I was surprised to see Thomas Walton was making regular donations to it. It doesn't appear on any list of legitimate charities, and it's not registered as a business."

"Did you track it down?"

Noah wolfed down a bite of his sandwich before replying. "Of course. The money was going straight into Chico's account."

"What!" I nearly knocked over my iced tea. "Are you sure?"

"The amounts and dates match exactly. But here's the interesting part. There was an intermediary. Walton actually wrote the checks to someone else who runs a dummy foundation and she funneled the money straight into Chico's account."

"Who?" I was stunned. Noah had said *she* and my mind raced through the possibilities and came up empty.

"Amber Locke." He looked at me searchingly. "Do you know her?"

"I met her at the fund-raising dinner that night at the Waltons." I remembered the dedicated young staff member with the silky hair and wide smile who didn't seem to be well liked by Jennifer Walton. She'd been so enthusiastic about her politically ambitious boss. She'd positively glowed when she talked about him. But how far would she go to support him? Was she dedicated enough to set up a phony charity to funnel money for him? Or had Walton somehow finagled things so it was done without her knowledge?

"Walton was paying off Chico through Amber Locke?"

"It sure looks that way. The Rossiter Foundation only has one officer. Amber."

"It had to be blackmail," I said, suddenly sure of myself. "All those rumors were true, and Jennifer really was having an affair with Chico. Walton was paying him off to protect his reputation. It's going to be a close race, and the last thing he needs is a scandal." I waited until a group of tourists moved by us. I was happy to see that the kiddies were holding helium balloons from the shop.

"This puts a whole new spin on things," I said slowly. "Walton must not have any regard for Amber if he's willing to involve her in something so shady."

"I don't think he has any regard for anyone," Noah said. "The word around town is that the guy's a complete narcissist. He uses people and discards them."

*Just like Chico*, I thought. "I think Walton has just moved up the ranks on the suspect list."

"It's certainly a motive," Noah agreed. "No one wants to pay a blackmailer forever. And it looked like Chico was getting greedy. The amount of the payments had steadily increased over the past few months. Maybe Walton thought it would be a one-time thing, but Chico had other plans."

"Probably because Chico needed the money to buy up the block of buildings on Ali's street," I offered. "He might have needed a large amount of cash to make a lump sum payment for the real estate deal. He was most likely gouging Walton, forcing him to cough up as much as he could."

"Exactly. And the way the money was going, the next payments were going to be huge. They were increasing by twenty percent each time."

"Wow," I said softly. "So someone put a stop to them." I raised my eyebrows. "But who? Was it Thomas Walton or Amber Locke?" Could sweet, sincere Amber be the killer, the mystery guest, or both?

"Women and poison," Noah continued. "Poison really isn't a popular murder weapon with men. If there was any way Amber could have had access to a bottle of High Test that night, I think she's the most likely suspect." He shrugged. "Unless there's another woman suspect, someone we haven't looked at yet."

"Jennifer Walton," I said. "But I can't imagine her getting her hands dirty." I thought of the edgy Savannah socialite with the pricey highlights and couldn't picture her as a killer.

We were silent for a moment. "What if Chico's death was just a lucky break for Walton, and it had nothing to do with the blackmail scheme?" I mused. "We still have several other suspects, you know."

*But no proof,* I added silently.

I knew there were a couple of leads I had to pursue right away. No matter how many times I went over the facts, the trail kept winding back to the Waltons.

"You've got that look in your eye," Noah said. A knowing half smile flitted across his face.

"What look?" I said innocently.

"The look that tells me you're going to do something reckless. Or dangerous. Or both."

"Nope, nothing like that at all. Just a little bit of old-fashioned detective work. I need to follow up on something."

"A hot lead?"

"Maybe." I had a hot lead all right. Thomas Walton. Could I get him to confess to making the payments to Chico? I could certainly rattle his cage. I'd struck out with my visit to Jennifer, but I hadn't tackled the senator yet.

"Look, Taylor, maybe this is the time to back off on the investigation," Noah began. A worried frown crossed his face, and he laid his hand on mine. "The closer we get to the truth, the more likely it is that someone could get hurt. I think it's time to turn this over to the police. You've already had one threat." Noah had taken the phone call more seriously than I did. The more I thought about it, the more convinced I was that it was just a prank.

"Oh, c'mon," I said, "that wasn't really a threat. It could have been kids fooling around."

"Or it could have been a murderer who sensed you were getting too close to the truth."

"Too late—you can't convince me to back off." I smiled and stood up. "Hate to cut our lunch short, but I have an appointment."

He rose, too, and gathered me for a brief hug. "Just promise me you'll be careful."

"Always." I tried to keep my voice steady. Feeling Noah's arms around me brought back a rush of feelings. Sometimes I let myself think that nothing had changed, and the old magic was still there.

I gently released myself, trying not to get caught up in Noah's dark, sexy eyes. They were gorgeous, hypnotic, even though they were clouded with concern for me. "We'll touch base tonight. Right after the Dream Club."

"I didn't realize you were meeting today."

"I'm asking Ali to call an emergency meeting. We have some things to sort out. Don't worry, I'll keep you posted."

**"I'm not sure** he has an opening this afternoon, Ms. Blake. Would you like to schedule an appointment?"

"Oh, I was just in the neighborhood and I thought I'd stop by," I said. I hoped she'd think I was a socialite with a lot of time and money on her hands. Actually, it wasn't a total lie. I had been in the neighborhood; I'd just left Noah half an hour ago back at Forsythe Square. "I met the councilman at the fund-raising dinner his wife hosted, and I'd like to find out a little more about his campaign. Maybe I could volunteer or host an event for him."

That definitely got her attention. "Well, let me see what I can do," she said, flashing me a million-dollar smile. "I'm Denise, by the way." She extended her hand. "Do you live here in Savannah, Ms. Blake?" She started flipping through her appointment book with long, polished fingernails.

"Oh, please call me Taylor, I'm sure we're going to be seeing a lot of each other. Yes, I'm new in town. I just moved here from Chicago to be near my sister. She's a local businesswoman and a great supporter of Councilman Walton." I paused. "I'd really like to get involved in local politics, and I know Mr. Walton has done so much for the community."

"He'll be so happy to hear it. I can give you some literature about the key issues. As you can see, we have a lot of young people involved in the campaign, both staffers and campaign workers."

I glanced at the glossy brochure she handed me. "Why, that's Amber Locke," I said, recognizing the pretty girl with the strawberry blond hair.

Denise smiled. "Yes, she's one of our most enthusiastic staffers. Amber does a lot of outreach with the Hispanic community for us. And that's her boyfriend standing next to her, Nick Hayden. They're such a nice couple."

"And good-looking," I couldn't resist adding. Politicians always made sure attractive people were featured on their campaign literature. It also occurred to me that the Harper sisters had heard raised voices coming from the dance studio the night of the murder. Chico had been arguing in Spanish with someone. Could it have been Amber?

"Have a chocolate mint," Denise said. "My aunt made them." She gestured to a small glass dish on her desk.

"Thanks, but I think—"

"Denise, did you ever get a hold of Morrison on the zoning commission?" Thomas Walton strode quickly out of his office, studying a sheaf of papers. His scowl turned into a smile when he saw me. "Well, well," he said heartily, "I didn't know we had a visitor." He walked briskly toward me and pumped my hand. It was obvious he didn't have a clue who I was.

"This is Taylor Blake," Denise said, scurrying around the desk in three-inch sling-back heels. "She met you at the dinner party Jennifer hosted the other night." She raised her eyebrows and gave him a meaningful look. I'm sure Denise was a human Rolodex, supplying the senator with capsule biographies of people he'd met.

"Oh yes, yes, of course," he said, turning a full-wattage smile on me. "How could I ever forget a pretty lady like you?" He was as phony as a three-dollar bill; there was absolutely no sign of recognition in those steely gray eyes. He looked me over appraisingly. "So glad you stopped by, always happy to see a constituent. What can I do for you?" His piercing gaze locked on mine, and I felt a little chill go through me.

"Why nothing, Councilman," I said coyly. "You've done so much for the district, and I'd like to help with your campaign. Georgia needs you in the United States Senate; you can help more people, on a broader scale." I stared at him and I saw his eyes widen with interest. I wondered if I was laying it on a little too thick, but that's practically an impossibility with politicians. Like actors and rock stars, they crave endless approval. Nothing is over the top.

"Denise, I think we need to make this young lady part of our team," he said, slipping an arm around my shoulders. It was supposed to be a friendly gesture, but it came off as creepy and I tried not to flinch. "Why don't you come into my office and we can get to know each other a little better? Can I offer you something to drink? Denise can get you a soft drink or some iced tea."

"Oh, no thanks, I can only stay a couple of minutes."

"Well then, let's make the most of them," he said with a wolfish smile. He was obviously flirting with me and I saw Denise frown. She was probably used to the senator's "shenanigans," as my granny used to call them, and she turned back to her computer. She was tapping on the keys as the senator ushered me into his private office and I wondered if she was doing a Google search on me. She probably was wondering how I'd snagged an invitation to an A-list event if I was new in town. Or she might have been checking my net worth, hoping to hit me up for a major donation to Walton's campaign.

Once we were in the office, he ushered me to a visitor's chair and sat on the edge of his desk, so our knees were almost touching. It looked odd and somehow artificial, as if he were posing for a *Vanity Fair* photo shoot. He smiled a big toothy grin at me, flashing an impressive set of veneers.

"So," he said, his smile never wavering, "we both know why you're really here."

*We do?* My stomach dropped to my toes. Could he really have figured out that I was on to him? Or was this some cheesy opening line he'd learned from *The Bachelor*? I wish I'd thought to bring a tape recorder. I figured this conversation was going to turn hinky very soon.

"You're new in town, you're an attractive girl, and you're probably looking for a business opportunity." He let his eyes scan over me again, lingering a little too long on my lips. I felt decidedly uncomfortable but kept a polite smile plastered on my face. "I figure you for real estate, or maybe a job in marketing or PR. Am I right?" He sounded supremely confident, the kind of guy who thinks he's never wrong. "I have plenty of connections, people who can help you," he said smarmily. "All you have to do is say the word."

"Actually," I said, lowering my voice, "I am interested in real estate development. And in contributing to your campaign," I added hastily.

His jowly face creased into a smile. "Tell me more, my dear."

"I happened to hear of a really interesting opportunity just the other day." I paused, wondering how much to reveal. "I'd like to follow up on a deal that Chico Hernandez was brokering. A string of commercial properties a few blocks from the Historic District? Perhaps you know about it?"

His nostrils flared and his jaw tightened at Chico's name. He swallowed hard, his eyes never leaving mine. "Sounds interesting," he said in an offhand way. "But I'm afraid I—"

"Surely you know Chico?" I cut in. I smiled innocently as he stood up. I felt unnerved with him looming over me, but I couldn't back down now. *In for a dime, in for a dollar.* "Your wife took dancing lessons from him." I lowered my eyes discreetly. "So sad about his passing. It must have been a shock to her."

A muscle was now jumping in Walton's jaw. The guy would make a lousy poker player; his emotions were too close to the surface and I'd hit a nerve.

"I don't know what you're talking about," he said coldly. "My wife never dances," he huffed. "And I've never heard of this Hernandez guy."

"Really? Because that's not what I heard—"

Before I could complete the sentence, Walton had slid his beefy hand under my elbow and pulled me to my feet.

"It's been a pleasure to meet you, Ms. Blake," he said curtly, "but I'm afraid I have another appointment. If you'd like to learn more about business opportunities here in Savannah, I suggest you contact the Chamber of Commerce. Denise can give you their phone number if you like. And of course, we'd like to see you volunteer for the campaign."

He was propelling me toward the door so quickly, my shoulder bag thumped noisily against my hip. I had really upset Walton, and we both knew it. Seconds later, I was deposited in the waiting room, where Denise gave me a curious look.

"Make sure you call ahead for an appointment the next time," he hissed into my ear. In a louder voice, he said, "Give Ms. Blake one of our volunteer applications, Denise." Then he turned and disappeared back into his office, closing the door with a loud thunk.

"Well," I said to a baffled Denise, "that went well." She blinked and went back to her keyboard. This time she didn't offer me a chocolate peppermint.

# 33

"You were crazy to meet with him," Sara told me. "What did you hope to accomplish?" Sara and Ali and I were sharing a quick take-out pizza from Luigi's later that night.

I shrugged. "I guess I wanted to see if he would completely deny knowing Chico."

"Of course he denied it," Sara said, rolling her eyes. "He's a politician. He'll deny everything and anything." We were sitting in our backyard patio, and Sara had looped Remy's leash around the table leg. Remy looked up with puppy eyes from time to time, begging for a piece of pizza, and Sara finally slipped her a small slice of pepperoni. That seemed to satisfy the friendly dog, who remained alert and curled up at Sara's feet. Barney and Scout were safely tucked upstairs in the apartment and glancing down balefully at us from their window perch.

"And now he knows you're on to him," Ali said disapprovingly. "Usually I'm the one who acts impulsively, not you. I think you took a terrible chance."

"What's he going to do, have me killed?" I joked. My words hung in the air for a moment, and both Ali and Sara looked grim. "A poor choice of words," I muttered. Even though it was a warm evening, I felt a little chill. Because the truth was that someone already *had* been killed, and it was entirely possible that Walton was the murderer. Ali was right—I'd acted impulsively and out of character. I'd been growing impatient with the slow progress of the investigation, and I figured I could speed things up by a direct confrontation. In hindsight, it was probably a bad idea. My visits to both of the Waltons had been unproductive and had tipped them off that I was interested in them.

"How will things turn out for Walton with the campaign?" I asked Sara. "Don't you think this investigation will stop him in his tracks?"

She dabbed her lips with a napkin. "You never know. Voters are unpredictable; he may come out of this smelling like a rose. He's got a loyal following, and as far as they're concerned, he can do no wrong."

I shook my head. "It seems unfair. We know he was paying blackmail money. Or hush money, or whatever. He's got to be guilty of something."

"I agree with Sara," Ali piped up. "Being guilty and having someone prove it are two different things. Walton may still come out on top. As Chico used to say, 'He who laughs last, laughs best.' "

I nearly dropped my fork in surprise. "Chico used to say that?"

"All the time. It was one of his favorite expressions," Ali said calmly. "Why so surprised?"

"Jennifer Walton has a little plaque with that saying posted right over her desk," I said. "I spotted it when I visited the mansion. She has the Spanish version: *"El que ríe último ríe mejor."* I knew it was significant but couldn't remember why."

"Interesting," Ali said wryly. "She probably thought about him every day."

"Going back to your visit with Walton," Sara said,

frowning, "I think you set yourself up as a target. Ali said you're going to be on your own tonight—will you be okay?" She glanced up at the apartment above the shop. Gauzy white curtains were billowing out the second-story bedroom window, and the antique bricks were bathed in a golden glow. It was a picture postcard scene, and the air was fragrant with flowers.

"Of course I'll be okay." I was going to be alone with the cats this evening. Ali was meeting a college friend in Charleston for dinner and staying overnight for a baby shower the next morning. I found myself looking forward to my time alone. I wanted to go over the list of "handheld desserts" Ali was planning to serve in the shop, and I hoped to drum up some more marketing ideas for her. Ali was on a roll, her enthusiasm was high, and I wanted to keep the momentum going.

Noah called and invited me out to dinner at seven but I begged off, telling him I was right in the midst of a marketing campaign for Ali and I didn't want to lose focus. He made a joke that I was always "on point," teasing me about my workaholic, type A personality. I told him about my visit to Thomas Walton, and he agreed with Sara and Ali, telling me it was a mistake. After we chatted for a few minutes, I spent the next couple of hours checking the shop inventory with Dana, and finally headed upstairs for a grilled cheese sandwich and a lemonade.

It was nearly ten when I turned in, propped up in bed with my notepad and pen. I was thinking of Dana's patience with the children in the shop the other day and wondered if we could do a promotion involving kids. Maybe a candy-making class on a Saturday morning? We could use the back of the store and keep the recipes simple, perhaps no-bake candies. And we could limit the number of participants, and only have eight kiddies in each class. I made a note to run the idea by Ali the next day. I scribbled *Kids Project?* on my pad. It was a definite possibility.

I also thought about bringing some candy baskets to nursing homes and assisted-living facilities in town. Seniors can certainly relate to candy from their childhood, and it might have some nostalgic appeal. Plus it would get our name out there.

A short time later, the pen and notebook slipped out of my hands, and I decided to call it a night. Cuddling Barney and Scout close to me, I fell into a deep sleep.

When I heard the noise in the kitchen sometime later, I wasn't immediately alarmed.

The room was pitch dark and the bedside clock read 2:06 a.m. Barney and Scout had left my side in the night and were probably snacking on crunchies in the kitchen. I thought I heard a pan fall to the floor and figured one of them was up on the kitchen counter again. Someone told Ali that spreading sheets of aluminum foil would discourage cats from leaping up on the counter, but it obviously hadn't worked. I remembered I'd left a small saucepan next to the stove, and from the sound of the metal "thunk," it had tumbled to the tile floor.

I was all set to snuggle back under the covers when my blood froze. My bedroom door was cracked open, and I saw a flash of light in the kitchen. It happened so fast, it was almost subliminal. For a second the light was on, and then quickly extinguished. I swung my legs over the bed, my heart pounding in my chest. Clever as they are, there is no way Barney and Scout could use a light switch. The reality of the situation hammered in my brain: *Someone is in the kitchen.* A deep, primal fear went through me, and I stumbled backward, reaching for my cell phone on the night table. My mind reeled with shock when I realized I'd left it in my purse in the living room. There was no other phone in the bedroom; Ali and I had decided to save money and use cell phones instead of landlines in the apartment. The only landline was downstairs in the shop. There was no way I could creep down the stairs without alerting whoever was in the kitchen. I was trapped, but determined to save myself.

I wondered if I could make it into the hall undetected and then lock myself in Ali's room. There was a small shed beneath her bedroom window, and I was fairly sure I could jump on the roof if I had to. I cautiously padded to the bedroom door, my hands trembling as I clasped the knob and opened it silently.

I flattened myself against the wall, inching my way down the hall to Ali's room, when a dark figure appeared in the shadows. Whoever had been in the kitchen was running straight toward me. There was no place to go, and I instinctively threw my arms around my chest to protect myself.

The intruder was too fast for me. A millisecond later, I felt a sharp elbow slam into my throat and a muttered curse. Was it a man or a woman? I had no idea. The figure was dressed in black, maybe sweatpants, and seemed well built. The first blow knocked the wind out of me, but the karate chop to the back of my head knocked me right on to the floor.

I heard a cat shriek as the figure barreled out of the hallway and down the stairs leading outside. My head hurt so much I thought I was going to faint, but I pulled myself to my feet, holding on to the wall. My arms and legs were weak and as rubbery as spaghetti. I tried to call out, but only a gurgling sound rumbled out of my throat.

*The cats!* I thought frantically. Had this monster taken them or harmed them? I willed my legs into motion and staggered into the kitchen, fumbling for the light switch. I was moving gingerly, silently, doing a quick search for Barney and Scout.

And then I heard a familiar voice in the downstairs hallway. "Yoo-hoo," a quavery voice called. "Are you all right, dear? It's Minerva and Rose."

*Minerva and Rose?* What were my elderly neighbors doing in the apartment in the middle of the night?

"I'm up here," I managed to say. My voice was hoarse, and my throat felt like it was on fire. Every word was an effort. I knew I sounded strange, distorted, and I hoped they understood me. "I'm trying to find the cats." My eyes swept the tiny kitchen and living room. No sign of Barney and Scout. My heart thudded with dread.

"Oh, don't worry about the cats, my dear. They're safe and sound. We'll bring them upstairs to you."

Nothing made sense to me. I felt a sudden wave of dizziness and dropped into a kitchen chair as the two sisters made their way up the stairs.

"Here they are, your very own kitties," Minerva said, puffing a little as she deposited a nervous-looking Barney in my lap. Rose was holding Scout like a baby and he nestled in happily against her until she put him down carefully on the sofa.

"How did you . . . what's going on?" I asked. I touched the top of my head and felt a lump forming. Apparently the intruder had done some serious damage with that karate blow.

"Why, we were up watching TNT, dear, when we happened to see the kitties in your front yard." Minerva turned to her sister and nodded. "Rose was getting up to get us some warm milk, when she looked out the front window and spotted them."

"Taylor, is something wrong?" Rose said, her voice soft with concern. She came over and bent down to look at me. "You're very pale—are you sure you're all right?"

To my embarrassment, I felt tears welling up in my eyes. Probably the stress of the home invasion and maybe the beginning of a concussion. I quickly wiped my eyes and sat up straighter.

"I've had a bit of a shock," I began uncertainly. "Someone broke in a few minutes ago. That's why the cats were outside. He must have run out through the front door and left it open."

Minerva gave a little gasp and raised her hand to her mouth. She and Rose exchanged a look. "Yes, it was cracked open; we thought you'd forgotten to close it. Good heavens, Taylor, this is terrible."

"What shall we do?" Rose chimed in, wringing her hands. "A break-in, my word. What's the world coming to?" she said, her voice rising to a nervous spiral.

"Pull yourself together, Rose," Minerva snapped at her. "It's lucky we happened to look out the window when we did."

"It certainly is, you saved the cats," I said, clutching Barney to my chest and stroking his soft fur.

"What do suppose they wanted?" Rose asked. She looked around the tiny living room. It was obvious there was nothing of value there.

"Who knows?" Minerva said irritably. "Let's stop chatting, Rose. It's time to call the police." She picked up my cell phone and handed it to me. "Taylor?" she said questioningly.

"I'll talk to them," I said quickly. "There's nothing they can do, but they do need to come over, you're right." I felt like my mind was working in slow motion. Maybe that crack on the head had done more damage than I realized.

I was relieved when Sam Stiles arrived a few minutes later. She was a composed, reassuring presence; her face was creased with concern. I heard Minerva greeting her in the downstairs hallway, and moments later, Sam came bounding up the stairs.

"Don't touch anything," she said to Rose, who was standing uncertainly near the kitchen sink. "Taylor, are you okay? The call came in just as I was going off duty." She peered anxiously at me and rested her hand lightly on mine.

"I'm sorry to be making a big deal out of this, but I feel a bit sick," I said. I told her what happened, and she whipped out her notebook. "I'm afraid I didn't get a good look at him," I explained. "Just a shadowy figure dressed in black."

"You're sure it was a guy?" Sam was back in cop mode, her voice calm yet commanding.

She'd already thanked Minerva and Rose for their quick action, told them they could go home, and closed and locked the front door after them. I noticed she'd slipped on a pair of gloves before touching the door handle.

"No, I'm not sure of anything." My head was throbbing and I had sharp twinges in my neck.

"Height and build?"

"I don't really know—"

"Use yourself for comparison," she suggested, with her pen poised. "When he stood next to you, did he seem taller or shorter?"

"Oh, well, he was about my height, I guess. I'm five-eight. And I think he was well built, but I couldn't tell for sure because he was wearing a heavy sweatshirt. He was strong, very strong." I gave a little shudder. "And I think he knows karate," I added, remembering that sharp, well-placed blow to the back of my neck. "He seemed like a pro."

Sam raised her eyebrows. "Interesting."

"How so?" I carefully moved my neck from side to side. I didn't have much range of motion, but I knew it could have been worse, much worse.

"A lot of women are taking up karate for self-protection," she said flatly.

"I suppose it could have been a woman." I winced in pain, and Sam quickly stood up.

"We're getting you to the ER," she said firmly.

"But—"

"No buts about it. You have a head injury, and they need to check it out." She grabbed my hand and pulled me to my feet. "I'll call Ali for you and explain what's happened." She glanced around the apartment. "I'll have a couple of crime scene techs sweep the place, but we may not get much."

"Okay," I said, feeling suddenly passive. My head hurt too much to think straight. "But can I ask you a favor?" When she nodded, I continued, "Please don't tell Ali until later this morning. There's nothing she can do here, the cats are safe, and I'm fine. I don't want to spoil her reunion in Charleston."

"If you insist," Sam said with a sigh. "But we're leaving for the hospital right now, and I don't want to hear any more objections."

"Whatever you say," I told her gratefully. It was good to have someone else make the decisions, and I was glad that Sam had taken control.

# 34

"I've been worried sick!" Ali exclaimed later that day. "Sam told me you wouldn't let her call me earlier." Ali had come flying home from Charleston and was by my side at noontime. "It's amazing you don't have a concussion—or worse," she said ominously.

"We've all been worried about you, dear," Minerva said. She and Rose had come over to check on me, and Ali had insisted they stay for lunch. I didn't have an appetite for the homemade cheese soup Ali had pulled from the freezer, but I managed to eat a few spoonfuls. I'd been given painkillers in the ER, and they were making me feel woozy.

"You weren't able to identify the attacker, were you?" Minerva asked, her blue eyes sharp and penetrating.

I shook my head. "Not at all. I'm not even sure if it was a man or a woman. I just know the attacker must have been a street fighter," I said, only joking a little.

"A street fighter, my word," Rose said. "That does sound alarming."

"It's just an expression," Minerva told her. "Don't be so

literal." She paused. "Or do you really mean it was a trained assailant, Taylor?"

I touched the back of my neck. Luckily I'd moved just in time to shield myself. The ER doc had said that if the blow had been a couple of inches either way, I could have been paralyzed.

"It could have been. It was someone who knew how to do a lot of damage in less than a minute." I was hoping we could change the subject. The attack was over and I didn't want to focus on it any more.

Minerva bit her lip. "Women are taking up self-defense, you know," she said thoughtfully. I nodded in agreement. That was exactly what Detective Sam Stiles had said. "I know how much Gina enjoys her Krav Maga classes."

She let the statement just sit there for a moment and waited a beat. "She's certainly gotten in good shape; she says it's quite a workout. Of course, she did all that dancing at Chico's studio. She's probably a natural at Krav Maga."

I conjured up a mental image of the fiery assistant with the long red hair. She certainly had a terrific figure and managed to be both toned and voluptuous.

"You're not suggesting Gina had anything to do with this," Ali cut in.

Minerva leaned back and smiled. "No, of course not, my dear." She helped herself to some rosemary bread from the basket. "It would be awful to think that someone you knew did something so terrible. I just meant that self-defense classes are popular right now."

"I suppose it was just a random act of violence," Rose offered. "You read about this happening all the time."

"Yes, you do." Minerva gave me a thoughtful look, and I knew she didn't believe a word of what her sister was saying. This wasn't random; this was personal.

"Has anyone seen Gina lately?" Ali asked. "I noticed she's missed a few of the club meetings." She was right.

Gina had been off the radar screen for the past few days, and I wondered what was up.

"She's been busy with community activities," Minerva offered. "Someone told me she's been at loose ends since the studio closed, and she's looking for another job. Right now, she's doing a lot of volunteer work down at the Hispanic Center. Since she speaks both Spanish and Portuguese, she's very valuable at the reception desk."

"That's nice," Rose said idly. "It's good to be bilingual. Or in her case, trilingual."

Someone who speaks English, Spanish, and Portuguese. A little red flag went up in my head. Why is that important? As hard as I tried, I couldn't bring the answer into focus.

"**I want** you to take it easy for the rest of the day," Ali said later, collecting the soup bowls and carrying them to the sink. She'd offered the Harper sisters dessert and coffee, but they said they had to be on their way. They were headed to an outdoor food festival at the Riverwalk this afternoon and were looking forward to sampling the goodies.

"Yes, Mother," I teased Ali.

"I mean it," Ali said, her eyes flashing. She looked around the apartment. "The whole break-in is baffling. There's nothing here to steal, so that means it was personal."

"I'm afraid so," I admitted. "Noah said the same thing."

"He must be worried out of his mind." Ali forced some cinnamon tea on me. It was a new item she planned to feature in the shop. It had a spicy aroma and was delicious with a bit of honey added. I held the cup with both hands, inhaling the tantalizing scent, feeling oddly comforted.

"He is. He's coming over later today, and I think he wants me out of the investigation." I waited a beat. "He can say whatever he wants, but I'm in for the long haul."

"Do you think the attack last night was related to Chico's

death?" She curled up on the wicker sofa next to me, her eyes thoughtful.

"I think it must have been," I said guardedly. "But it won't happen again. Noah is having the locks changed on the front door, and we'll be safe and sound." I didn't want to alarm Ali, but I wondered if it really was safe to stay in the apartment. Sara, our investigative reporter friend, had offered us the use of her extra bedroom, but I felt it was important to stay where we were. If someone was really out to find us, we weren't safe anywhere. I'd rather be on home turf if we were facing another attack.

Ali went down to the shop to help Dana, and I stayed on the sofa with a throw over my legs. I made a few notes about the case. I hadn't considered Gina as a suspect before, but I wondered if it was time to take another look.

Suddenly I remembered the raised voices Minerva and Rose heard the night of the murder. Chico was arguing with a woman, and the sisters heard either Spanish or Portuguese. I'd originally thought Lisa Ortez was the woman arguing with Chico in the studio on the night he was killed, and later considered Amber. But what if it was Gina?

What would her motive be? Could she have been in love with Chico and found out that he was seeing Jennifer Walton? Or did she have another reason to be angry with Chico?

When Noah arrived a couple of hours later, Ali ushered him upstairs with a smile. "Your gentleman caller," she said, grinning.

Noah was carrying a bunch of bright yellow tulips, my favorite flower. "For you," he said, swooping down and kissing me on the cheek. Ali hurried to put them in a vase filled with water and then disappeared back to the shop.

"They're beautiful," I said, burying my face in them. "I'm surprised you remembered how much I love yellow tulips."

"I remember everything about you, Taylor," he said, his gray eyes locked on mine. He pulled a chair over next to the couch. "Okay, start from the beginning and tell me what happened. I already talked to Sam, and the techs didn't get anything. No trace evidence, no fingerprints. Whoever attacked you was good."

"I know," I said ruefully. "It was a blitz attack. I was sound asleep, and suddenly, there she was."

"She?" His eyebrows inched upward in surprise.

"Did I say *she*?" I asked, flustered. "I don't know why I said that. It was impossible to tell if it was a man or woman." I quickly filled him in on the details of the attack.

"Go back to the bedroom," Noah said quietly. I must have looked puzzled because he said, "Just bear with me, I want to try something. Let your mind go back to the bedroom. You're sound asleep and something wakes you up. What was it?"

"I guess it must have been the sound of the pot falling off the kitchen counter. I figured it might be the cats because they weren't in bed with me." I hesitated. Something felt off, but I couldn't put my finger on it. I remembered being startled out of a sound sleep. The sound of the pan dropping on the floor came a few seconds later.

"What's wrong, Taylor? Don't overthink it. Just let the memories come to the surface."

I shook my head to clear it. These pain pills had stalled my brain, I decided. "Something woke me up—"

"You said it was the sound of a pan falling off the kitchen counter."

"Something happened before that," I amended. "Another sound. I just can't place it."

"Yes you can," Noah said gently. "Close your eyes and take a minute. Take a deep breath and imagine yourself back in the darkened room."

I closed my eyes and tried to visualize the scene. I was lying in bed, and a little frisson of fear went through me. I'd been sound asleep and then I'd heard a sneeze. "Someone sneezed!" I said, my eyes flying wide open. "That was what woke me up. Someone sneezed in the kitchen."

Noah smiled. "You see, you remember more than you think you do."

I nodded. The sneeze didn't seem significant, but maybe more details would come back to me. The ER doc had told me that I had a mild concussion and that some memory loss was to be expected. He predicted that the memories would return in a day or two.

"What's new with the investigation?" I asked a few minutes later. Noah had been flipping through his notebook and frowning.

"Nothing as dramatic as what happened to you, but I did come up with a few facts," he said. "Did you ever suspect that Gina Santiago had violent tendencies?"

"Gina? She's a member of the Dream Club." I remembered Minerva telling me about Gina's proficiency in Krav Maga. "I can't imagine her hurting a fly."

"That's not what the records show," Noah said confidently. "Her ex-husband took out an order of protection on her."

"Wow, I wasn't expecting this." I blinked. Gina was experienced in martial arts, was about my height, and had shown a propensity for violence. Could I have been on the wrong track all along? Was Gina the prime suspect? I still didn't know why she'd want to kill Chico.

"There's more," Noah went on. "Gina knew that Jennifer and Chico were involved, and she was furious. She hinted that there'd be 'payback' for his actions. The word on the street is that Gina had a longtime crush on Chico, and I don't know if he encouraged her or not. Maybe it was all in her head, or maybe he really was having an affair with her, but in any case, she could be a woman scorned."

"Hell hath no fury," I said quietly. So Gina had a crush on Chico? And Noah had found out about it? I knew that Noah had sources everywhere. His diligence had paid off.

"Exactly." I told Noah about the Krav Maga classes and

he scribbled a note. "This moves her up the list, I think." When I mentioned she spoke Portuguese and Spanish, he put a little star next to her name.

"I need to rethink everything I believed up to this point," I said.

Noah left shortly afterward, and I was helping out in the shop when Amber Locke strolled in. I hadn't seen Amber since that dinner at the Walton estate, and I wondered what had prompted her visit. Somehow I didn't think she was here because she had a sudden craving for retro candy.

"Taylor," she said, taking both my hands in hers. "How are you? I heard about someone breaking into your apartment. That's just awful."

"I'm fine," I said, gently pulling my hands away. There was something a bit unsettling about the woman's cool, unflinching gaze. I felt her eyes boring into mine like a drill, and I wondered what she was up to. "How did you find out about the break-in?"

She smiled. "The councilman likes to look out for his constituents," she said smugly. "We have ears everywhere."

*Ears everywhere?* That sounded pretty intrusive. "He asked me to stop by and see how you were doing," she went on. Her tone was patently false, and I felt a touch of annoyance. If she was going to succeed in politics, she was going to have to learn to lie more convincingly.

"Well, that's very kind of him, but as you can see, I'm all right," I assured her. "Would you like some candy?"

"There's quite a selection," Amber said, staring at the display counter without any real interest. "It's very colorful." She seemed distracted and was checking out the shop, glancing at the stairs that led to the second floor.

"Why not some peppermint chocolates?" I asked innocently. "Denise loves them."

"Denise?" She gave a puzzled smile.

"Denise from the councilman's office."

"Oh," she said softly, "yes, she does. I'll take a pound." I was sure Walton had told her I'd visited the office, but I knew she'd never admit it.

I scooped out the candies and watched as Amber fumbled for some singles in her bag. A small inhaler was nestled next to her change purse. "Do you have asthma?" I asked solicitously.

"What? Oh, the inhaler. No, I have allergies," she said, just as Barney and Scout walked toward us, tails held high. They like to wander around the shop and greet the customers. "You have cats!" she said in dismay. "I can't stand to be around them. My throat closes up and I become severely congested." She gave a delicate sneeze and thrust the money at me. "Please hurry with the candy, I have to leave immediately."

"Of course," I said soothingly. "Sorry about the cats. I brush them every day but the dander gets in the air. When people are really allergic, it's hard to escape it."

"Yes, yes, I know," she said, grabbing the bag of candy. She sneezed again, zipped her purse shut, and headed for the door. "Glad you're okay, I'll be sure to tell the councilman."

"What was that all about?" Ali said, the moment Amber was out the door.

"That was a woman who's allergic to cats." Ali continued to stare at me, but I didn't offer any other explanation. Gina, Jennifer, Thomas, and Amber. They all had a motive for killing Chico, but did they have the means and the opportunity? I had some serious thinking to do.

# 35

"I don't understand," Ali said later that afternoon. "How did Amber know about the break-in? It couldn't have made the papers so fast, could it?"

"I don't know. She said that Councilman Walton 'has ears everywhere,' whatever that means."

"It sounds kind of sinister," Ali said. "Almost threatening."

"I agree." I didn't tell Ali about Amber sneezing. It could have been entirely a coincidence that the intruder had sneezed in the kitchen.

Noah called just after three. "Feeling okay?" Ever since I'd been bopped on the head, Noah felt obliged to inquire about my health.

"I'm fine," I assured him. "What's up?"

"There's an interesting development," he said. I recognized the excitement in his voice. "Not exactly a break in the case, but it's moving in a different direction." I could hear the sound of paper rustling as he flipped through his notes. "Does the name Nick Hayden mean anything to you?"

"No, should it?" I mouthed the name to Ali, who shook her head.

"Nick Hayden is a grad student from England doing a teaching assistantship at the university. I found out that he's one of the few people in Savannah who has access to potassium cyanide." *Potassium cyanide. The chemical that killed Chico.* "His boss is doing a big research study on it. It's not easy to buy the stuff, you know. The cops got an anonymous tip that Nick ordered a batch of it from a lab outside town. They ran a computer search of recent sales and his name came up."

"But what does Nick Hayden have to do with Chico?"

"Maybe nothing," Noah admitted. "The cops tried to talk to him, but he'd already left the country, headed back to the UK. And Nick's boss is away at his cabin in Maine for a month, and there's no way to get in touch with him. "

"So it's a dead end?" *Nick Hayden, Nick Hayden*, why was that name familiar to me?

"Not necessarily. I was hoping we could link him to someone involved in the case, but so far, I'm drawing a blank." He paused. "Taylor, I'm just passing along this information because I promised to keep you in the loop. I don't want you doing any more investigating, remember?"

"I remember," I said, my mind racing. "I'll stay on the sidelines and let you do the heavy lifting."

"I wish I could believe you," he said after a moment. I smiled to myself. I knew how to pick up on the trail of Nick Hayden if I could just get one more piece of information out of Noah.

"This lab," I said, trying to sound casual. "Is it Atkins Pharmaceutical in Charleston?"

"No, it's Northern Georgia Tech Supplies, right outside of town. Why?"

"I was just curious. Someone had mentioned Atkins to me, that's all." Nothing like throwing a little red herring in Noah's path. "So what's the next step?" I asked.

"The trail is cold for the moment, unless the police can figure out how to find Nick Hayden. Or figure out who he is."

I grinned. Things were moving in a totally different direction than I'd anticipated, and it was exciting. We ended the conversation a few minutes later, and I grabbed my purse. "Going out on an errand," I called to Ali, who was cooking a pan of Kahlúa brownies. "Can I borrow your car? I'll be back soon."

"Yes, of course, but be careful," she said, adding a hefty swig of Kahlúa to the mixing bowl.

"I always am." I grabbed Ali's car keys and a map. I was fairly certain I could get to Northern Georgia before they closed for the day. It was barely four o'clock and it looked like it was only a few miles outside town. And I was pretty sure I knew who Nick Hayden was and how he played into all this. Nick Hayden was Amber's boyfriend, the young man standing next to her in the campaign brochure on Denise's desk in Walton's office. Things were falling into place, and all I needed now was proof. It was just a matter of connecting the dots.

The guy behind the counter at the tech company had a good memory, it seems. When I asked him about a recent sale of potassium cyanide to the university for Nick Hayden, he remembered it.

"You must have a steel trap mind," I joked.

"Nah, I sat through my daughter's piano recital that day and she played Hayden. That's why the name stuck in my head when he called it in," he said with a grin. He brought up the shipment on the computer and glanced at the entry. "But he didn't pick it up," he said. My hopes crashed but then he added, "Someone else did. It looks like it was a cash sale, and we don't get too many of those."

"Really?" I couldn't believe my luck. "Do you have a signed invoice?" He flipped open a ledger and passed it across the counter to me.

"Here it is, two weeks ago. It's really hard to read the signature, though."

The signature looked like a chicken scrawl; it was indecipherable. "Someone has really bad handwriting," I muttered.

"Yeah." He laughed. "But my friend Joe said she sure was a pretty girl, though."

"Joe?"

"The other guy who works the front counter. She told him she worked with Nick at the university. Anyway she had strawberry blond hair and was really a looker." He glanced at his watch. "Joe will be here in an hour or so if you want to talk to him."

Amber Locke. It had to be. "I can't wait," I said, "but could you do me a favor? Could you ask him if she looked like this and give me a call?" I pulled the brochure from Walton's office out of my purse and scribbled my name and phone number on the front. Amber Locke was smiling out at me.

The moment I was out the door, I pulled out my cell and called Sam Stiles at the station house. This was the kind of news that couldn't wait. After being put on hold for a full three minutes, a dispatcher told me that Sam was out investigating a homicide and would return my call later that day. I thanked her and jumped back in the car, eager to get home. I thought of calling Noah, but that would mean explaining how I'd happened to go to Northern Georgia. I powered back toward town; there would be plenty of time to tell Noah tonight.

**Ali called me** when I was ten minutes away from home. "Taylor, thank God I got you," Ali said, her voice racing over the wire. "The most awful thing has happened." I pulled over to the shoulder and turned off the ignition.

"What's wrong?" I asked, my pulse hammering. "Are you okay?"

"I'm all right, but Gina Santiago is dead. Someone killed her late last night."

"Gina Santiago?" I hadn't seen this one coming. "What happened to her?" I thought of Chico's fiery-haired assistant, so vibrant and full of life. I felt a guilty pang remembering that I'd recently considered her a likely suspect in Chico's murder.

"One of her relatives found her this morning. She didn't show up at a family breakfast, and she didn't answer her phone." Her voice wobbled a little. "Poor Gina. First Chico and now this."

"I'm coming right home. I can be there in a few minutes," I said soothingly.

"There's no need to rush," Ali said. "I gave Dana the rest of the day off, and I'm closing the shop. I'm too rattled to think straight. I just finished talking to the members of the Dream Club. Everyone is so upset."

"It's very sad," I agreed. *And baffling. Who would want to kill Gina?*

"I'm heading over to Gina's apartment with Dorien and Lucinda right now," Ali went on. "There's probably not much we can do, but I want to talk to Gina's aunt and her niece. They're the ones who called it in, and they're still at her apartment. Sam Stiles is over there, taking their statement." *Sam Stiles. That was the homicide she was rushing to.* "The whole thing is tragic, and the least we can do is show our support. I feel so helpless," Ali went on.

"I know. Everyone does at a time like this. I'll stop by the house and then come on over to Gina's."

**The closed sign** was hanging in the front window, and the shop looked dark and unwelcoming with the shades drawn. It was nearly dusk. The street was bare, except for a few tourists sitting at Luigi's outdoor tables. I let myself in with my key, still thinking about Gina. Who had killed her and why? Her murder must be connected to Chico's death, I told myself, but I couldn't figure out how the two crimes were connected.

As soon as I opened the front door, I felt something was different. But what? There were no cats to greet me, but that wasn't unusual—they were probably snoozing upstairs. Still, I felt a strange feeling of foreboding slip over me. I paused at the bottom of the stairs leading to the apartment, sure that I heard a faint rustling noise upstairs. I hesitated, counted to ten, and then shook my head at my foolishness.

There was nothing to fear; the place was empty and still. The words "as still as the grave" went through my mind, but I brushed them away. Gina's death had clearly unnerved me, I decided. Coming on the heels of Chico's murder, it was enough to unsettle anyone.

As I climbed the stairs, I heard a scuffle in the kitchen. Was it a chair scraping on the kitchen floor? No, it was probably Barney and Scout, vying for face time with the catnip mouse. I reached the landing, surprised to see neither cat in sight.

An even bigger surprise was in store for me. Amber Locke was sitting at the kitchen table, calmly smoking a cigarette. "I didn't think you'd mind," she said airily, blowing a puff of smoke my way. "The shop seemed to be closed, but luckily the back door was open."

I staggered backward in shock, mentally kicking myself for forgetting to lock the downstairs door leading to the garden. One stupid mistake and I was face to face with someone who could easily be a murderer. *This is how Chico and Gina must have felt.*

"Amber," I said in a hoarse voice, "what are you doing up here?" The fight-or-flight instinct stabbed into my brain. I wondered if I could make a run back down the stairs and decided against it. Amber was wearing a sleeveless top with shorts, and I noticed how muscular her upper arms and calves were. She could have been the ninja whose powerful punch had connected with my head the other night.

"We need to talk," she said bluntly. "Why don't you come over and sit down." It was clearly a command, not a request. It seemed odd, being ordered around in my own house, but this wasn't the time to discuss etiquette. I had to wriggle my way out of this one.

"You've been asking a lot of questions," she continued. There was a hard, glittery light in her eyes that I'd never noticed before, and I wondered if she was becoming unhinged. Or maybe she'd always been unbalanced and I'd never noticed it. She didn't look like the sweet, idealistic political staffer I'd met at the Waltons' dinner party. Her eyes shone with a kind of evil delight.

"Is that what's troubling you?" I asked, stalling for time. I figured Ali might wonder what happened to me and come back to the house, or even call Noah. I had to keep Amber talking, though. "I guess I've always been a curious person."

"You know what they say about curiosity," she said, narrowing her eyes. "It kills cats and it kills people, too." She glared at me. "I thought I told you to sit down."

I let out a long, slow breath and tried to compose my features into a friendly look. I pulled out a chair and sat across the table from her. "Would you like something to drink? We have iced tea, lemonade, and cider."

"You sound like a flight attendant!" she said with a hoot.

"Sorry." I cast my eyes downward as if I were embarrassed. "What do you really want, Amber?"

"Information," she snapped. "You've got it and I want it." She stubbed out her cigarette on a wooden coaster.

"I don't think I can tell you anything."

She reached into her Prada bag and pulled out a shiny black gun. "This Beretta says you will." She stared at me without blinking. The kitchen was silent except the cat's tail swishing back and forth on the wall clock. She gave me a quick, appraising glance, and my heart rammed inside my chest. "Where did you go today? That's a good place to start. I started to follow you out of town and then I got sidetracked."

"I went for a little ride in the country."

"Really?" She gave a dismissive little gesture of her hand. "You're lying through your teeth. I think you were up to something."

"No," I said vehemently, "I didn't go anywhere important. I just wanted to drive around and look at the scenery." It sounded like a lame excuse even to my own ears. I was trying to think of how to distract her so I could slip downstairs when the phone rang. The ringer was set on high, and the shrill noise pierced the quiet room.

I nearly jumped out of my seat, but Amber waved me back down.

"Don't answer it," she barked. "Let's see who it is," she said in a dangerously soft voice. "Maybe we should invite some of your friends over for a tea party."

My pulse jumped as the answering machine switched on. "This is Joe," the message began. *Oh no!* My heart squeezed. It was the guy from Northern Georgia Tech Supply. "Gary left this picture for me to look at, and yeah, this is the girl who picked up the potassium cyanide. This is her, all right. I never forget a face." He rambled on for another minute while I sat frozen in my chair.

Amber gave a strange laugh. "So you *were* checking up on me. My instincts were right. I wonder how you happened to have my picture. It doesn't matter. I knew you were going to be a problem from the first moment I met you."

"Really?" I pretended to be shocked. "I was struck by how sweet and idealistic you were. I remember thinking that Councilman Walton was lucky to have you on his staff."

Her mouth twisted in a frown. "I have a sweet deal with Walton," she said, her voice harsh and guttural, "and I'm not going to let anyone mess it up. That's why Chico and Gina had to go."

"You killed both of them?" I asked, my voice barely a whisper.

"I had to. Chico was blackmailing Walton because of his slut wife, but you probably already figured that out, didn't you?"

I nodded, afraid to say yes or no.

"Then you're not quite as dumb as I thought," she went on. "She was an idiot to get involved with Chico. Why risk her husband's career over a dance instructor? So I knocked off Chico. He never knew what hit him. That's the advantage of potassium cyanide. It's quick and hard to trace."

"How did you get him to drink it?"

"Easy. I just slipped into the back door of the studio, pulled out a bottle of that swamp water he drinks, and poured it right in. I screwed the top on tight and stuck it back in the fridge. I figured if I was lucky, it would be the first bottle he reached for."

"But they never found the empty bottle."

"Of course not," she cackled. "I watched while he drank it and tossed the bottle in the trash bin. I did a little Dumpster diving and retrieved it. It takes ninety seconds for the cameras to do a sweep of the alley; I had plenty of time."

"Very clever," I admitted, and she rewarded me with a sneer.

"It's pretty easy to kill someone; you just have to be smart," she said smugly.

"And you were the guest for dinner that night?"

She grinned. "Yeah, I thought that was an inspired touch. He invited me to dinner, hoping to get more money out of Walton. I was the go-between, but I guess you already know that. I stayed long enough to eat a few bites and watch while the potassium cyanide hit him."

"And Gina?" I prompted. "How is she involved in all this?"

"Gina tried to pick up where Chico left off. She figured Walton would pay her hush money, too." Amber chuckled.

"No way, José. I surprised her in her apartment. She didn't put up much of a fight."

"Walton had no idea that you were killing his blackmailers, one by one?"

Amber shook her head. "He might have had his suspicions, but there was no way to prove anything. He should have thanked me or given me a promotion." She gave me a hard look. "Who else knows about all this? I've seen you around town with that reporter and the private detective. I figure they've both been sticking their nose in my business. And you're friends with a cop. You really do like looking for trouble, don't you?" She waved the gun in a lazy figure eight in the air just a couple of feet from my chest. If she was trying to intimidate me, it was working.

I was beginning to wonder if I'd ever get out alive. Now that Amber had confessed to everything, she'd have to get rid of me.

And then I saw a shadow flickering in the hall. Amber had her back to the hallway that led to the bedrooms, but my view was unobstructed. The shadow moved cautiously, hugging the wall. I didn't dare stare, but I took a quick peek out of the corner of my eye. The shadow was moving steadily forward, and my heart nearly leapt with joy.

"What's going to happen now?" I asked, hoping to distract Amber.

"You're going to be the victim of a home invasion," she said coolly. "I screwed up the first time, but this time will be easier."

"So that *was* you, prowling around in the dark, the night that Ali was out of town?"

"You must have a thicker skull than I thought," she said, giving me an appraising look.

"You gave me a concussion," I said irritably.

Amber grinned. "Well, this time it's going to be a lot worse."

Barney strolled into the kitchen just then, and before I

could stop him, he rubbed against Amber's leg. "Get that cat away from me!" she hissed. Her nose twitched and she gave a gigantic sneeze. She squeezed her eyes tightly shut, trying not to sneeze again, and this time she rested the gun on the kitchen table. I saw my chance, reached across the table, and with one sweep, the gun clattered to the kitchen floor.

The shadow moved quickly then, almost a blur, covering the few steps to the kitchen and stopping a foot away from the oak table. It was Sam Stiles. Gun drawn, cop face on, she was a formidable figure. She held her gun in her right hand and reached for a pair of cuffs with the left.

She deftly yanked Amber to her feet while I watched in astonishment. "You're under arrest for the murders of Chico Hernandez and Gina Santiago," she said, calm as you please. "You have the right to remain silent, you have the right to an attorney." She pulled Amber's arms behind her, and I heard the cuffs clicking into place.

Amber was squirming furiously, but two deputies moved swiftly into the kitchen. One scooped up the gun from the floor, and the other grabbed Amber by the upper arm. Sam finished reading the rights, and the deputies led Amber down the stairs to the street. Barney and Scout, fascinated at the real life cop show unfolding before them, jumped up on the window seat, their eyes wide.

"Are you okay?" Sam said solicitously. She rested her hand on my shoulder, her eyes searching mine.

"I think so," I said. I'd jumped up when Sam barged into the kitchen, but my legs felt rubbery and I sank back into my chair. My heart was slamming like a jackhammer in my chest, and I could feel a muscle jumping in my jaw.

"Then I have a few questions for you," Sam said, slipping into a seat at the table. Her expression turned serious, and I figured she was going to read me the riot act for doing my own investigating.

"Well, I have a question for you, too." I swallowed hard,

wiping away the beads of sweat that had sprouted on my forehead.

"You go first," she said, pointing at me with her pen.

I took a deep, steadying breath and grinned. "What took you so long?"

# 36

"I don't understand," Rose said, adding a touch of honey to her tea. She was perched on the edge of the sofa, balancing a plate filled with lemon squares, brownies, and thumbprint cookies. "Amber had to kill Chico and Gina because Councilman Walton was paying them hush money?"

"Yes," I said. "She didn't want anything to interfere with Walton's career. All she wanted to do was see him elected senator so she could go to Washington with him. When Chico started squeezing Walton for more money, she decided it was time to pull the plug on him."

"It's hard to believe," Minerva said, shaking her head. "I wouldn't put anything past Chico, but I can't imagine Gina blackmailing anyone."

"Maybe we didn't know her as well as we thought," Lucinda said thoughtfully. "She always seemed a rather flamboyant type. She had that fiery temper, the same as Chico."

She flushed a little when she said his name, and I wondered if she regretted her brief encounter with him. She'd only taken one dance lesson from him, but she felt her reputation was sullied.

"It's amazing how many people got caught up with Chico," Dorien said. "I never should have brought dinner over that night. It's going to take years to live that down. I just hope my catering business can recover."

"The newspapers never should have mentioned that dinner, my dear," Sybil said soothingly. "Your food had nothing to do with his death." She looked carefully at the selection of pastries Ali had set out on the coffee table and reached for a napoleon. "They just want to sell papers, so they sensationalize everything."

"I know, but once the idea is planted, it takes root," Dorien said miserably. Everyone knew Dorien was in tough shape financially. Her tarot card readings were on the decline, and her catering business never got off the ground. The negative news about Chico's death certainly didn't help.

"You were very brave," Minerva said admiringly. "When I think of you all alone in the kitchen with the killer, I feel faint. I don't know how you kept your head."

"Taylor always keeps her head," Ali said, grinning at me. "Sam told me she played it exactly right, keeping Amber talking until she confessed to both crimes."

"I'm not sure how much credit I deserve," I said ruefully. "Talking was the only thing I could think of to do."

"Nonsense!" Persia exclaimed. "You managed the situation perfectly."

We were silent then, tasting some new selections Ali had added to the shop menu. She has a real flair for creating "handheld desserts," and I was proud of her. With the new marketing in place, business at Oldies but Goodies had taken off, and we'd attracted a lot of attention in the local press. "So Amber targeted this young chemist and befriended him, just to have access to the potassium cyanide?" Persia asked. "Is that what happened?"

"The cops aren't sure about that part," I said. "Sam said

it might have started as a real friendship and then she realized she could use him, or maybe she planned the whole thing from the start."

"Persia," I began uncertainly, "there's been something I've been meaning to ask you—"

"I know," Persia said, flushing, "I'm afraid I didn't tell the truth about Kevin Moore the other day."

"We spotted you having coffee with him," I said. "What was all that about?"

"My big mouth got me into trouble," Persia admitted. "I didn't know Kevin Moore from a hole in the ground, but he called the office and said he was looking into some real estate deals in Savannah." She paused, fingering an opal ring the size of a walnut. "We talked on the phone a few times, and I agreed to meet with him when he came to town. I should have been suspicious—all he wanted to talk about was the hush-hush development deal that Chico had going. I started blabbing about it, and he asked a bunch of questions. In the end, he was just using me." She gave a sad little sigh. "I guess I was flattered by his attention. You'd think I'd know better at my age, wouldn't you?"

"You were too embarrassed to tell us?" I asked. "That's why you pretended you didn't recognize him in the photo?"

Persia nodded. "There's no fool like an old fool," she said sadly.

"So he had nothing to do with the murders?" Minerva asked.

"No, nothing," I told her.

We were all silent for a moment.

And then Rose spoke up. "Going back to Amber Locke, how could such a sweet-looking little thing be a killer?" Rose mused. "She looked so pretty in that newspaper photo."

"Councilman Walton certainly has some explaining to do," Minerva said. "It's going to be embarrassing when everything comes out at the trial, both for him and his wife."

"It probably won't go to trial. I'm pretty sure Amber will

make a plea deal. There won't be any more secrets, that's for sure," Ali offered. "The newspapers will have a field day with the story. The truth will out, as they say."

"I think it always does." Lucinda's tone was sad. She'd been shaken by her interview with the police and had decided to put her Internet dating plans on hold. She and Dorien had been cleared immediately, but such a close brush with murder had sent Lucinda back into her shell. I figured it would take weeks to coax her out again.

"I wish Sam Stiles could have been here tonight," Minerva said. "We owe her a lot, don't we?" She gave me a broad smile. "You're here with us, safe and sound."

"It's a good thing Noah had his suspicions," Ali said. "Somehow he knew you were headed out to that tech supply place. And he figured Amber would be hot on your trail, so he called Sam to look out for you."

"Maybe he's psychic," Sybil said, clasping her hands together.

"I don't think so," I said, laughing. "Noah just knows me too well." Noah had been at the airport when he had a premonition I was doing something "reckless," and had called Sam and asked her to check on me. Sam sent a couple of her deputies to the shop, and when they spotted Amber's car parked down the street, they ran the tags. Sam told them to get inside the house immediately, and said she'd be there in a few minutes. Luckily Amber had left the back door open so the deputies could easily slip inside.

"Shall we start on a dream interpretation, ladies?" Sybil glanced at her watch. "This murder has taken up most of the meeting." She tsk-tsked.

"Who wants to go first?" Ali asked.

Dorien was silent, idly petting Barney, who'd jumped up next to her on the sofa. Her abrasiveness had vanished; now she had a perpetually worried frown on her face. Lucinda looked demure, wearing a classic gray sheath with matching pumps. The Harper sisters were happily munching on Ali's new desserts, cheerful as ever, and Minerva looked up with a bright smile.

"Taylor," she said, her eyes beaming, "you look like there's something you want to share with us?"

I smiled and hesitated. So much had happened in the past couple of weeks that I barely had time to make sense of it. "I . . . well, it's not a dream, but I do have some news," I began.

Rose clapped her hands together. "I bet I know what it is. You're going to stay in Savannah!"

"Honestly, Rose," her sister chided. "Let the poor girl tell her story her own way. Go ahead, Taylor," she urged.

"Yes, tell us," Ali said, slipping into a seat next to me.

I looked around the circle. I felt connected with all these women; along with Ali, they were my family. "I've decided to stay," I blurted out. "I'm selling my condo in Chicago and moving in with Ali. We're going to run the shop together."

"I knew we could win you over!" Ali said, reaching over and giving me a quick hug. "This is what I've always hoped for," she said, her eyes moist with happy tears.

The meeting went on for another hour, and it was dark when we ushered the last guest down the stairs to the front door. It had been an emotional evening for both of us, and Ali decided to turn in, Barney trailing after her.

I was making a cup of chamomile tea when Noah called.

"I go out of town for a few days and look what happens," he teased. Sara told me that after learning that I was all right, he'd immediately left on a business trip to Atlanta. Apparently a Fortune 500 company was trying to recruit him to head up a new threat management and risk assessment division. I was sure the pay was tempting, and I wondered what he'd decided.

"I have news," we both blurted out at the same time.

"You first," Noah said, his voice husky.

"I've decided to stay in Savannah," I said quickly. "Ali and I are going to be co-owners of the shop." I hesitated. "It's a big leap, but I'm going to start a new life here."

"Wow," he said softly. "Not what I was expecting but I'm glad to hear it." A beat. "I had an interview in Atlanta—" he began.

"I know, Sara told me," I cut in fast. "What did you decide?" My pulse jumped. Was I going to lose him again? I felt a ripple of regret over the time we'd gone our separate ways in Atlanta. Our work lives had taken up our whole existence, and our relationship had ground to a halt. Was this a case of history repeating itself?

The silence stretched out for a moment, and then he said, "I decided to stay here." His voice was strong, firm. I hadn't realized I'd been holding my breath, and I let it out in a little sigh. This is exactly what I'd been hoping for.

"When did you decide?"

"Just now," he said, his voice slipping over me like a caress. "I can't leave Savannah because I can't leave you." A long pause. "I think we need to talk. In person," he added. "Is it too late to come over?"

I swallowed and managed to find my voice. Scout jumped on my lap, and I looked around the cheerful kitchen. The black cat with the rolling eyes was swishing his tail on the wall clock, and all was right with the world. I grinned, and a little curl of desire fluttered in my stomach.

"It's never too late," I told him.

# Dream Symbol Guide

What are your dreams trying to tell you? Do you ever dream of being stranded in a strange city in the dead of night, alone and afraid? Do you dream of wandering through a beautiful house, discovering hidden rooms filled with treasures? Dreams are our passport to the unconscious. Understanding dream symbols can help you unlock their secrets.

* Being lost and alone is a frequent theme in dreams and suggests that you feel powerless and vulnerable in some area of your waking life. You literally "don't know where to turn" and there is usually a strong element of danger in these dreams.

* Finding yourself in a beautiful house filled with hidden rooms is another common theme. The hidden rooms represent your potential, parts of yourself that you have never explored, skills and talents you have never developed.

* Standing on the edge of a cliff is another well-known dream feature. You might be facing a turning point in your life, facing a momentous decision. Sometimes in the cliff dream, you see a canyon across the way. The distance is insurmountable; there is no way you can bridge the gap. This usually means that there is an

obstacle to an important goal in your waking life; the gap represents the barrier you must overcome.

* Dreaming of driving a car—or riding in a car—features prominently in dreams. Are you driving or is someone else driving? If the car is careening down the road, it could mean that some element of your life is spinning out of control and needs to be addressed. If you are in the backseat, or unable to reach the pedals, it could mean that you seriously doubt your ability to control your own life and destiny. You may be overly dependent on others to make decisions for you.

* Cellars in dreams represent the deepest level of your unconscious. There is usually an element of darkness and danger in these dreams. Dreaming of being in a cellar can signify there is something in your conscious life that is hidden, something that you are afraid to face.

* Drowning in dreams usually means you are having trouble "keeping your head above water," and water is a very powerful symbol of the unconscious. A flood represents the notion that you are about to be overwhelmed by a force more powerful than you are.

Symbols in dreams embody our greatest hopes and fears; understanding their significance can help uncover material that is useful in our waking lives. There is no single way to interpret your dreams because you are the architect of your life. Sharing your dreams in a dream club can offer valuable insights into dreams and the power of the unconscious.

***First in the Family Skeleton Mysteries from***

# Leigh Perry

# A SKELETON IN THE FAMILY

Moving back into her parents' house with her teenage daughter was not Georgia Thackery's "Plan A." Neither is dealing with Sid, the Thackery family's skeleton. Sid has lived in the house for as long as Georgia can remember, but now he's determined to find out how he died—with Georgia's help of course.

## PRAISE FOR THE SERIES

**"You'll love the adventures of this unexpected mystery-solving duo."**

**—Charlaine Harris, #1 *New York Times* bestselling author**

**"[A] charming debut . . . Just plain fun!"**

**—Sofie Kelly, *New York Times* bestselling author**

leighperryauthor.com
facebook.com/TheCrimeSceneBooks
penguin.com

M1490T0514

FROM THE AUTHOR OF *A KILLER PLOT*

ELLERY ADAMS

*Wordplay becomes foul play . . .*

# A Deadly Cliché

A BOOKS BY THE BAY MYSTERY

*While walking her poodle, Olivia Limoges discovers a dead body buried in the sand. Could it be connected to the bizarre burglaries plaguing Oyster Bay, North Carolina? The Bayside Book Writers prick up their ears and pick up their pens to get the story . . .*

The thieves have a distinct MO. At every crime scene, they set up odd tableaus: a stick of butter with a knife through it, dolls with silver spoons in their mouths, a deck of cards with a missing queen. Olivia realizes each setup represents a cliché.

Who better to decode the cliché clues than the Bayside Book Writers group, especially since their newest member is Police Chief Rawlings? As the investigation proceeds, Olivia is surprised to find herself falling for the widowed policeman. But an even greater surprise is in store. Her father—lost at sea thirty years ago—may still be alive . . .

penguin.com

M896T0511

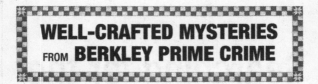